To Aunt De____

Find Y____

THE
SANCTUARY

Sara E Santaha

**SARA ELIZABETH
SANTANA**

OFTOMES PUBLISHING
UNITED KINGDOM

To Daniel, Shelby, Nathan, Erik, Alyssa, Allison, Andrea, Jenna, Allison, Holly, Lauren and all the rest. Thank you for letting me into your family. Thank you for showing me what true friendship and love is.

PROLOGUE

IT FELT GOOD to be back in the sunlight again. After months underground, it was like waking up. Everything about being out in the open air was perfect. I could smell the pine in the forest and my cheeks were cold from the breeze. I wished Zoey had been on duty with me this morning. It was hard to leave her, especially when she was in my bed. Even knowing I would see her at the end of the day didn't make it any easier to get my ass out the door.

The two guards with me were quiet. It wasn't as if we needed to talk while patrolling, these two were just so serious. They definitely weren't the type to joke with.

I was completely bored.

I knew I shouldn't be. This job was to be taken seriously and I was lucky enough to get to do it. A few months ago, I wouldn't have imagined that I would be allowed. People were constantly dying and I was given a chance to try and prevent it. I felt guilty for being bored.

The sun was high in the sky and I could feel the sweat underneath the heavy black uniform I was wearing. I wasn't sure how long I was on patrol today; that was up to the captain. Seeing as he hadn't said a word in an hour or two, I wasn't really feeling inclined to ask him.

I was on my third pass of the east side of the front entrance when I heard it. A branch snapping clean in two. The three of us spun in the direction of the noise, guns out. My heart was beating a loud rhythm in my chest. We waited but there was nothing but quiet around us.

"Maybe it was just an animal," the other guard said. The barrel of his gun lowered a fraction as he stared in the direction that the noise had come from.

Just as he said this, there was movement in the trees and we froze. There was something out there. There was a distinct sound of footsteps. Someone was coming our way but they were doing nothing to conceal their presence.

Awakened. It had to be.

Before any of us could make a move, shots rang out. I ducked, rolling to the ground, one of my hands coming up to cover my head. I waited and then my head rose. Panic went through me. My two companions were on the ground, both of them with a clean shot to the head. Their eyes were empty. They were dead.

I scrambled up and immediately was yanked backward by a pair of powerful arms. My gun went flying out of my arms. I couldn't see who had me but I fought, I kicked my legs backward and connected with something. There was a loud grunt but the kick did nothing to free me from the grip that I was trapped in. Arms snaked around me and I did the only thing that I could think of. My teeth sank into his arm.

My captor howled and stepped backward as his hold on me loosened and I took advantage of it. I yanked hard and he went spinning away from me. I moved towards him but he was already recovering and his fist collided with my face, my world going blank for a moment. Blood was pouring from a wound in my forehead. I couldn't see.

A kick landed in my gut and I fell to the ground. I knew my gun was close by. I rolled onto my stomach and spotted it, just a few feet away. I crawled over to it, ignoring the pain that was shooting through my body. I was only inches away from it. I reached out and my breath caught in my throat as a heavy boot came crashing down on my hand, shattering the bones underneath.

A hand yanked the fabric of my shirt, pulling me toward them, and a punch landed on my face. Then there was another and another. The world around me was a haze. I couldn't even see who was attacking me.

Another punch landed on my jaw. The world spun and right before I blacked out, right before the pain was too much for me to stay awake any longer, I saw it. The dark brown uniform and the woman etched on it.

A woman with a lion's head.

I was in big trouble.

BEFORE

RAZI CYLON'S HANDS clutched the firm wood of her son's casket. She was unwilling to let go; her grip firm on the cold and unforgiving wood. There were so many people in attendance at his funeral. It was hard to believe that such a beautiful soul that was loved by so many people, could have been killed in such a hateful act. Just the thought of it made her angry. She was not a person known for letting her anger show. It was not how she was raised. From the time she was a little girl, she was taught to be still and silent. She was to be a stone, never showing anything more than calm. This was, simply, how things were done. This was how things were accomplished. Nothing came from flying off the handle.

Razi had never felt like this before. Like she could rip into every person that dared look in her direction. They offered condolences, kind words, but they didn't know. They had no idea. They had no idea the hurt that burned through her veins. She was a doctor. She prided herself on her wide variety of knowledge. Razi Cylon was anything but stupid. She was confident in her ability to have answers. But this…this, she didn't have an answer for. She couldn't bring herself to admit that she had no idea how to deal with this.

So instead, she started to plan. She started to tell herself that she could do other things. She would make it better. She would fix it. She would take this and attack it logically. Taking action was the only thing she was ever good at.

Something needed to change. She was tired of seeing this world crumble to pieces around her, life was a gift that too many people did not appreciate and Razi Cylon was ready. She was ready to teach them a lesson. If they wanted to take life for granted, she was ready to take that life from them.

Something needed to change.

Everything needed to change.

AFTER

CHAPTER ONE

SHE ESCAPED. SHE escaped. She escaped.

I kept repeating the words in my head. It gave me a dash of hope as the nameless doctor stuck a needle into my vein, taking blood. I had no idea what they were doing with all the blood they were extracting, but I had since gotten used to the slight poke in the skin and the way I always felt like sleeping after they were done. I had been trapped in Sekhmet for nearly four months and I was beginning to forget what the outside world looked like.

But it was okay. It was going to be okay. Zoey escaped.

The entire place was in an uproar. No one had ever left Sekhmet, not without permission, and not only had Zoey managed to escape, but she'd freed her boyfriend Ash as well. Security had been increased and I was kept in my room more often than I ever had been before.

I was going insane. There were only so many hours a guy could stare at the wall.

But Zoey had escaped and she'd done it with the one person I trusted more than even myself to keep her safe. She was going to be okay. She just needed to run, and never stop running. I knew she would. She was a survivor. She was feisty and stubborn and had the worst temper of anyone I had ever met, but she was the only friend I had left. She was keeping me alive, though she didn't know it.

I missed her so much. I hoped to god that she was safe.

Razi Cylon walked into the room, interrupting my thoughts. This was the first time I'd seen her since Zoey escaped and I immediately noticed the difference in her demeanor. I had heard whispers that she had been shot, had hoped and prayed that she wouldn't make it. Against all odds, she had survived.

She had changed though, in the few short days since Zoey had escaped. It was obvious, and I didn't only mean the white bandage that was wrapped tightly around her neck. Her calm and confident façade had slipped. Her skin had paled and her hands shook as she reached for me.

I flinched away from her. Her fingers clutching the stethoscope as she leaned forward to listen to my heart were cold against my bare skin. Sometimes I wondered what she heard when she did that. Surely she could hear the way my heart sped up every time she came near me. I was man enough to admit that the woman terrified me. I wasn't fond of admitting it, but it was true. Everything that happened was because of her. Everything was her fault.

And there was nothing I could do about it.

Dr. Cylon concluded her examination and spent a few minutes looking over the chart that the previous doctor had handed her. She made a few noises, eyes roving over the page like this was any other day in Sekhmet, but I was not stupid. I could see it in her eyes. Panic.

Hope filled me again.

"Did you know about Miss Valentine's plan to escape?" She finally spoke. Her voice was low, so low I could barely hear her. The doctor at her side flapped his hands, worriedly, reminding her that she shouldn't talk, but she waved him aside. She leaned forward so that our faces were mere inches apart. "Answer me, Mr. Garrity."

I cleared my throat, urging my voice to be steady as I spoke. "You must be referring to my father."

Her hand came out so fast that I barely had time to register the slap until it was over. My face stung but it felt gratifying. She was losing her cool. She was losing her confidence. This wasn't as good as her lying dead on the side of the road like Zoey had probably intended, but I would take it.

"Don't test me, *Liam.*" The words dripped off her tongue like venom and I swallowed hard, my hands gripping the armrests of my chair tightly. I leaned backwards, away from her, but there was nowhere to go. "Did you know?"

I shook my head. "No. I didn't know," I lied. Zoey's tear stained face from the night we almost had sex flashed through my head and I closed my eyes tightly. "She never trusted me enough."

There was a long silence before she finally spoke again. "Lies," she hissed. She backed away from me and I was surprised to see a smile stretch across her face. Her voice remained low, barely above a whisper, but every word spoken with directness. Confidence. "Losing Miss Valentine is not what I wanted. I will get her back. Keep that in mind, Mr. Garrity."

A wave of panic swept through my body but I schooled my features to show nothing. I would never show anything to this woman other than complete indifference. I refused to let her know that she had such an effect on me. That she scared me "I'll do that," I replied.

Another smile stretched across her face. "Good. I have a surprise for you today, Liam."

"I'm not really interested," I managed to say. Whatever she had for me...well, it couldn't be good. And the abrupt change in subject threw me off. I hadn't seen her in days and yet she still had me on my toes. It was hard to feel in control when it was so hard to keep up with her.

"Put your shirt back on," was her only response.

I yanked the stiff brown scrub shirt over my head and ran a hand through my damp hair. It had grown so long since I had been there. It was the only indication that time had passed at all. My fingers clenched for a moment in the long strands. Razi was speaking to someone on the other side of the door. Her voice remained low so I couldn't hear anything.

She finally opened the door wider and stepped aside. I wasn't quite sure what I was looking at right away.

The girl was younger than Zoey, but not by much. Zoey had passed her nineteenth birthday while in Razi's clutches and this girl looked to be about sixteen, maybe seventeen. She was tiny, with deep, dark black hair, falling in a messy, wavy curtain down her back. Her skin was a creamy brown, and her wide brown eyes were darting around in shock. They fell on me. She immediately skittered back, looking alarmed.

I didn't want to know what caused her to have such a fear of strange men.

Razi, on the other hand, looked like Christmas had come early.

"Liam, meet Astrid," she said, sounding happy for the first time today.

Astrid's eyes met mine again and I knew she had no idea where she was or why she was here. She was completely terrified.

I knew why she was here. I knew exactly why. Razi Cylon hadn't wasted any time at all.

And I knew we, Astrid and I, were royally screwed.

CHAPTER TWO

"WELCOME TO SANCTUARY."

The first words that went through my head were *we made it*. Ash's hand slipped against mine. I wasn't entirely sure which of our hands were so sweaty but it didn't matter. We were both excited. Nervous. Scared, though neither of us would actually have admitted that. We were finally here. This was real.

And we had finally made it.

The lady stared at us for a moment. I couldn't quite figure out if she wanted us to say something else but before I could speak, she stepped forward, gesturing toward herself. "Follow me."

She turned around and started walking away, not pausing for a moment to see if we were following her. Ash's hand squeezed mine and it sent a shock of confidence and certainty through me. If Ash was with me, I knew that everything would be okay.

It had to be okay.

The two of us followed the woman as she headed down the hallway. It reminded me of Sekhmet, the top-secret medical facility I had just escaped from days before, but I tried hard not to think of that. Thoughts like that were not going to keep me sane in this unfamiliar place.

She led us through a few doors, but all it took was a few twists and turns for me to completely lose my sense of direction. There were so many doors and the hallways seemed endless. It made me nervous. Ever since the Awakened had hit, I always looked for the way out. You never knew when you needed to escape. I had lost track of our route almost the moment we had started following her. I didn't like the feeling.

I could tell Ash felt the same way. His eyes darted around, noting every detail as we took a sharp left and came face to face with a large concrete door. It was enormous and overwhelming, taking up the entire wall. The woman slid a card through a nearly invisible slot and it glided open soundlessly. Ash tugged me closer and together; we stepped through.

It crossed my mind that I should stop, ask this lady who she was. This place was unfamiliar and despite what I've heard about it from both Liam and Bert, it was still unknown. It was still scary. I opened my mouth to say something but the woman continued on and the two of us scurried to keep up with her. I exchanged looks with Ash, hoping that we weren't being led into a trap.

I gasped, when we left the short hallway leading away from the large door and entered an open corridor. It was raised high above a huge chasm. There were people everywhere, walking on different levels, moving quickly. We were in a cone, everything turning in a circle, everything made with thick, sturdy concrete. There were several levels below us stretching further and further down into darkness, and my head spun at the frightening drop. I never thought I'd had a fear of heights before this. I had grown up in the city of skyscrapers, but this was something else. There were small walls along the walkways to prevent anyone from falling over, but they were small, waist height. Not reassuring in the slightest.

There was no time to dwell on this, however. The woman moved immediately to the right and we hurried to keep up with her. Several people stared curiously as we passed by, all of them in the same black uniforms. We stood out in our neutral blues and whites. However, no one said anything. They just nodded at the woman and repeatedly said "Director" in hushed voices as they did so. This woman was obviously someone to be respected.

It was incredibly bright in the center of Sanctuary and it was a natural light too. I glanced up and saw that there was a large dome at the top, the only reminder that an outside world still existed. I knew we were underground but it felt good to see that the sun had not disappeared, not here.

It felt like ages, walking in circles, down the corridors before she finally led us into an extremely large room.

The lights in here were even brighter, so much that they were nearly painful, and came as a total shock. My hand rose to cover my eyes. When they had finally adjusted, I looked around and realized she had brought us to what looked like a hospital emergency room, an infirmary of sorts.

She led us through the main room and opened the door to a much smaller room, gesturing for us to enter. She shut the door behind her and smiled thinly, her hands clasped tightly in front of her. "Thank you for your patience. Not many get to this point without a fight."

Ash and I exchanged glances before looking back at her. "I think we're still trying to process everything," I admitted.

She nodded, understanding. "You've been through a lot." Her eyes roamed my face. A bright flush filled me, which I knew made the scar on my face stand out that much more. It stretched from just above my right eyebrow, across my nose down to the bottom of my left cheek. It was hard to miss. "You are safe here."

Neither of us answered.

"My name is Octavia. I am the director here at Sanctuary and, for the most part, people address me as Director." A small smile curled on her full lips again. "This place has existed for quite a long time, as I'm sure you've heard if you've made it this far. How did you get here?"

There was a long silence before Ash finally spoke. "We were brought here by a man named Bert Washington."

Octavia's cool demeanor faltered for a moment but she moved forward, without commenting. "We work hard here. This place was designed to sustain human life in the event of a catastrophe. This is not an easy thing to do, not with most of the outside world a mess of radiation and martial law. Everyone contributes in Sanctuary. "

Her smiled stayed in place, genuine, but her eyes stared at both of us, hard, making sure we were paying attention. "You both will be given full medical exams, to make sure you are healthy. If you aren't, we'll do our best to get you back to good health. You definitely look like you've missed a few meals. We can fix that. You'll be educated and you will work. It's not an easy life in Sanctuary, but it *is* life. We are grateful every day to have it, and we are happy to have you here."

Words got caught in my throat. We were alive and so lucky to be. The scars the two of us bore showed that struggle. I would work as hard as I needed to if it meant that I was finally safe.

Octavia stood up, wiping her palms against the clean fabric of her simple black dress. "I will leave you now. Doctors will be coming in shortly to examine you."

My heart immediately picked up its beat, slamming hard against my ribs. Going to the doctor had never bothered me before; they were just doing their job. I had never had this fear until Razi Cylon and her band of doctors. They had poked and prodded me for over a month, studying me like a bug under a microscope. I shrank back. My breaths coming short, panicked. Octavia paused in the doorway, her brow furrowed.

Ash turned, his hands reaching out for me. He gripped my face between them, forcing me to look at him. "It's fine. It's okay. You're going to be okay. I'm not going to leave you. It'll be over before you know it."

I tried to shake my head but it was stuck between his warm hands, and I felt a sense of calmness from his grip. "I don't want to."

Ash's voice came out stronger than before. "I will not leave your side. You can do this. You are the strongest person I know, Zoey. They want to make sure we are safe, and I agree. I want to make sure that after everything that has happened, you are okay. That's all that matters."

We stared at each other for a few moments, probably long enough for Octavia to feel slightly uncomfortable. She cleared her throat loudly, and Ash dropped his hands from my face.

"You were...you were at Sekhmet," she said, shock filling her voice.

There was a large lump in my throat, and I was afraid what would happen if I tried to speak so I nodded in response.

"But how?" She was looking at both of us, disbelieving. "No one gets out of there. No one does."

"We escaped," Ash explained. Octavia opened her mouth to protest but he immediately cut her off. "We had help. That's really all there is to know."

Octavia's lips pressed tightly together and her shoulders tensed for a moment. "You are safe here," she repeated. "I can promise you that." She turned again to leave, pausing to quickly look back over her shoulder. "If you two ever need anything, do not hesitate to ask. We have rules and we cannot provide everything. But we will try our best." With those words, she left the room, leaving the two of us alone.

Moments later, a doctor entered. He was young, much younger than I had expected and he smiled at the two of us, approaching carefully. I wondered if he had ever been attacked by anyone in this room before. My bets were on yes, definitely.

"I know you are both scared," he said, immediately. Neither of us said anything and he continued. "But I promise that I'll try to make it as easy as possible. For both of you."

Ash looked over at me and I nodded, swallowing hard. "Okay," I finally said. "Let's do it."

NOW

CHAPTER THREE

WHEN THE END of the world came, I doubted anyone would have ever thought that a little thing like snoring would still bother people.

News flash: it still does.

The numbers on the wall above the door reflected the only light in the small room, blinking the time at me, mocking me. It was 3:45 am and I was still not asleep. Another loud, grunting snore filled the room and I sighed, giving up. I kicked the covers off the bed and sat up, running a hand through my hair.

We had been at Sanctuary for nearly three months now and I still hadn't gotten used to the constant snoring of my roommate, Kaya. I was hoping I would eventually adapt to it and get a decent night's sleep but I wasn't holding my breath.

The nightmares probably weren't helping either.

I was safe though. I was in Sanctuary. That was all that mattered. The Awakened couldn't reach me here, even when they were haunting my dreams every single night.

They were like zombies, but worse than any nightmare we had ever conjured up. The Awakened retained the memories of when they were human, and they were clever as hell. They worked together in packs to get the one thing they craved more than anything else: human flesh. And they were fast, incredibly so, able to outrun a normal human easily. They were frightening, former versions of themselves, their skin a pale blue hue, their teeth sharped into points that could tear through skin and flesh, and eyes that were endless pools of black. They had taken nearly everyone I loved away from me leaving me scarred and beaten. I would be happy if I never had to see one ever again.

I sighed again, looking back up at the clock. Time in Sanctuary seemed to pass so slowly, the minutes ticking by felt like hours. In just a few hours, the bells would sound and I would need to wake up for another long, long day in this place.

Don't misunderstand me. I was happy to be here. Despite the fact that Sanctuary hadn't quite turned out the way I had expected, I was grateful to be safe. The alternatives were much worse than being bored all the time. I didn't want to be back on the road, fighting to survive, fighting for my next meal, running away from the endless hordes of Awakened. But I also didn't want to be under the clutches of Razi Cylon, the woman behind everything that had happened over the past year. If she'd had it her way, I would be pregnant by now, ready to repopulate the earth for her utopia. I shivered underneath the thin blanket covering my body, even though it was far from cold in this place. Everything here was regulated: our schedules, our meals, even the temperature of our room. Everything was calculated to an exact science, perfected for survival and not much else.

For so long, I had been only concerned with one thing: surviving. Seeing my best friend, my dog, my father, my mother and countless others die in front of me...all I wanted to do was live. I had a fierce obsession with living. Making sure that I had enough food in my system, making sure that I had a place to sleep, making sure that I woke up the next day...those were the priorities in my life. That's all I needed.

But now? Now I had all those things. I had to work for them, but I gladly worked for the comfort of knowing that I would receive three meals a day and that I would climb into a bed at the end of the night. I had nothing left to obsess over, nothing that seemed to give me a purpose. Instead, all I could think about was how ridiculously boring it was to live in Sanctuary.

The entire world felt like it had stopped living. We were surviving, but we weren't living anymore. A year ago, I was a senior in high school, getting great grades, waiting for college letters in the mail, cheering for the football team every Friday night and listening to bands with my best friend, Madison. Now, I was waking up every day and eating and working and learning but I wasn't going anywhere.

I was nineteen years old and I felt like I was basically dead.

But what else was I supposed to do? There was nothing left. The entire country had turned into a complete wasteland. The United States had bombed their own country into oblivion and from what I had heard since arriving at Sanctuary, the rest of the world wasn't much better. The virus had spread, jumping continents and oceans, and with no clue where it had come from or what to do about it, the world's population dwindled and turned to chaos. World leaders were dead. Marshal law was common all over the place. People were fighting to survive.

I knew I should have been focused on that, on how the world was literally crumbling from underneath itself but it was so hard to when I spent my life with the white and gray walls surrounding me at all times. I wanted to bang my head against the wall. I wanted to DO something, anything.

"Zoey, are you awake?"

I took a deep breath, closing my eyes briefly, before responding. "Yeah, I am."

There was a long pause and I wondered if Kaya had fallen asleep again. I hoped she had. She was a nice enough roommate but she had been born and raised in Sanctuary, she didn't know anything other than these walls. Which meant that she found me completely fascinating. She was shy as hell but that didn't stop her from asking me everything there was to know about the "real" world, including shopping malls, frozen yogurt and a multitude of other things I hadn't thought of in months.

She was sweet as hell and she drove me absolutely insane.

"Are you okay?" Her voice was super high-pitched, squeaky almost, which completely clashed with her Amazon stature. The first time she spoke, I thought she was kidding and had to stop myself from laughing.

I sighed, yanking the covers over my head, ready for the blinking numbers to stop staring at me. "Of course I am. Go back to sleep."

"Okay." I waited a few beats and sure enough, her snores filled the room once more. I shook my head, turning over to face the blank wall on the other side of me, ready to stare at it all night if that's what it took to fall back asleep again.

I missed Ash.

I hardly ever saw him anymore. Sanctuary had strict rules when it came to boys and girls spending time together. You could sort of see their point. While this place was absolutely gargantuan, there was still a population concern. They could not and would not allow it to run rampant. Everything here was under a strict control.

Which was why I had a stupid birth control implant in my arm, whether I wanted it or not. This had pissed me off to no end. Don't get me wrong. There was no way on earth that I actually wanted a child. I was nineteen years old and there was the whole problem with the Awakened and all that. We weren't exactly in the prime time to bring a child into the world. But putting an implant in, taking away my choice, that had pissed me off.

When we had arrived, it was immediately apparent that my relationship with Ash was weird. It was unusual because that sort of thing wasn't normal for those who had grown up in Sanctuary their whole lives, like Kaya. The older generations had fallen in love, married, and had children. But for their children, love and companionship and dating were foreign concepts. Relationships were more business deals than emotional connections. Ash and I obviously fell into the latter category.

Kaya was absolutely fascinated by Ash as well, which amused him to no end. She was a nervous wreck around him too. She usually dropped whatever it was that she was holding if he came anywhere near us and he didn't make it any easier on her either. He teased her and made her blush like crazy.

But despite the fact that Ash was my boyfriend and I was implanted with the tiny device to keep little versions of me and Ash entering the world, I wasn't allowed to spend too much time with him. Girls and boys were kept separate most of the time, and we definitely were not allowed to enter each other's dorms.

I missed being able to touch Ash, kiss him, do things we had been able to do before we arrived here….

I shifted uncomfortably in my bed as a flush filled my body. There had been too many nights like this and I was so tired of it.

CHAPTER FOUR

"YOU LOOK LIKE shit."

Ash's voice was loud in the large cafeteria, which was full of Sanctuary citizens.

I rolled my eyes. I would have preferred much sweeter words coming from my boyfriend this early in the morning, especially before I'd had breakfast, but I couldn't deny the shivers that went up my spine at the sound of that deep voice. It had been months since I had finally figured out how insanely in love I was with Ash Matthews, flaws and all, but it was still new and exciting and perfect.

Well, almost perfect.

Which made staying away from him most of the day completely awful.

"Thanks, baby. You're so sweet." The sarcasm dripped from my lips and he laughed loudly. A few heads turned our way and his smiled stretched across his face even wider.

Kaya and I slid into seats next to Ash and his roommate, Corbin. They both had half empty plates in front of them. Kaya's face was a brilliant shade of puce and I resisted the urge to scoot my tray away from her. I didn't wanted to be anywhere near the splash zone if it came down to that. Why she always seemed to look like she was about to vomit around this boy was beyond me.

Technically, according to the never-ending rules of Sanctuary, girls and boys were supposed to sit on opposite sides of the table. The two of us weren't eager to break rules here. Though no one had ever said that you'd get kicked out for breaking rules, I wasn't about to take the chance and end up on the run again. However, this small act of rebellion was Ash being Ash. Even when he was trying to follow all the rules, he still couldn't help but break just one or two. His arm snaked around my waist, pulling me in closer to him, and his lips pressed against my neck, just below my ear.

"Didn't sleep well?" he whispered in my ear. I shook my head, and he placed an affectionate kiss against my forehead. He turned back to his tray of food but the tingle of his kiss still lingered and I couldn't help the stupid goofy grin on my face.

Kaya fidgeted next to me, her mouth screwed up. She was always incredibly uncomfortable around us. Affection wasn't super common in Sanctuary and sometimes it was hard to remember that the public displays of affections needed to be kept at a minimum around her.

But to be fair, judging by the way her eyes constantly darted over to Corbin, I knew she wouldn't mind those kinds of displays if it were between the two of them...

"She kept waking up last night," Kaya cut in. She reached for the salt sitting in front of us, and knocked it over, sending a spray of white crystal across the linoleum table. Her face flushed a brilliant tomato red and her eyes darted toward Corbin, who was too busy reading the book he had propped up against his orange juice. He was always so wonderfully clueless.

Corbin had come to Sanctuary much in the same way that Ash and I had. His parents had died in the bombing of Seattle while he and his friends had been driving home for the holidays. The four of them had survived for a few months before coming across someone from Sanctuary who brought

19

them in. there was no college system in Sanctuary, just a basic education before you went on to be trained in some sort of job field within the community, but that didn't stop Corbin from reading every single book he could get his hands on.

I took a deep breath. "I just couldn't sleep. No big deal." I shoved a spoonful of oatmeal in my mouth. Everything in Sanctuary was healthy. No more hamburgers or tacos or any of that. Not that I had had a lot of that in the past year anyway but I was tired of oatmeal and grains and flavorless chicken and salmon.

I know. Perspective. I was working on it.

Despite all that, I had gained weight back again. I was still much smaller that I was back in New York, before all of this. I was practically skin and bones. Occasionally I would run my fingertips across my stomach in the shower, amazed to feel the bones underneath my skin. I had never been able to do that before.

"That's true. She didn't wake up screaming. That's definitely a good thing, right?" No one answered and Kaya looked up from her oatmeal at the rest of us. "What?" Her eyes grew wide. "Oh, that was a bad thing to say, right? That was rude, wasn't it? I am so sorry, Zoey!"

My fingers clenched around my spoon but I forced a smile. "It's okay, Kaya. Really."

It was embarrassing enough to have nightmares all the time. It was even more embarrassing to have them around your completely clueless and tactless roommate. It hadn't happened in a few nights, but most nights I woke up screaming, coated in a cold sweat that never seemed to go away.

The doctors at Sanctuary said that I had posttraumatic stress disorder. I wasn't so sure but I wasn't the expert here so I took their diagnosis with what I could. All I did know was that sometimes it felt like the walls were closing in on me and I couldn't breath and I couldn't get out. It wasn't normal behavior and I'd never felt like that before but I didn't know what else to do about it. I didn't want to drown underneath all the panic.

"Where are you working tonight?" Ash asked me.

I swallowed and looked up at him. He looked so different from the boy I had grown up knowing my whole life. The boy who was popular and roamed the hallways in designer clothes made to look like he didn't care at all. The boy who smiled and winked at girls and no one thought it was cheesy in the slightest. That boy was gone.

But Ash Matthews was still there, despite all that he had gone through. His deep dark brown hair was not styled to perfection anymore. It had grown long and unruly since being on the run. His eyes were still bright and impossibly blue. Even in the mundane black uniforms that we were all given to wear, he looked like the boy I loved. He was beautiful, plain and simple, scars and all. "Laundry. What about you?"

The smile that stretched across his face was anything but innocent. "Laundry as well."

"Well, isn't that a coincidence," I said, under my breath. My skin tingled where he was pressed against me on the bench. Now I would be anticipating chores all day.

After breakfast, I headed out with the rest of them toward class. Everything was basic and essential, or so they said. We took history, economics, politics, English and math. We even took different languages, like Spanish and mandarin, which didn't feel so basic or necessary but I fumbled my way through them like everyone else. Everything here had a purpose, even if I didn't know that purpose.

Classes dragged. They always did. Most of the things they were teaching us were things I had already learned back at home at St. Joseph's. There were no grade levels; there was no need for that. All the children were grouped together, all the preteens, and all those high school age.

Which meant reading *The Scarlet Letter* again, even though I'd been through that horrible monstrosity before.

"Miss Valentine?"

I startled in my chair and looked up at the teacher. My eyes narrowed as they always did in this class. "Yes?"

Caspar looked at me with those sad eyes and I deflated a little. He missed my mom, a lot, and I knew he sometimes saw her in me. It must have been hard sitting in front of me, knowing that his wife was dead, buried in a grave back in Nebraska, and the only remnant he had left of her was me. I tried to hate him less but it was an ongoing battle.

Imagine my surprise, when I arrived in class a few days after arriving here, learning that the teacher in charge of English was none other than my stepfather, who my mom had been convinced was dead. He had managed to get out of Los Angeles before the bombs hit and was making his way to Nebraska, to the house he and my mother had shared, when he was picked up by Sanctuary.

I had yet to ask him what kept him from continuing on to Nebraska. He had no idea of she was alive or dead until I had arrived here and it drove me insane not knowing why he hadn't just left Sanctuary to go and get her. Sure, it would have been a fruitless mission but he didn't know that.

I hadn't had the courage to ask him yet. I was afraid that I would just start yelling if I did.

Apparently, though, being a published author gave him enough credit to teach English and now I had to see him every single day.

Every. Single. Day.

I had to give him this, though. Whatever history had existed between myself and my mother, and by default, him, whatever drama had been caused by their affair and eventually marriage, he had loved her very much. Having to tell him that she had died, that she was buried in the backyard of their farmhouse in Constance, was one of the hardest things I'd ever had to do. It had put a sort of unspoken truce between us but it was hard not to feel unhappy when I was around him.

"What" I asked, my voice low. There were titters and whispers around the room and I rolled my eyes. "I'm sorry. I must have missed your question, sir."

"We were discussing the idea of fault in the novel. Who do you think is at fault for the events that take place in the novel?"

I wished for a moment that I still had my notebooks, tucked in a drawer, back at home. Those were nothing but bits of rubble and radiation now, just like everything else I had left back in New York. "Nobody. Everybody. You could argue for any of them."

Caspar's eyebrows rose. "Why do you say that?"

"Because you can argue that its Hester's fault or Arthur's or even just place the blame on the archaic Puritan ideas they had. But then maybe it's no one's fault. And also why place blame on anyone? Sometimes shit just happens and we deal with it. Move on."

"Language, Zoey," Caspar said. "Although, that's an interesting idea you bring up; moving on. Do you think it's easy for a person to move on from something that hurts a lot of people?" He stared at me, pointedly, and I flushed. There were a few silent moments before he turned away from me and engaged in conversation with someone else.

Lunch was a mundane meal, as per usual. A cup of tuna mixed with light mayo, carrot and celery sticks, some crackers and a small glass of orange juice. It was just enough to get us through the rest of the day until dinner before chores.

I was folding shirts in the corner of the room when Ash walked over to me, grabbed a shirt from the pile and started folding with me. He stayed like that, in silence, as he folded three or four shirts before he finally whispered, "Follow me."

I dropped the shirt in my hands and followed him through the room. We snuck out the door and down the hallway. Ash's fingers circled my wrist as he opened a nondescript door and pulled me through.

We were in a supply closet. It looked like mostly medical supplies. It was dark until Ash flipped the switch and a low glow filled the small space.

"Well, this is cozy," I remarked, looking around.

"Hey, it's the best I could do under short notice," Ash shot back. "I scoped this place out all week." We stared at each other for a long moment before we both burst out laughing and I practically launched myself at him. It felt damn good to be in his arms and I couldn't help how happy I felt.

It wasn't the first time we had snuck off and had these moments with each other but it was getting harder and harder to make it happen. There weren't a lot of places in Sanctuary for privacy and it was hard to get away from the endless duties we were committed to by living here. We took every single moment that we could to spend with each other. I never knew when I would get another one.

"God, I miss you," Ash said, his cheek pressed tightly against the top of my head.

"How is it possible that I see you every single day but you feel miles away?" I asked, folding myself tighter into him. "Sneaking off every once in awhile just isn't enough."

"I know we're safe and all that, but god I hate that I can never see you or spend time with you or even just hug you."

"Agreed."

"How are you doing? Really?" Ash asked, pulling away from me a little bit so he could look me in the eye.

"I'm fine," I assured him quickly. Ash was there when the doctors talked to me about PTSD so I wasn't surprised that he looked doubtful, his eyebrows jumping high on his forehead. I laughed. "Really, I am."

"No more nightmares?"

I squirmed uncomfortably. "Not…often."

"Zoey…"

"Don't 'Zoey' me. You're the only person here that doesn't look at me like I'm suddenly going to go on a bender or something. I'm fine. I'm not going to break."

"I know you're not," he inserted. "Sometimes I just…I forget that. But that doesn't mean I'm not worried about you, Zoey. That doesn't mean I'm not going to care that you're still alone in that bed, scared."

My lips pressed tightly together and my fingers clenched tightly at his waist. "I'll be okay. I promise."

"I know you will. If there's anything I'm sure of, it's you." He winked at me and I smirked. The fact that the Ash Matthews charm was still in full force, even after the awful year that we had just had, meant that there was some normalcy in the world. "Now come here."

His lips came down on mine and I answered with enthusiasm, my hands wrapping tightly around the back of his neck. A low rumble went through his chest, as his hands reached for the hem of my shirt. His hands were cool on my warm skin and I pressed myself tighter to him as my tongue traced a quick sweep of his lower lip. He groaned loudly, and lifted me up easily, placing me on a cart tucked against the wall. Supplies went everywhere, but neither of us really noticed.

My heart was beating fast in my chest as he placed a few light bites across my collarbone. A low moan escaped my lips and a smile stretched across his face as his hand pressed tight against my ribcage. My skin burned at the contact, even with the clothes between us. I grabbed the hem of his shirt and started yanking it over his head, tossing it somewhere behind him. My hands skimmed over his hard chest, loving the way the goosebumps raised under my fingertips. Ash deepened the kiss, his fingers tight on the back of my neck.

"Ash?" I managed to say in between the ridiculously amazing kisses he was laying on me.

"What is it, beautiful?" he whispered, his lips tracing an impossibly sweet trail along my jawline.

"I love you," I said, my fingernails digging into his skin as my hands gripped his arms.

The smile he gave me was like a thousand fireworks in the dimly lit closet. His hands ran down my spine, causing little gasps to escape my lips, before they landed on my waist. He tugged me closer to him. "I love you. Always."

There was no more space between us after that. His hands slipped below the waistband of my pants and I lost my breath as he brushed over exactly the right spot. I could feel him pressed hard against me and I panted as his tongue danced with mine. I raked my nails against his skin, causing him to moan against my mouth.

My hands were in the middle of tugging his pants down when there was a sudden flood of light in the supply closet. We pulled away and looked over in the direction of the door. There were several people peering in the doorway at us, one of them the old cranky man who was in charge of the laundry room.

"We were looking for you. So glad we found you both safe and sound." The sarcasm dripped off the old man's lips like vinegar and I had the decency to look a little ashamed. "Mr. Matthews, please put your shirt back on, and both of you return to your duties."

The door slammed shut and we were left together for a moment longer, though I knew they would give us thirty seconds at the most. I pressed my palms flat against his bare chest and sighed, frustrated. "This sucks."

Ash pressed his lips back against my mine and laid a kiss on me that nearly had me saying "screw the rules" before he pulled away and found his shirt where I had tossed it. "It won't always be like this, Zoey." He offered his hand to me and I smiled, sadly, taking it and letting him lead me out of the closet.

CHAPTER FIVE

"ZOEY, DID YOU ever see the ocean?"

I closed my eyes briefly, putting down the book I had been attempting to read in my lap. I'd read it a million times. It had meant the world to me when Ash had stolen Bert's copy of *The Mists of Avalon*, knowing that it was my favorite book, but it was hard to read when it was all I really did in here.

We were in our room, enjoying what Sanctuary liked to call "free time". Basically, this was a two-hour block after dinner and chores where we could do whatever we pleased, which was a loose interpretation of what it actually was. We were mostly limited to reading, staring at the ceiling, playing board games in the library or staring at the wall.

I was glad that I really, really liked to read.

"Of course I have."

Kaya thought about that for a moment. "What is it like? Is it cold? What does it smell like? Are the waves really loud? All we have are pictures and videos and I've always wondered what it was really like and…"

"Do you think you'll ever actually say anything to Corbin?" I asked, interrupting her babble. I had to cut her off. If I didn't, she would ramble on for ages and I simply wasn't in the mood for it tonight.

She startled in her bed and turned to me, her face pale. Her tongue peeked out between her lips as she regarded me nervously. "What are you talking about?"

"Don't act stupid, Kaya. You're one of the smartest people I've ever met."

This was definitely not a lie or even an embellishment. When you lived in this sort of sheltered underground society, there wasn't much to do besides work and learn. Kaya may have been clueless on a lot of things, like talking to a boy, and anything involving the outside world, but she was insanely smart and it was sometimes incredibly intimidating talking to her.

Until she asked about MTV or something. Then I just wanted to smother her with my pillow.

Kaya sighed, covering her face with her hands. "I hate being obvious."

I couldn't help it; I laughed. Kaya looked up at me and chanced a smile. It was not often that I smiled or laughed in this place, especially around anyone that wasn't Ash, so I knew it made her happy to see it. "You *are* obvious. Luckily enough for you, Corbin seems to be pretty damn clueless."

"He's just so…perfect. He has those honey colored eyes and those cute brown curls and I just…" She sighed again, and flopped backward on her bed. "I've never felt like this before. It's definitely an unusual feeling."

"You have a crush on a boy," I pointed out. "It's really normal, I swear."

"Not in Sanctuary," she replied.

I rolled my eyes. "We have a stupid implant in our arm to keep us from having babies, not feelings. What do they think is going to happen?"

Kaya shrugged, as much as she could, considering she was lying down on her bed. She stared at the ceiling for a long moment. "What does it feel like?"

28

My feet dangled over the side of the bed as I regarded her. "What does what feel like?"

She fidgeted nervously for a moment. "You know, being with someone?"

I felt a flush fill my cheeks. "I don't know if I want to talk about that."

Kaya sat up quickly, looking horrified. "Oh, no, not like that, Zoey. Oh, I'm so embarrassed! That's not what I meant!" She covered her face again and groaned loudly, her squeaky voice echoing in our room. "Sanctuary *does* teach about that, you know."

I slumped in relief, immensely glad that I did not have to talk about sex with Kaya. It was bad enough having to describe what prom was like to her. "What did you mean then?"

She contemplated it for a moment. "Ash loves you."

A flush filled my cheeks again and I smiled, despite my efforts not to. It had been a few months since Ash had first told me that he loved me but it didn't get old. "He does."

"What does it feel like?"

I didn't miss a beat. "It feels incredible. The last year has been awful. It's just been...so awful. I've lost everyone I've ever known except him. He's always been there. And we've stuck together through all of this and still ended up together. He protects me and I protect him. He's what keeps me pushing to survive. I don't know if I would have ever survived without him."

"I'm jealous." The words were simple, and easy to miss, even in the near silence of our room. But our room was small and there was nowhere else for the sound to hide. She brought her knees up to her chest and regarded me with her large coffee colored eyes. She was so different from Madison, my best friend, but there were things that reminded me of her. Her deep black hair, her almond shaped eyes, turned down at the corners, the way her lower lip was just a tad fuller than the upper. She was taller, quieter, but she sometimes reminded me so much of Maddie, it hurt.

"Don't be. I'm so lucky to have Ash, Kaya. I am so lucky. And I wouldn't trade him for anything," I said, firmly. "But both of us would have killed to have the safety that you've had for your entire life. We've lost our parents, our friends, everyone. You've been very lucky to be tucked away, never having to see the Awakened."

Her eyes grew wide at the mention of the creatures that were still ravaging the entire country. "Are they scary?"

I took a deep breath and when I released it, it came out shaky and uneven. "They are the scariest things I've ever seen in my life."

Kaya didn't say anything after this and I wondered if she was done with the conversation. She had changed the subject away from her and Corbin, and I knew she was confident that I'd forgotten. I'd noticed though but I decided to let her off the hook, at least for the night.

I was going to bring it up again eventually though. Watching the two of them circle each other was sometimes the only form of entertainment I had, and I would continue to take advantage of it.

Instead my mind was on the Awakened. I hadn't seen any since I was at Sekhmet. when I had learned that they were actual creations, accidental, but still created by Razi Cylon to take down everyone in her path to create a utopia. They were terrifying, monsters from every worst nightmare. I had killed so many of them but they had taken so much from me as well. They had killed both of my parents, they had taken my body and turned it into something I barely recognized some days. My fingers stroked the raised scar on my face, absentmindedly.

When I arrived at Sanctuary, all of the doctors and nurses had clucked over the ravaged scar on my face. It hadn't healed cleanly and my mom hadn't quite known what to do with it. It was a miracle that I hadn't experienced any infection, though I felt like that was due to the doctors at Sekhmet. Those guys had created the virus that had wiped out most of the population. They'd created the Awakened. A large scar on a girl's face was nothing compared to that.

But despite that, my face had been sewn back together by an eighteen-year-old boy who had no idea what he was doing. At the time, I hadn't been picky. I was more concerned about not bleeding to death. The doctors here had stared at it, poked and prodded it, but they couldn't do anything about it. It was there to stay and I was slowing learning to get used to the stares from the Sanctuary-born residents. It was hard sometimes to look at my own reflection in the mirror though. It was not a pretty sight.

"Zoey?"

I closed my eyes, trying as hard as I could to resist picking up my pillow and tossing it at her. "Yeah?"

"Is Ash a good kisser?"

I laughed again, and my eyes flew open. She smiled sheepishly at me, and my irritation disappeared, like it always did. She was just too easy to like, even when she was driving me up the wall. "He's an excellent kisser."

Kaya smirked at me. "Yeah, I'm sure. I heard you guys got caught in a supply closet the other day."

I shrugged, feeling a jolt in my stomach at the memory. "Totally worth it."

It was Kaya's turn to roll her eyes. "Right. Maybe just be a little more careful next time you guys sneak off…"

"Thanks, Kaya. I'll do that." My words were punctuated with our lights flickering on and off. The clock on the wall showed that it was exactly 9 pm. "Right on time."

She reached for the pad on the wall that turned off the lights. "You'll get used to it."

I tugged at the thin comforter on my bed and climbed underneath, pulling it up to my chin. "I certainly hope so."

"Good night, Zoey."

"Good night, Kaya."

***

"ZOEY? ZOEY, WAKE up."

There was a hand shaking my shoulder and I startled when I woke, throwing my hands out. My fingers made contact and I grabbed on tightly, and yanked.

"Hey, it's me! Kaya. It's Kaya."

The light switched on and I blinked rapidly in the sudden brightness. The clock above the door read 4 am and I was momentarily surprised that I managed to fall asleep at a decent time. Which made getting woken up like this that much worse. "What is going on?"

"There's someone at the door for you." Kaya looked nervous, biting her full bottom lip. Her hands were fidgeting with the hem of her regulation pajamas; a long sleeve gray shirt and white sweatpants.

I blinked a few more times, staring at her. "Excuse me? There's someone at the door? For me?" I ran my fingers through my bedridden hair and stared at her. "Who?"

"The Director," she whispered, her eyes wide. Her expression told me that the Director visiting someone's private quarters was not a regular occurrence. I hurried out of bed, pushing back the covers. I made sure my pajamas were at least on straight before heading to the door and pressing my wristband to the plate.

The wristband was my life at Sanctuary. It contained all of my personal information, including everything about my health. It gave me access to my room and other places that I needed to be and it was the device that kept me updated with my daily schedule. When I had been granted one, after my original medical examinations, I learned that it didn't come off and it was water resistant, amongst other things. The first few weeks, it had chaffed and I had rolled on top of it in my sleep many times, but now I was used to it.

The doors slid open. Octavia was standing just outside the doorway. She looked perfect as usual, not at all like it was four in the morning. She wore black, the way everyone else wore black in this place, but she didn't wear the same nondescript shirts and pants we did. She always managed to be in a dress or skirt, not a wrinkle or rumple in them.

"Director," I addressed her. "This is a surprise. Is there something wrong?"

"I apologize for waking you at such an hour, Zoey," she said, a concerned look on her face. "But this is an urgent matter. Please follow me."

I looked over my shoulder at Kaya, who looked frightened. My stomach dropped but I turned back to Octavia and nodded. "Of course."

She led me down the hallway and out of the resident floors. We turned down into an unfamiliar corridor and ended up at a door, with a special access pad. I hadn't seen one of these since arriving at Sanctuary. She pressed her thumb to it and it opened soundlessly. Behind the door was an elevator and we hurried inside.

The elevator traveled up and up until it finally came to a halt. When we exited, we were met with Octavia's second in command, Patrick, who was standing with a rumpled Ash. My stomach dropped even more.

"What's wrong? Are you okay?" I asked, rushing toward him.

Ash's arms reached out and quickly wrapped around me. I pressed my face against his chest, inhaling his scent. "I'm fine. I didn't know you would be here. Are you okay?"

I pulled away slightly and looked up at him. "Yeah. Yeah, I'm fine." I looked over at Octavia and Patrick. "What is going on?"

"Please, follow us," was the only answer we received as we rushed after them. We didn't have to go very far until we turned into a very large office. Octavia crossed the room and sat down at the chair behind the desk, while Patrick perched on the edge of it. Two empty chairs were in front, obviously for us. Ash collapsed in one seat and pulled me into his lap. Both Octavia and Patrick stared at us, but I took comfort in Ash's warmth. Whatever was about to happen, I was happy he was there.

"We received a...package an hour ago. It was accompanied with a note. The note was addressed to you. We took the package immediately, and you will receive that in just a moment." Octavia reached for an envelope on the desk and handed it to me.

My fingers shook as I took the envelope. My name was written in perfect handwriting on the front. I stared at it before using a fingernail to break the seal. A note fell out, on a small square of cardstock. My hands gripped it tightly as my eyes roamed the page. They widened and I gasped. "No. NO. This can't be real."

"Zoey?" Ash's voice was low in my ear. When I didn't answer, he grabbed the note out of my hand and read it out loud. "Zoey, I hope you enjoy my gift. I am so looking forward to seeing you again. Fondly..." He paused and his face paled. "Razi Cylon." Ash's fists clenched, the note crumpling in his hand. "What the fuck?"

"Language, Mr. Matthews," Patrick said, but Ash didn't listen.

"This is a joke, right? It's not real. Dr. Razi Cylon is dead. She can't be writing notes to Zoey because she's dead. I saw her die. I saw her get shot."

"You yourself were shot at the moment that this happened, Mr. Matthews," Octavia pointed out. "Forgive me if your witness is not taken as fact."

"I, however, was not shot," I cut in, my voice shaking. "I saw her get shot. Bert shot her in the *throat*. How could she even survive that?"

"Razi Cylon has some of the best doctors in the world at her facility. It would not be impossible that she survived. This is also her handwriting. That much is true."

My breathing grew erratic and for a moment, the world went black. It was like every nightmare came to life. She was alive. The past three months of safety were nothing but a farce. She was alive. She would never stop. She would never stop until I was dragged, kicking and screaming, back into her underground hellhole. She would never stop until I was in her control again. "She can't be. She just can't be."

Ash's hand rubbed my back again and again in circles. His warm palm against my back was a source of comfort and I focused on that, not on the fact that my world was crumbling down around me. "What was the package? What is this gift?"

It was the only moment that Octavia showed anything more than complete calmness. "I think it would be better to show you. Perhaps we can understand the meaning of it more." She gestured toward the guard at the door and he opened it. Someone stepped in and I nearly fell off Ash's lap.

He was beaten, broken. There were bruises along his jawline and he looked much smaller than the last time I had seen him. His hair was longer and he was barely standing. But I knew him. I would never forget that face.

I jumped up, nearly sprinting across the room. "Liam. *Liam.*"

He looked up at me, as if he didn't recognized me. His eyes were blurry and unfocused and I wondered what on earth they had done to him at Sekhmet since I had escaped. I looked up the guard who had escorted him accusingly but he didn't even flinch.

Liam started to lose his balance and I reached for him, catching him before he fell to the ground. The guard remained unhelpful as I struggled to keep Liam upright.

Ash jumped up from his seat and rushed over to rescue me. The two of us each grabbed an arm and helped Liam into one of the chairs we had just vacated. He collapsed in it, slumped over.

"What's wrong with him?" I demanded, looking over at Octavia and Patrick.

"We think he was given a heavy sedative," Octavia explained. She looked neither upset nor concerned about this. "He was unconscious when we found him at our entrance."

"You think?" My voice rose even higher. My fingers were in a vice grip around Liam's wrist, relieved that I still felt the steady beat of his heart beneath the pad of my thumb. "Why wasn't he given a medical examination as soon as he was found?"

"We didn't know who he was or what his purpose was in being here. He's wearing a Sekhmet emblem on his clothes." Octavia showed no emotion at my raised voice. She simply studied me from over the desk as I glared.

"He could be hurt! He could be sick! And you just dragged him in here. What is wrong with you?"

"Zoey."

I looked up at Ash, who was shaking his head. I could see my own anger reflected in his ocean blue eyes, but his features remained smooth and calm. He gestured ever so slightly to Liam and I immediately understood. This was about Liam. Liam and Sekhmet were the things I needed to focus on. I nodded in response and scooted myself closer to him.

"Liam, honey, can you hear me?"

Eyelashes fluttered for a moment and his eyes met mine. There was a brief moment of confusion and then a flash of recognition shone through. ""Zoey."

36

Relief flooded through my veins at the simple sound of my name leaving his lips. "Yes, it's me. Zoey. It's Zoey."

Liam took a couple deep gulps of air before he raised his head a bit more. "Where the hell am I?"

I hesitated. "What do you remember?"

He frowned. He looked so lost, like he wasn't sure of anything. "I was at Sekhmet with...but now I'm not. I was going through a routine check and then...then I woke up here." His hand scratched his thigh absentmindedly. His blonde hair was long, longer than I had ever seen it and was sticking up in all directions. Brown Sekhmet scrubs hung loosely on his thin frame.

I looked over at Octavia and Patrick. "He was knocked unconscious at Sekhmet. They did that to us all the time. But now he's awake." Liam swayed and I winced. "Well, mostly awake. How is this possible? How long has he been here?" Neither answered and annoyance filled me. "How long has he been here?"

"Since the afternoon."

"The afternoon? As in, hours ago?" I shrieked. "And you still haven't taken him to a doctor? And you woke me up at 4 in the morning to show me that he was here? What on earth is wrong with you?"

"We were waiting for him to wake up," Octavia said, slowly, as if to a child. "We wanted to question him first."

"And did he give you anything useful in his drug stupor?" I asked, sarcastically.

"Zoey. Zoey, where am I?" Liam repeated, his voice clearer than before.

My mouth opened and then closed. I sent a pleading look over at my boyfriend, who nodded.

"Hey. Liam. Do you remember me?" Ash asked.

Liam looked between the both of us and there was a ghost of a smile on his lips. I was surprised he remembered how to

37

do it. "Of course. You guys are together. I'm glad. I'm glad you made it out together."

"Not without a few hiccups," Ash remarked, drily, his hand running over his ribs where he had been shot during our escape. I wondered if he even realized he was doing it. "You're at Sanctuary. You made it."

Russet colored eyebrows shot high up on his forehead. "I made it." There was a super long pause before he spoke again. "My parents?"

My heart sunk in my chest. One of the first things I had done when I arrived at Sanctuary was inquire about Liam's parents. I had been so pleased to find out that the two of them had both made it here. Sadly, not both of them had survived. "Your mom is here. She's safe, even works in the infirmary, which apparently is a big deal here. But Memphis…" My eyes squeezed shut. I never thought I would have to deliver this news to him. "I'm so sorry, Liam."

I wasn't sure what I had expected but when Liam stayed silent, I looked at Ash, worried. Then I remembered. Ash, coming over to my house, collapsing on my staircase, beyond words. He had reacted so similarly when his parents had died.

Liam moved suddenly, his hands gripping the armrests tightly. His eyes looked wild and they darted around the room in panic. "We have to go to Sekhmet. We have to go now."

The words caused a rupture of fear to go shooting from my heart all the way through my veins and down to my toes. It had been nearly four months since I had escaped from that literal hell on earth and I still felt like throwing up every time I heard that word. The last thing I ever wanted to do was go back to that place.

"Why on earth would you want to go back there?" Patrick asked, his pale gray eyes narrowed in confusion as he regarded Liam.

The note that had been addressed to me was still a crumpled mess in Ash's hand and I reached for it, smoothing it out the best I could. I handed it to Liam, who took it wordlessly. "Is this from her? Is she alive?"

He studied it for a long moment, reading it over more than once, judging by the way his eyes roamed over the page. He pulled his wrist out from under my grip and slipped his fingers between mine, squeezing tightly. "She's alive, Zoey. She is very much alive."

I felt my knees give in a little and I nearly collapsed on the chair beside him. "We can't go back in there. I can't go back there, Liam. Why would you even want that?"

Liam's eyes were desperate as they met each of ours in turn. "We need to get there. You don't know the kind of control she has." He sighed, raking his shaking hands through his hair. "And I need to get Astrid out of there."

CHAPTER SIX

LIAM DIDN'T SPEAK for the rest of the night. He had exhausted all that was left inside of him. Octavia had him cleared to be escorted into the infirmary and the reunion between him and his mother was enough to make tears spring to my eyes. One of the Sanctuary doctors looked him over, with Julia hovering the entire time. They determined that he wasn't seriously injured in any way and he was taken to the room he would be sharing with his mother. We were all cleared from breakfast and morning classes.

I didn't see him again until I finally woke up and got ready to go down to lunch.

I had a nightmare. It was much of the same, like most nightmares I'd had since I had come to Sanctuary. I dreamt of the small room I had been locked in at Sekhmet. I dreamt of needles and treadmills and Razi Cylon's cold, calculating stare. I dreamt of Liam and the way we had desperately clung to each other. I dreamt of Ash's blood all over my hands, and the way he shook in my arms as he went into shock. I dreamt of the tiny black teeth dripping with flesh. I dreamt of a sharp knife cutting into the softness of my face.

I woke up, screaming. Luckily, I was in the room alone so there was no way for Kaya to know and there was no way for her to tell anyone about it. I splashed cold water over my face in our shared bathroom before dressing for the day. Everyone in Sanctuary wore the same uniform. We were given two sets of clothes each week; a basic black shirt, short or long sleeve, our choice. Long black pants that absorbed heat but kept you cool at the same time. Sturdy black boots. Sometimes I felt like I would fit in quite well at a punk concert back home or something.

Liam was waiting right outside my door when I was finally ready to lave and I shrieked as I bumped into him. No one stayed in the resident corridors during the day and I hadn't expected to see anyone here.

"Boys aren't exactly allowed in the girl's residence halls."

He raised one eyebrow. "So I've heard. I didn't realize that until I left the room I'm sharing with Mom. Family areas, male areas, female areas…this place is not what I thought…" He trailed off, looking pensive for a moment.

I studied him. He looked like he had gotten some much needed sleep but he still bore dark circles under his eyes, and there were still the yellow marks of fading bruises in several places that I could see. And I didn't even know what lay beneath his clothing. "How much did you know about this place before you came here?"

He lifted one shoulder slightly before it fell back into place. "Not much. Just what my grandfather told me. I don't know how much I believed but he was so sure. I kept wondering if there was more that he just never told us." A breath escaped his lips, and his long bangs fluttered in the movement. "And here we are."

"Here we are." I hesitated. I had so many questions for him. I wanted to know how Razi had survived being shot in the *freakin'* throat. I wanted to know who Astrid was. I wanted to know what Sekhmet had planned. I had been worried and anxious about what they could accomplish without Razi Cylon but now that I knew she was alive…I was terrified.

Liam, however, didn't look like he was ready to talk about it so I kept my mouth shut. I shuffled in place for a moment, not sure what to do or say. It had been so long since I'd seen Liam, and we'd had an interesting time together to say the least. Razi had forced us together and I had taken complete advantage of the situation. I glanced at Liam, whose bright blonde hair and blue eyes stood out against the darkness of his clothing, my cheeks burned with embarrassment.

"So," Liam finally said. "Want to show me where a guy can get some food?"

I shook my head, clearing my thoughts. "Right. Of course. Let's go."

We made our way out of the resident dormitories, which were the fifth floor of Sanctuary. All the residents that lived here ended their days in these rooms. They were divided into three sections; one for families, one for men and one for women.

Sanctuary was large, and everything was divided perfectly. Each floor had a purpose and went in descending order from the top dome, which let in the only source of sunlight. The first floor held all of Sanctuary's vehicles, which were a lot more than I had expected. Cars, SUVs, large passenger vans, even some bulletproof cars that were just the cherry on top of the large supply of transportation options that were housed there. There were even a few small planes and a handful of helicopters. Sanctuary was prepared and it reminded me a lot of the aboveground level in Sekhmet.

The second level was where the cafeteria and kitchens were. All the food production took place on that level, mostly because it was the one closest to the surface. They used synthetic sunlight in Sanctuary for the most part but if they could get the real thing, they did it. It only made sense to have that level as close to the outside world as possible. Refrigerators, freezers, livestock pastures and a lot of crops took up majority of the level. Everything Sanctuary needed to feed its population was housed there.

The third floor was the weapons artillery. Or so I had heard. Most of the doors on the third floor were closed off to everyday civilians like me. Part of surviving should the worst happen involved protection, so this was where weapons were stored and where the guards and patrols were trained. Guards stayed mostly indoors while patrols kept an eye out above. Patrols kept Awakened from wandering too close to Sanctuary, corralled those looking for it on purpose and kept an eye out for Sekhmet soldiers.

Fourth floor was for the classrooms where everyone went to learn. And it was more than just the children learning. This is where adults could learn skills as well, whether it was learning more about politics and government to help run Sanctuary, to become a teacher or to learn medical skills to be a part of the infirmary. All the learning took place on this level.

I was explaining all of this to Liam as we made our way up to the cafeteria. There were elevators in Sanctuary but they weren't used unless necessary. They were a great source of energy and were avoided for the most part. There weren't a lot of stairs so it was just a lot of spiraling walkways. I spent the first few weeks feeling nauseous from all the spinning and my legs protested at the amount of exercise they were getting. Now they still burned but the muscles I had built up were getting used to it.

We pushed our way through the double doors leading into the cafeteria. There was a hush when we walked in and I remembered the whispers that had broken out when Ash and I had made our way into this room for the first time. I held my head high and walked forward with purpose, hoping that Liam would follow me.

He did. He stayed right behind me as I made my way to the trays. He copied my every movement, picking up a tray and utensils. He was right behind me as I made my way to the window where they dispensed our food. The cafeteria workers there held out their hands for our wristbands, and scanned them, before dispensing lunch onto our trays.

When Liam's wristband was scanned, the cafeteria workers added a little extra to his tray. He looked over at me questioningly and I shrugged. I led him through the crowd of tables to the one that I usually occupied with Ash, Kaya, Corbin and some of the other younger people here. Eyes followed us as we passed but no one said anything and almost everyone returned to their food once we'd cleared their view.

I slid onto the bench next to Ash, and gestured for Liam to sit across from me next to Corbin, who didn't even notice. Kaya's face flushed at his arrival and she looked over at me curiously. I shook my head, ducking to pay attention to the food. I would have to explain Liam to her later. Which meant I also had to explain Sekhmet and my role in all of that too. Dammit. I had been doing everything I could to keep that personal information away from my innocent roommate.

"I was worried about you. You didn't show up for lunch on time," Ash whispered in my ear as I scooped a spoonful of applesauce into my mouth. "I didn't know you were with *Liam.*"

I looked up at him, noticing the slightest difference in tone when it came to Liam's name. He was focusing on his food, his expression smooth and calm but I could see that he was tense by the way his fingers clenched around his own spoon.

"Ash. Don't," I whispered fiercely back to him. His eyes shot up to mine and I held them for a long moment. "Don't do that."

"Do what?" Ash asked, his eyes wide in feigned innocence.

"Act that way." I could feel the other's eyes on us and it made me want to immediately drop the subject. The last thing I needed was a fight with Ash, witnessed by Kaya, Corbin and Liam. Ash and I rarely fought, though I didn't know if that

44

was because we had nothing to fighting or because we didn't see each other enough to actually fight about anything. "And don't ask me 'what way' or I'll punch you."

A smile broke out across his face, cocky and sure. It didn't quite match the darkness that clouded his blue eyes but it was reassuring to see at least. "You wouldn't."

"Try me," I answered, rolling my eyes. "Liam, this is my roommate, Kaya. And the one who *still* hasn't looked up from his book is Ash's roommate, Corbin."

At the sound of his name, Corbin finally looked up from his book and did a double take when he saw Liam sitting next to him. "Who are you?" he asked, confused, and I resisted the urge to laugh at the perplexed look on his face.

"Corbin, this is Liam Garrity. I knew him from...outside. Liam, this is Corbin Kovalski."

Corbin stared at Liam and I doubted he would even remember shaking Liam's hand. He was studying him as if he were something he could learn from a book and I cleared my throat. He jumped back and ducked behind his book.

"Where are you from, Liam?" Kaya ventured bravely and I nearly spat out my milk in surprise.

Liam glanced at me before turning his attention to her. "I'm originally from Atlanta, Georgia. What about you?"

Kaya flushed. "I actually grew up here."

Liam looked surprised at this. "What, you were born here?"

She nodded, and I noticed there was something different about her around him. She seemed comfortable and I knew how she felt. Even when Liam was a complete stranger to me, I felt that connection, that ease. He was an easy person to like. I remembered how he made me feel when we were both trapped and wondered if he had that sort of effect on everyone.

Kaya continued. "There aren't a lot of us. Sanctuary really couldn't be a place of refuge for people if there were already a lot of people here. But there are people that have lived here for ages and you know, they get married and have children and grow old and live their lives, just like you guys did on the outside. That's how I was born."

Ash, Corbin and I stared at Kaya, flabbergasted. It was the most she ever had said at one time, in the entire short period that we had all known her; Corbin having arrived at Sanctuary just a week or two before Ash and I. She blushed and smiled sheepishly.

"That is…incredible," Liam finally said. He looked uncomfortable, eyes darting around. His hands shook when he picked up his spoon but his eyes were steady as they met mine from across the table. He reminded me of myself when I first came here. It was a shock, coming from the outside world, where things were chaos, and landing in here. He would get used to it. We all would. I hoped. "Where are your parents?"

"They're here," Kaya was saying. "They're both geneticists so they spend most of their time on their research and seeing what sort of effect living down in Sanctuary has on future generations."

Liam looked impressed and the two of them immediately launched into conversation. I sagged a little with relief. I was afraid of what Liam would be like. I was already a mess on my own and I didn't know if I could handle anyone else's messes right now. I kept to myself here, other than Ash, and I didn't speak much unless spoken to. I had no desire to get close to anyone, even Kaya and Corbin.

Everyone I knew ended up dead anyway. My parents. My best friend. God, even my dog. Now Liam was in here in front of me, safe, and I was afraid of losing him too. I was even more afraid of him losing himself.

He seemed to be holding it together though, despite the fact that he had spent months inside that hellhole just to be delivered here and find out that his father had died. He was stronger than I knew and I admired him for that.

"Aren't you a little worried about him being here?" Ash whispered to me, breaking into my thoughts.

I looked at him, confused. "What?" My eyes darted back to Liam, but his focus was still completely on Kaya. "What you rather he was still at Sekhmet?"

"Of course not," Ash cut in quickly. He fiddled with his fork, before laying it down on his plate. I waited patiently for him to continue. He sighed. "I just...why would Razi just give him to us? It doesn't make any sense. I can't think of any reason for him to be here. Maybe he's a play. Maybe he's a tool. Maybe he's here to convince you to go back?"

I nearly spat my water everywhere. "On what planet, in what universe, in what totally alternate point of being would I actually agree to go back to that place, Ashley Matthews?"

He winced at his full name but didn't comment on it. "I'm just saying, Z. it's not that I'm not glad that Liam is safe. I obviously am." I nearly snorted at that. "But no one has stopped to think about why Razi gave him back. She wanted him just as much as she wanted, and still wants you. Why would she let him go?"

He was asking questions that definitely needed answers. But I couldn't think about that right now. Razi was smart as hell, and angry, and that made for an incredibly dangerous combination. She didn't make any moves unless there was a reason for them. Liam was here for a reason. I was willing to bet that she hoped we would be so happy to have him back that we wouldn't focus on the reasons why.

But I also knew that while Ash had a point, there was also something else brewing under his skin.

"I get what you're saying," I said sharply before he could continue. "But you also need to refrain from this jealousy in the future, okay? We'll figure out why he's here, why Razi gave him to us, but nothing is going to be accomplished if you act like a brat about it."

Ash's mouth dropped open to protest but Kaya shot a question our way and he was saved from having to respond. I was immensely grateful for Kaya in that moment. Ash's hand reached out to squeeze my thigh and tingles flooded through my veins, all but dissipating what little irritation I'd had with him.

CHAPTER SEVEN

"**DID YOU SEE** Peter's hair this morning. I'm pretty sure he could give Einstein a run for his money..."

I looked over at Ash who grinned at me, and I shook my head. If there was one thing I could always count on, no matter how weird and crazy the world got, it was his ridiculous humor and that even more ridiculous smile.

Liam had been in Sanctuary for about a week and was adjusting much better than I expected. He was working and spending time with his mother and reading a lot. He had told me once that he wasn't much of a reader but I think the books were keeping him distracted.

Every once once in awhile, he would zone out during a conversation, disappear off somewhere, a place where none of us could follow. When he did that, I would exchange worried looks with Ash and Kaya. He would eventually return to us, like nothing had happened, but I didn't like it. The only time we had spent together was the night we had met, when our families shared a campfire in the middle of nowhere, and the month we'd been together at Sekhmet. But I knew him. I knew him better than I had known some of my friends back in New York. He was a survivor and it scared me every time he disappeared into his own head. It wasn't like him.

I would find him asleep in the library sometimes. He slept fitfully, twitching in his sleep. He would mutter while passed out but most of the time, I couldn't tell what he said. Occasionally though, there would be one coherent word, and it would send shivers down my spine. *Astrid.*

I sighed. Anytime I asked about Astrid, Liam would change the subject, and usually turn the attention away from him to Ash. Since, Ash, god bless him, liked to be the center of attention and also liked when Liam didn't pay attention to me, it usually worked quite well.

"Does it make you feel normal to tease people in here like you did back at St. Joseph's?" I asked him, dryly.

"Aw, come on, Z," Ash laughed. "You know you agree with me. "

Peter was the old cranky man who was in charge of the laundry. Sometimes I thought the only reason he had the job was because nobody else wanted it. And while he did have crazy white hair that bore some resemblance to Albert Einstein, I was pretty sure that Ash's comments came from the fact that had Peter had been particularly grouchy toward the two of us since catching us in the closet making out. The corners of my mouth twitched up a bit and Ash's grin grew wider. "I hate you," I finally said.

"You really don't," was his only reply.

"I really don't," I groaned. "Just promise me you won't put glitter in his locker or something." I recalled the memory of walking around in my school uniform, covered head to toe in glitter, looking like a character from an anime or something.

"I only reserve those kinds of things for you, baby doll," Ash answered, winking at me. I rolled my eyes at him and he laughed again. "Pass me those plates, will you?"

The two of us were on kitchen duty, my least favorite chore here in Sanctuary. It mostly consisted of washing dishes, putting them away and mopping and wiping down the entire kitchen and cafeteria. There were several others with us though, so at least the job went by quickly.

I handed him a stack of plates and he dumped them into the soapy hot water. Our fingers brushed as I passed them over and I was distracted from my work for a moment. It was amazing that he still had the ability to drive me so crazy. He smiled widely at my reaction and I turned away.

"Zoey."

I turned around and saw Liam standing there. A small smile stretched across my face. "Hey there."

"Can I talk to you?"

Ash's head shot up fast and his eyes met mine, pleading with me. The words *I told you so* were written all over his face and I wanted to stick my tongue out at him, as childish as it was. I glared at him, before wiping my hands on a towel, and turning to Liam. "Of course," I answered.

I followed him out of the kitchen; aware that Ash's eyes were burning a hole in my back as I left. Liam collapsed on one of the benches and cradled his face in his palms for a moment. "Liam?" I asked, immediately worried.

"How do you get the nightmares to go away?" he whispered. I barely heard him. His hands muffled his words. He raised his eyes to mine and they were wide and tired, and the bags underneath them were dark and scary.

I felt the tears prick the corners of my eyes. I practically fell onto the bench next to him. "Can I be honest with you, Liam?"

"Of course," he immediately answered. His hand slipped into mine and it felt natural. It felt comfortable. It didn't feel like it did with Ash. When Ash held my hand, it felt like he was holding me down, keeping me attached to the earth. He was my gravity. With Liam, it felt like…the most comfortable thing in the world. He was my friend, the closest friend that I had, and he knew. He just knew.

"They don't go away," I admitted. "They haven't gone away in a very long time. They've just…changed their nature. I used to dream about Awakened and my best friend, Maddie, and my dog and the bombs and now? Now I dream about Awakened and Razi Cylon and you and babies that turn blue and tear at my skin…" I trailed off and shuddered. "I would do anything in the world to make them go away, Liam. Anything."

"All I do is dream of her. I dream of her and I dream of what is happening to her right now, what I imagine is happening to her and how I can't stop it because I'm here, in this stupid place. I'm safe and she isn't and I hate it." His words were rushed and quiet but I was sitting next to him and I heard every word he said.

"Who? You dream of who, Liam?" I asked, hesitantly, my voice soft.

He looked worn out and I squeezed his hand. He constantly looked like he was going to fall apart, but he was pushing through each day, going through the motions.

Surviving. He was a damn survivor.

That's all any of us were trying to be.

"Liam?" I repeated. "Who are you talking about?"

"I don't want to talk about it," he murmured after an extremely long pause. "I don't…I can't…" His breathing was picking up and I could feel the tremors going through his body. "I think and I think and I think and I can't breathe, Zoey. I can't breathe."

I reached for him but his hand pulled out of mine. His breathing got faster and faster and I stood up, staring at him, unsure of what to do. He was panicking, he was experiencing some sort of attack but I'd never dealt with this before. "Liam, it's okay. It's going to be okay. I promise…"

"It's NOT going to be okay." His voice was sudden and loud in the empty cafeteria and I took a step back. There were tears rolling down his cheeks and he was choking on his breaths. I reached for him again but he recoiled. My heart was beating quickly in my chest. I didn't know what to do.

"Hey, man, it's okay."

Ash's voice startled me. He was standing behind me, and he stepped around me, looking at Liam, who was falling apart in front of me. Ash leaned down but didn't touch Liam. He just looked at him. "It's okay, Liam. Breathe, okay?"

"It's not okay!" Liam's voice was loud, and it didn't even sound like him. He always spoke in calm tones, even when he was scared. God, even when he was flirting. He stayed calm. He had been my rock for so long. My arms circled my waist, as if this could keep me from unraveling as well.

"I know. I know it doesn't seem like it's going to be okay. But it is. I promise. Just focus on breathing, okay?" Ash's voice was steady and confident and I clung to it.

Liam let out a shaky breath, slow and focused.

"There you go," Ash praised. "Try it again for me, okay?"

Liam gulped down more air and then let it out. It was still shaky but he looked calmer. He focused on his breathing for a few more minutes with Ash as his coach. Liam's eyes stayed fixed on Ash's as he took him through each breath until finally Liam had calmed down.

The three of us stayed quiet for a while. I chewed nervously on my thumbnail, staring back and forth between them. Eventually Liam's eyes met mine and I saw that they were swollen and red. He looked embarrassed, though he had no reason to feel that way.

"I'm sorry," was all he said, his voice hoarse.

"Don't be," Ash and I chorused at the same time.

Liam's shoulders were hunched and he looked more exhausted than he was before.

"Go back to your room," Ash instructed. "Get some sleep. You deserve it."

Liam nodded at Ash gratefully, before pulling himself off the bench and making his way back out of the cafeteria.

Ash turned back to me, and it took no time at all for me to throw my arms around his waist. His hands came up to my shoulders, pulling me against him.

"God, that was so scary. I didn't know what to do and I...thank you, Ash," I managed to say, my face pressed against his chest.

"He had a panic attack. It's not unusual considering what he's gone through. You've had them. Maybe you didn't realize but you had a couple when we got here. I kept waiting for you to fall apart but you just bottle everything inside," he said. I raised my eyes to him, and he gave me a small smile.

"How did you know how to handle that?" I asked him, ignoring his comments about me.

"Heather used to get panic attacks."

"Heather...Carr?" I asked, disbelieving, referring to his ex-girlfriend from New York. Heather Carr was every mean girl multiplied by ten. Over the past few months, I'd learned more and more about her, though I'd gone to school with her since kindergarten, and it was still hard learning that she was a normal human being when she had been so cruel to me.

"Do we know another Heather?" he asked, wryly.

I made a face. "I guess not. I didn't realize perfect Heather wasn't so perfect after all."

Ash sighed. "Come on, Zoey. Heather is dead; do you really want to be jealous of her now?"

A flush of shame rushed through me and I looked away. "You're right. That was wrong of me. Just because she was a bitch doesn't give me the right to be a bitch about her now that she's dead." Ash raised an eyebrow at me but didn't say anything. I looked in the direction that Liam had left. "Do you think he's going to be okay?"

Ash sighed again, running a hand through his hair. He shrugged. "I honestly don't know. He's got a lot to work through. But I think he'll be okay." He turned away from the door and faced me. "I'm more worried about you."

'fused.

'ghtmares, even though you told

were   listening   to   our

', firmly. "I came to see
...king about it. Why would
when you're obviously not?"
... closed it. "Because I *am* fine."
...nin line on his face and he stared at the
...nally raising his eyes to me again. "I don't
...at." His voice dipped lower, almost pleading. "Why
...n't you talk to me?"

"I talk to you all the time," I insisted.

"Not the way you just talked to Liam…" I barely caught the words; they were barely a whisper. Our eyes met and no more words were said.

I didn't know what else to say.

CHAPTER EIGHT

"ZOEY, CAN YOU please stay after class?"

My eyes closed briefly in irritation. I hadn't argued with Caspar that badly about *The Great Gatsby,* not nearly as badly as I had argued with him in class before, though I wasn't surprised. He was probably getting really tired of my attitude.

Ash paused at my desk before leaving, giving me a look. *Do you want me to stay?* I shook my head and waved him away, more than a little thrilled that we had reached the level of communication without having to say a single word. Things had been strained between the two of us over the past few days since we had talked, so I was glad that he had stopped to check.

The classroom cleared out quickly and I remained at my desk until the room was empty. Caspar walked over to me, leaning his hip on the desk. I studied him. I had never been a big fan of Caspar and it wasn't just because he had helped in the breakup of my parents' marriage. He had always seemed pretentious to me. Yes, he was an author, and a good one at that, landing not one but two books on the New York Times bestsellers list. He was obviously smart. But did he always have to talk using big words? Did he always have to dress like he was expecting to run into F. Scott Fitzgerald himself at a salon somewhere? Did he have to act like anything mainstream or commercial was so below him?

The answer? Yes. Always yes.

So seeing him in the plain black uniform of Sanctuary gave me a sort of thrill. He can't have been that comfortable, and it certainly was beneath him to teach English to a bunch of ragtag teenagers with attitude, because I was definitely not the only one in that room that had an attitude.

I was just probably the worst one.

"What is it, Caspar?" I asked, propping my chin up with my hands, looking up at him bored. "Care to dissect Gatsby and Daisy's relationship further?"

His eyebrows rose so high, they nearly disappeared under his hair. "I'm just checking in with you, Zoey. I want to make sure you're okay?"

The surprise flashed across my face before I had a chance to hide it. "You're asking me if I'm okay?" I questioned slowly.

"Of course," Caspar responded. "Zoey, you are my daughter."

"Step-daughter," I corrected, hissing through my teeth.

He nodded his head. "Even so. I've known you for the past seven years. I care about you and we are all each other has left."

I glared up at him, my lips pursed. "We are not. I may have had to put up with you when you were my mom's husband but we don't owe each other anything anymore. You are not my father. My father died, protecting me. Saving my life. *You* are not the only person I have left."

Caspar's mouth opened and closed a few times before he finally replied. "I don't think your mother would agree."

Tears sprung at the corner of my eyes. "I have no idea if she would agree, Caspar. She is dead. She died. I appreciate your concern; I do. But you owe me nothing. And I'm an adult now. I've spent months taking care of myself and that's not going to change any time soon."

We stared at each other for a few moments. It was still hard to see my stepfather here in Sanctuary. I'd had no love for him and it hurt to think that he really was all I had left of my mother.

Finally, he spoke again. His was low and his eyes dropped to the ground. "You're right. We don't know and I hate it. But I'm pretty sure she'd want us to take care of each other."

When I didn't answer, he sighed. "You can go now, Zoey."

I hurried out of my chair, nearly tripping over my own feet in the process. I was nearly out the door when his words reached me again.

"You can always come to me, Zoey. Anytime."

My hand gripped the doorway before I let go and disappeared down the hallway.

***

"WHY IS EVERYONE whispering?" Ash asked, squeezing into a seat next to me at breakfast a few days later.

"No one is whispering," I said, rolling my eyes. "No one has been whispering since Liam arrived and he's old news now." Liam's eyes met mine and I nearly laughed. "No offense."

"None taken," he replied, easily.

"Um, Zoey?" Kaya said, looking around. "People *are* whispering."

My head shot up and my eyes darted around the large cafeteria. Now that Kaya had pointed it out, I noticed all the whispering. There was a low hum throughout the room and more than one worried face.

"What do you think is going on?" Kaya asked, nervously, chewing on her thumbnail.

"I have no idea," I admitted, turning back to my food. I could feel the whispers behind me, like invisible spiders crawling up my spine. I resisted the urge to turn around.

"There's probably a shortage of turnips in the kitchens," Ash answered, wryly. "It's probably no big deal. Nothing exciting ever happens here, remember?"

I didn't necessarily agree. Liam's arrival just a few weeks ago was definitely something exciting. I said nothing though. I just nodded, tossing one more look over my shoulder before dropping the subject entirely. Ash was probably right.

The whispers, however, continued for the rest of the day. Everywhere we went people were huddled together, talking hurriedly under their breaths. I started to notice they were all adults, and they almost always fell immediately silent when we drew near.

Of course. We were considered children in Sanctuary.

"I can't handle this anymore," I burst out, as we left the laundry room.

"Zoey..." Ash started to say but I spotted Octavia walking through the spiral and I took off after her. She looked up at me as I approached and sighed.

Me too, Octavia. Me too.

"I'm not sharing classified information with you, Miss Valentine, so I wouldn't bother asking," Octavia said tiredly when I reached her.

"And that's why everyone in Sanctuary has been whispering all day? Because the information is *so* classified."

"You really don't give up, don't you?" Patrick spoke up, looking at me appraisingly.

"She really doesn't," Ash cut in, cheerfully. His hand reached for mine and squeezed it tight in warning. "She's nosy, my Zoey."

Octavia's eyes closed briefly for a moment. Some days, I was sure she regretted letting the two of us in this place. "Come."

We didn't end up going far. Octavia lead us into an empty supply room and shut the door behind us. I had to admit; she looked a lot less impressive under the dim glow of what was basically a closet.

"One of our patrols is dead," Octavia announced, bluntly.

I froze. Whatever I had thought was going to come out of her mouth, this was not it. Deaths didn't happen in Sanctuary; not as far as I had seen. "What...who...how...?"

Octavia's mouth barely opened as she replied. "He was separated from the rest of his group last night but there was no cause for worry. It happens and Captain Bruin has been here for decades. We were going to send out a patrol this morning when he didn't return." She paused, unable to continue.

Patrick picked up where she left off. "His body was found dumped at the main entrance, completely ripped apart. It was almost too hard to identify him...there was blood everywhere." He swallowed hard. "Luckily we have data on every citizen in Sanctuary so we were able to confirm that it was him."

I didn't want to think what sort of state Captain Bruin had been in for them to need DNA or fingerprints to be entirely sure of his identity. There was a bitter taste in my mouth and I had to control the urge to vomit.

"What happened?" Ash asked.

"We are pretty sure it was an Awakened," Octavia answered him. Her face was very pale, even more so in the lack of light, but her tone was even. "No one else could have done this." She reached for something in her pocket and held it out to us. "This was pinned to his chest with a knife."

I took the paper with a shaking hand. It was dirty and stained with dark blood but you could still see the symbol printed there. It was a woman with a lion's head. Sekhmet. The bile role further in my throat and I shoved the paper back into her hands.

"What happens now?" I asked, grateful for Ash's hand in mine. The room was spinning and I wasn't sure how I remained upright.

Patrick opened his mouth to reply but Octavia quickly cut him off. "That is information that you are not privy to, Miss Valentine. IT will be taken care of."

I rolled my eyes. "And why don't I believe that? She already gave us Liam without any explanation. Now she's left a dead man on our doorstep. How long will you allow her to do as she pleases?"

"Enough!" Octavia said, sharply. She opened the door, her hand indicating that we should leave. "I have indulged you long enough. You need to go."

The two of us exited, though I did so begrudgingly. I barely registered where we were going. I only felt the comforting pressure of Ash's hand against mine as he guided me through the crowd. It wasn't until I was in his room and sitting on his bed that I woke up out of my stupor.

"I'm not supposed to be in here." I pointed out. "Especially if Corbin isn't here."

"What? You think I can't keep my hands off of you?" he asked, innocently.

"I know you can't."

He laughed but almost immediately sobered up. He sat on the bed next to me. My head rested on his shoulder. "Are you okay?"

I shrugged and then nodded. "I'm fine." I paused. "She's not going to stop, Ash. I'm not safe here. No one is. And I don't think anyone here is going to do anything about it."

Ash sighed. "I don't think so either. They are comfortable, Zoey. They think they're completely safe underground."

"They're not," I interjected angrily. "Someone died. And someone at Sekhmet drove a knife through his chest just to pin a note. And it was because of *her*. It was on *her* orders and you know it. She did it just because she could, just to let us know that she's still in control."

"I'm starting to think that it's going to take more than just one dead patrol for Octavia to take action."

"Oh god," I shuddered. "I hope it doesn't come to that."

We sat like that for a while, enjoying the silence of each other's company. It had been so long since we'd been able to do that. I knew both of us were thinking of what else we could do in the room but neither of us made a move and I was relieved. I just needed him there, to keep me grounded and connected to reality. After a bit, he pulled me closer and we laid next to each other, our hands intertwined and my head listening to the easy rhythm of his heart in his chest.

The dinner bell rang out eventually, bringing us out of the spell we had put ourselves under. I lifted my hands sleepily and allowed myself a small smile. We rearranged our rumpled clothes before setting out to dinner.

We wasted no time at all telling Liam and Kaya about what we had heard from Octavia. Presumably Corbin heard too but it was always hard to tell with him. Kaya's face went very pale and Liam gripped his fork tightly. His eyes met mine in understanding.

"Did she say what she was going to do about this?" Liam asked, through clenched teeth.

"Well, if she's going to do anything, she certainly isn't going to tell me," I replied.

Liam's lips pursed but he didn't say anything.

Ash was studying Liam intently. "What happened there after we left, Liam?"

Liam shook his head, shoving food in his mouth. Ash stared at him a bit longer and Liam sighed, frustrated. "I'd rather not talk about it, Ash."

Ash scowled. "Look, I don't know why you're here. I don't know how the hell Razi is alive considering that she was shot in the goddamn throat. And now the bitch is dropping bodies on our doorstep. So forgive me for being a *little* curious about what the hell is going on."

It was Liam's turn to make a face. "I'm just as in the dark as you, Matthews. All I know is that I was there…with…" He swallowed hard and continued. "With Astrid. I went to sleep, like normal, and then I woke up here. I don't know what she's planning, and if I did, I wouldn't be sitting here, eating turnips. I'd be *doing* something."

Liam's words were met with silence after his rant. I looked down at my own sad little cup of turnips and frowned. I looked back up at Liam. "But Liam…"

He wiped his mouth with a napkin and stood up abruptly. "I'm done." He made his way out of the cafeteria, weaving his way through the tables and out the swinging doors.

I stood up, dropping my fork with a clatter on the table.

"Come on, Zoey," Ash started to say, but I shook my head in response. He ducked his head, looking miserable. Whatever progress we had made in the last few hours seemed to disappear. I ran my fingers through his soft hair and his eyes closed briefly. By the time he opened them, I was gone.

I'd taken too long to go after Liam. He was nowhere to be found. I searched everywhere for him but finally gave up. It was clear that he wanted to be alone. If he needed me, he would come and find me.

Kaya was in our room by the time I returned. She was sitting stock still, staring at her folded hands in her lap. She didn't move when I came in and I wondered if she'd even noticed my return. I approached her cautiously. "Kaya?"

She jumped, startled, her eyes wide. "Oh. Zoey. Hi." Her voice squeaked even higher than normal.

"Are you okay?" I asked, sitting on the bed next to her.

"Oh, yeah, I'm fine," she waved me off, her voice still unusually high. "Totally. Completely. Absolutely."

My eyebrows raised and her shoulders slumped. "You're a terrible liar, Kaya."

She didn't respond right away and when she did, she spoke so softly that I barely heard her.

"What if they get in here?"

My brow furrowed in confusion. "Who?" I asked.

"The Awakened," she whispered, sounding terrified. Rightfully so. I had seen them, had my face cut into pieces by them and escaped them several times, and I was still seeing them in my nightmares nearly every night. Kaya had only ever heard stories, and stories were the scariest thing.

A shiver went through me. "They won't," I heard myself answer.

"But how do you know that?" she asked, desperately. "How can you possibly know that, Zoey?"

"You're right. I don't," I answered, honestly. "But this place is supposed to be a sanctuary, right? I mean, it's in the name. You're safe here, Kaya."

The words didn't feel sincere. Once I'd believed this place to be a stronghold, where nothing bad could happen. I'd since learned differently. This place was nothing more than a place to hide. But I had to say this. I had to believe it for Kaya. She hadn't known any different. To her, this place would always be safe because it always had been.

Kaya nodded at my words and reached into her drawers for some pajamas. It was not until we had showered, brushed our teeth and tucked ourselves into bed that she spoke again.

"I don't think I believe that anymore."

CHAPTER NINE

THE SECOND BODY was found at the main entrance just days later. This guard was younger, or so I heard, not much older than I. He was even less recognizable than the first guard. The rumor was that actual body pieces had been found as opposed to a whole body. I had spent quite some time bent over the rim of a toilet bowl after that. There was no hiding the news this time; it had been found during the day while everyone was awake. This time, Octavia called the citizens together, to make the announcement.

There was a large amphitheater in one of the lowest levels of Sanctuary. I had never seen it before and was surprised to find it. It was almost like a full football stadium, buried deep below the ground. Kaya explained that it was rarely used. It wasn't often that Sanctuary needed all of its citizens in the same place. It was also used as the sort of evacuation area in case of any disaster, which hadn't been necessary since the bombs went off over a year ago, at which point I had been on the road out of New York City. It always seemed sort of odd to me that the citizens of Sanctuary just buried themselves further underground in emergencies

Octavia spoke calmly during her entire speech, not deterred at all speaking in front of countless faces looking to her for answers. She explained about the murders of the two guards, and ensured us that they were doing the best they could to prevent this from happening again. There were worried looks on several faces but most seemed at ease after the speech. The Director had that sort of effect on the people of Sanctuary.

I, however, had seen the sweat glistening on her brow. She was nervous.

"Did anyone else buy that load of bullshit?" I asked loudly as we filed out.

"Zoey," Liam warned, tiredly. Several people glared at me as they passed and I rolled my eyes. Octavia was not faultless or flawless, despite what people here thought.

"I'm just saying," I lowered my voice. "I doubt they're doing anything at all."

"Zoey." Ash's voice was stern. "Stop."

I looked at him, confused. I followed his line of sight and my heart fell. He was looking at Kaya. She looked like she was barely keeping herself together. Tears were silently streaming down her face.

I took a step closer and she looked startled, like she'd forgotten that all of us were still there next to her. Her fingers wiped her cheeks hastily. "I'm fine," she said.

"You are clearly not," I pointed out. "You're crying. Did you know him?"

"Of course I knew him Zoey! Before the Awakened, there weren't many of us around here. I knew everyone. These people are my friends, my family, and now they are dying! And no one seems to care because at least it's not them!" Kaya snapped. She breathed heavily for a few seconds, unaware that several people were staring at her in shock. Her eyes widened and her face turned an attractive puce color. "Oh my…Zoey. Ash. Liam. I'm…your parents and…I'm so sorry." She looked ashamed.

I, on the other hand, probably looked impressed. I had never seen Kaya use a tone louder than a slightly loud whisper. She was soft-spoken and kept mostly to herself, unless she was asking me about a Kardashian or something equally as useless. "Damn, Kaya, I didn't know you had that in you."

"I'm sorry," she repeated, wringing her hands nervously.

I shook my head. "Don't be. It's healthy to get angry. And it's nice to see someone else yell besides me."

The corner of her lip turned up slightly but she still looked miserable. "People shouldn't be dying," she said, softly. "We're supposed to be safe here. If we aren't safe here, then where are we?"

"I'm starting to think there's nowhere that's one hundred percent safe. Not with the Awakened out there. Not with Razi Cylon," Ash spoke up. His hand was resting gently on my waist but I could see the tension in his shoulders.

All around us, people looked calm. They were reassured by Octavia's speech and I didn't blame them. It was easy to fall into that sort of hope. Most of these people had been driven from their homes and seen loved ones die. They were tired and broken down. They were beaten. These people needed to believe that it was finally over.

I was starting to believe that it was never going to be over.

In the next two weeks, four more people were found dead, each body more gruesome and torn apart than the previous. Sanctuary was in a frenzy. Octavia doubled the amount of patrols and then tripled them but there simply weren't enough people. People didn't leave Sanctuary often; people hardly went outside unless necessary. Now, no one was leaving. Whispers filled the corridors and there were worried faces everywhere.

Every time I saw Octavia, she looked worse than she had the last time. I tried to corner her but she always seemed to disappear when I got near. I didn't chalk that off as a coincidence. She spent more and more time in her office and there were definitely no more speeches.

Two weeks and three days after the first death, a total of six bodies were found by the back entrance, scattered amongst the ancient cliff dwellings of Mesa Verde that were the cover for Sanctuary. One of those bodies belonged to Kaya's brother.

I felt awful. I felt truly horrible. I had spent almost five months in the same room as Kaya and I'd no clue she'd had a brother, let alone known that he worked in the military sector of Sanctuary.

Kaya spent a few days with her parents, sleeping on a cot squeezed into their living quarters. I didn't like the silence and solitude of our room. It gave me way too much time to think. I actually missed the sound of her snores and her incessant questions.

I walked into our room a few days after her brother's death and found her sitting on her bed, legs crossed, her eyes fixed on the wall in front of her.

"Kaya?" My voice was soft. "Are you okay?"

Her face titled and her eyes met mine. They were tired but there were no signs that she had cried at all. She looked like a ghost. Her hair was hanging dirtily around her face and she looked as if she hadn't slept in days. She probably hadn't.

"Kaya?" I repeated.

She blinked a few times and then recognition flickered across her face. "Zoey." Her voice was rough and broken, like she hadn't used it in a while. "I haven't cried. They kept telling me that I need to cry but I can't. I'm angry and I'm *scared.*" Her voice broke on the last word and I felt it deep in my stomach.

"I am so sorry, Kaya. I am so incredibly sorry."

She nodded once, biting her lip.

I didn't know what else to say or do. It seemed wrong that after so much loss, I still had no idea how to deal. I had cried more in the last year than I had cried in my life. But I hadn't been given a chance to grieve, not really. After every death —

my best friend Madison's, my dad's, my mom's – I hadn't had the time to process. It had always been about the next move, the need to keep going, to stay alive and survive. Dwelling on what had happened had not been a luxury I could afford.

Kaya had nothing but time for thinking and dwelling and, until she cried, I was afraid it would sit in her chest like a tumor and fester.

I opened my mouth to say something – though I had no idea what I could possibly say – when the door to our room slid open. The two of us jumped, startled and my eyes widened as Corbin came rushing into the room.

I had never seen Corbin like this before. He was always well put together, his head tucked behind a book. I had never seen him this aware of what was going on around him. His hair was a curly mess on his head and his eyes were darting around the room. His clothes were rumpled, like he had just thrown them on hastily, and there was no book to be found. His eyes landed on Kaya and his shoulders sagged in relief.

"I've been looking for you everywhere," he said, not taking his eyes off of her. I had never seen him look at a person this long before and I had certainly never seen him look at anyone the way he was looking at Kaya. I might as well have been invisible.

Kaya's face flushed. "You have? Why?"

Corbin crossed the room and stopped in front of her. His hands twitched at his sides, like he wanted to reach for her. "I've been so worried about you. Kaya, I'm so sorry." Sincerity rang through his voice and a little something else. Maybe I had been crazy to write Corbin off. It was always the quiet ones that surprised you.

Kaya stared at him for a long time, almost as if she wasn't sure if she was really seeing him. Then in a split moment, she grabbed the front of his shirt and yanked him toward her. Corbin stumbled as their lips met and I nearly laughed. It was awkward but absolutely perfect for them. I wouldn't have expected anything less.

My face burned red. Now I was *definitely* intruding. "Okay, so I'm just going to go now…" Neither one of them acknowledged me. My embarrassment increased when I heard Kaya sigh. "Okay then! Bye!"

I fled the room. I wasn't sure how long they would need privacy – and I had no desire to even think of what they would do with that privacy – but for now, I was banished. I wandered the corridors for a few minutes before ascending the spiral walkway to the library.

It was fairly abandoned, as it tended to be, especially late at night. I flitted through the shelves aimlessly but nothing was really calling out to me. I was about read to give up when I spotted Liam in the corner, his head bent over a book.

I tilted my head to read the title as I approached him and my eyebrows rose high on my forehead. "*Co-Parenting in the 21st Century,*" I read aloud. "Interesting read, there."

The tips of Liam's ears turned red but he smiled slightly. "It's a nice distraction. None of it means anything and so it means everything."

I hopped up on the table in front of him, my feet dangling. "And what exactly do you need a distraction from?"

His lips were practically glued together as he gave me a knowing look.

"You can't blame me for trying," I shrugged. "Well, I've been banished from my room because Corbin and Kaya are currently making out in there."

"What?" Liam's voice carried but there was no one around to even care. "Damn. It's about time. Who kissed who?"

"Kaya kissed Corbin. I'm just as surprised as you," I laughed at the incredulous look on his face. "Corbin came rushing into our room, looking for Kaya. Shocked the hell out of me, and then Kaya just grabbed and…." I laughed again. "I didn't know either one of them had it in them."

"Damn," Liam said, shaking his head, disbelieving.

I nodded, agreeing. "Everyone seems to be pairing up," I spoke carefully.

"So it would seem," Liam answered, his face blank again.

I nearly growled in frustration. Instead, I placed my hand on his forearm. His blue eyes lifted to meet mine, his mouth a thin line. "Just tell me, Liam. Hiding it from me is just stupid."

"Zoey, I don't want to talk about it. I've continually said that and you just don't listen, do you? You never listen. You push and you push and you push. Why do you think Octavia runs in the opposite direction every single time she sees you? Because you can't just leave it alone!"

I opened my mouth, my face flushing, but I was interrupted.

"Don't yell at her."

The two of us turned around. Ash was standing there, his fists clenched at his sides. He was looking right past me, glaring at Liam, who glared right back. They both looked ready to punch each other and I was getting seriously tired of it.

"Ash, he wasn't yelling. Okay, well, he was yelling but…"

"Zoey, stay out of this. This doesn't concern you," Ash cut me off, not looking at me.

I rolled my eyes. "Right. Sure. This doesn't concern me."

"You're wrong about it concerning Zoey, but you're not wrong about her staying out of it," Liam said, seeming unconcerned. "We should have had this out ages ago."

"Have it out?" Ash burst out angrily. "Shit, I don't want to fight with you, Liam. I'm just tired of not knowing why you're here. Razi Cylon doesn't just let people go, not when she wants them. Hell, she didn't even want me and I have a damn scar from the bullet wound I got escaping that stupid place. And you're spending a lot of time with my girlfriend and I'm not comfortable with that."

"You worried, Matthews? Worried she might want a Southern taste instead of the Brooklyn muck?" There was a lazy smile on his face, which only seemed to enrage Ash more.

"You are so not helping, Liam," I scolded him.

"Maybe I am helping, Zoey. Maybe it'll be helpful to talk to Ash and about his jealousy issues."

Ash stepped closer to Liam, his eyes burning. His eyes were normally a dark, ocean blue but now they flashed a deep black. "I am *not* jealous. This is not what this is about. I know who Zoey is. Zoey is mine. She belongs to me."

"Or I don't belong to anyone," I spoke up, irritably, but neither of them noticed.

"You keep repeating yourself. Maybe you don't actually believe that. Maybe you're worried that Zoey wants to spend more time with me than you."

Ash moved even closer, his fists raised and I hopped off the table and stepped in between them. Ash's hard chest bumped into my shoulder, his eyes focused on Liam. "Both of you. Stop it."

"She doesn't want you. She wants me. I love her and she loves me and you just need to deal with that."

Liam looked bored and irritated. "Trust me, I know that, Matthews. And I'm more than okay with that. You're the one that needs to deal with the fact that Zoey and I are friends."

"I don't care if you're friends!" Ash yelled. "But I don't trust you! I don't know why you're here and you keep saying that you have no idea, but you won't tell us at all. You won't even tell us about Astrid, and yet I'm just supposed to be okay with you being alone with Zoey all the time. I don't trust you and I don't want anyone I don't trust around her. I'm supposed to protect her! I promised her dad that I would protect her and I'm not going to let you get in the way of that!"

My fingers gripped the fabric of Ash's shirt tightly and tears sprung in the corner of my eyes at the mention of my dad. It had been so long since he had died, but it didn't make his death any less painful.

"Ash," Dad said softly, looking around at the Awakened surrounding us. They were so silent and so still. They looked dead, more so than they already were. I kept waiting as the seconds passed by. "Ash, whatever happens, you take care of Zoey. You protect her, no matter what."

"Ash," I whispered, looking up at him.

"You've done a really great job of protecting her. Where were you when she got her face cut up?"

I gasped, my fingers letting go of Ash's shirt as I turned around. Liam had stood up, and his face was bright red. I was the only barrier between the two of them, and considering I was a good foot shorter than both of them, I wasn't sure what good I could do. Even with my pretty legit fighting skills, I couldn't really take out both of them at once. But I was definitely going to try if it came to that.

"How dare you?" Ash growled, his voice low. One of his hands unclenched and wrapped tightly, but gently around the back of my neck. He pulled me closer to him and I hid my face in his chest. I could feel the raised scar on my face against the soft fabric of his shirt and my face burned. Most days I forgot that it was there, but it hurt to remember that my face would never look the same again. "She is beautiful. No matter what, she is beautiful. How dare you bring that up?"

"She *is* beautiful," Liam cut in. "But every time I see that on her face, I want to punch you in the face. How could you have let this happen to her? You want to protect her? You shouldn't have let anyone even *touch* her!"

"I *did* protect her!" Ash shouted back. He moved closer to Liam, close enough that I was sandwiched between them. I pulled back, one palm against Ash and another pressed against Liam. "You think I like that she has that scar? Don't you think that it kills me every single time I think about how I couldn't

73

prevent it from happening? But she's here and she's with me and she's *alive* and that's what matters."

Liam laughed, loud, but there was no humor in it. His own blue eyes were staring daggers at Ash. I had never seen Liam be this cruel before. He had always been so nice, so polite, so perfect. I couldn't figure out if he really meant what he said or if this was yet another distraction from the things he didn't want to think about.

"Face it, Ash. You can't protect her. You could never protect her. The only reason she is here is because she's strong and she's tough and she saved *your* ass in Sekhmet! You can't do anything for her, and it kills you! You're useless. You just sit there in your stupid room and you're useless. You can't protect her because she isn't safe!"

Liam's voice grew louder and louder as he yelled at Ash, and he sounded angry, upset and desperate. The more he yelled, the more that it seemed to make sense. Liam wasn't talking about me. Okay, maybe he was talking about me a little bit. He was the closest thing I had to a best friend anymore and he did care about me. And I did think that he wanted to get under Ash's skin a bit. But he wasn't talking about Ash and me. His eyes were wild and I realized exactly who he was talking about: Astrid.

Ash, it seemed, had realized the same thing. "Don't you dare talk to me about Zoey? I do everything I can to make sure she is safe and protected. And that's with me knowing that she can damn well take care of herself. But at least she's here, with me. Don't take out your inability to take care of Astrid out on me. You may not have told me anything but trust me, I know. It's not my fault that you left her there."

Liam moved so quickly that I almost missed him, but I was fast, even if massively out of practice. My hand reached out, landing a punch in his stomach, and I had him flipped on his back before he could reach Ash. The table next to us crashed on its side. I was surprised no one had come to see what was going on by this point. Liam lay on the ground, motionless for a moment, before groaning.

"Shit, Liam, I'm so sorry," I apologized, reaching for him. He pushed my hand away and pulled himself into a sitting position. He winced, rubbing his arm where I had grabbed him.

"Damn, I forgot how hard you could hit…" Liam said.

"I'm sorry," I repeated.

"Don't be," Liam cut in, shortly. He looked up at me and I felt horrible. I hadn't wanted to throw him like that, especially when he looked like a kicked puppy. His eyes traveled to Ash, who was still staring at Liam like he still wanted to hit him. "Besides, I wouldn't want to break your boyfriend's pretty face."

"Goddammit, Liam," I spit out. "Don't make me flip you again."

"No need," he said, bracing his hand on the overturned table and standing up. "I'll let myself out."

"Good," Ash snapped. "Go think about how you can't save Astrid and leave Zoey alone."

Liam's face broke for just a moment. I saw the despair and the worry and the utter desperation on his face. I didn't know who Astrid was – though I was damn determined to find out – but he cared about her and it was tearing him apart. The expression was gone in an instant though, and he sighed. He gave Ash a mock salute and walked away from us, disappearing between the shelves.

"Shit!" I cried out. I whirled on Ash. "Why did you do that?"

Ash was surprised. "Me? You heard him!"

"Of course I did," I admitted, angrily. "The difference, Ash, is that you know better. Or I thought you did." I spun on my heel and stomped out of the library.

CHAPTER TEN

I RAN DOWN the corridor, hoping to catch up with Liam. My anger at the two of them was still burning in my chest and I was so tired of this feud going on. They needed to gain a little perspective if they thought fighting over me – though I knew Liam had no feelings for me whatsoever, was a priority. Ash was my boyfriend. Liam was my best friend. I was tired of them acting like love interests in a cheesy love triangle. It was driving me insane.

And the last thing they needed to be doing in times like this was turning on each other.

I finally caught up to Liam as he was about to enter the family compound of the residence corridors. I sped up to catch him. My wristband didn't have proxy to that area and I didn't want him to escape.

I grabbed his arm and practically sent him flying into the wall with the force that I yanked him with. I cringed. I really needed to stop throwing him around like a ragdoll. "Stop. You need to stop right now. Tell me what's going on."

Liam was leaning against the wall, looking defeated. His hand covered his face and I almost wanted to back off. Almost. "Zoey," he pleaded. "Please. Just leave it alone."

"No. No way," I said, stepping closer to him. "I'm tired of all the secrets. My boyfriend is mad at me, and mad at you, and bodies are turning up everywhere and you won't tell me anything, except that Razi is goading us and that we need to go back. But you won't tell me why."

Liam didn't answer and I was frustrated. I was angry. I was tired of spending all this time with him, sitting next to him in silence, and losing time with Ash when I had no idea what was going on. I was tired of them saying ugly words to each other.

"Liam, is it Astrid?"

He looked at me and his eyes were wild, just like they always were when Astrid's name came up. His expression was desperate and he couldn't seem to get the words out. The expression I had just seen in the library was on his face again. I felt a pain in my chest at the sight of it.

I took a step closer to him, my hand resting on his arm. "Tell me about her. Please."

His legs gave out and he sunk to the ground. His knees were bent and he rested his forehead on them for a moment before taking a deep breath. "She's your replacement."

I jolted back, surprise shooting through me. "My what?"

"You didn't think Razi would wait for you forever, did you?" Liam asked, sarcastically, but the tone didn't match the look in his eyes. "She wants you, Zoey. She wanted you even more after you escaped. She's crazy. It's been…terrifying."

Liam took another deep breath before continuing. "But she can't wait for you. She couldn't. So she brought in another girl. Astrid. And Astrid is still there. She's still in there, Zoey, and she's alone and I'm not there with her!"

I was taken aback by the passion in his voice and then it suddenly hit me. It made sense. It explained why he was overprotective of me even though I was safe. It explained why he kept telling Ash that he couldn't protect me. It was because he couldn't protect Astrid. He was helpless. "You're in love with her," I whispered, sliding down to sit next to him.

"Of course not," he protested, his eyes meeting mine.

"Liam."

"Zoey."

"You're in love with her. You've fallen in love with her."

"I care about her, that's all. I couldn't be in love with her. I barely know her. We've only known each other a few months, I couldn't…" He stopped, contemplating for a moment. He swallowed hard and continued. "I just care about her, Zoey. And she doesn't deserve it. None of it. Just like you didn't."

And I got out. I escaped. The words were unspoken but they lingered between us anyway. Liam was a huge part of the reason that I was safe, that I had escaped the clutches of Razi Cylon and the evil Sekhmet Industries. When I finally spoke next, my words came out slowly. "I don't know what you want me to do, Liam…"

His eyes met mine. "We need to go get her."

"Liam…" The realization hit me hard and I went cold. "Is that why Razi let you go?" My fingers clutched at the hem of my shirt tightly. "She had to have known, that you would want to come back for Astrid. She had to have known that I wouldn't let you do that, not without me."

He was silent. "I don't know," he finally admitted. "Maybe. But I can't leave her there, Zoey. I can't do that to her."

"And I can't go back there," I cut in. "And neither can you. But we'll have to do something. I just don't know that I can convince Octavia to do something about it. She won't launch anything against Sekhmet, not when she hasn't already. Not when the only reason is that you're in love with Astrid."

Liam snorted but ignored my statement. "I don't understand why they aren't doing anything. Don't they know what's going on over there?"

I shook my head, closing my eyes briefly. "I think they know exactly what is going on there, but they don't care. They're safe here, Liam. They think they're untouchable here. They're willing to let the entire world burn around us because they're underground and safe from everything."

"This is not what I expected of this place. This is not what my granddad had told me," Liam admitted. "I knew it was a safe place but I didn't think it was going to be a place that didn't give a shit." He looked thoughtful for a moment.

"They give a shit. Just not enough to do anything about it."

He shook his head. "I just don't feel safe. I know I should. I know that that's the whole purpose of Sanctuary but the longer I'm here, the more I don't feel safe Zoey. Sekhmet is still out there. Razi Cylon is still doing her best to take over the world and with the country a complete ruin...she is completely capable of doing it. Most cities are nuclear wastelands...and those that are left are barely hanging to life as it is. I don't feel like I'm safe. I feel like I'm hiding."

Liam hit the nail exactly on the head. Being underground at Sanctuary felt exactly like hiding. We weren't safe, not really. We were under the illusion that we were safe. Outside of these walls, above our heads, were rogue societies, and an entire company bent on taking over the world with horrible, deathly creatures ready to tear us apart at any moment.

"I don't know that we have any other options," I said, sadly.

His blue eyes met mine. It was so strange that both he and Ash had blue eyes but I saw such different things in them. "There are though, Zoey. There are other options."

"What options?" I asked him, confused. It was just as I was asking this that my entire world exploded.

Ash came sprinting down the hallway, his eyes darting each and every way. When they landed on me, he looked relieved. When he saw Liam sitting on the ground next to me, his eyes narrowed. I wanted to throttle him, or throw him against the wall and kiss him until he remembered that it was him that I wanted. Both sounded equally appealing at the moment. I glared at him. I knew that Liam had said things he shouldn't have said but the loathing really had to go away.

Liam, however, looked alarmed. "Ash? What's wrong?"

Ash threw a scathing look at Liam and focused on me. "There are Awakened on level one. No one knows how they got in but the entire level is an absolute chaos."

Ice struck my heart and for a split-second I was frozen, pressed against the wall. There was a rushing sound in my ears as I took in the words I had just heard. The last time I had come face to face with Awakened was when my mother was killed by one of them. The thought of facing those pale blue faces intent on killing me, didn't sound like a fun time.

Ash held his hand out to me. "Let's go."

My palm slipped easily into his and he hoisted me to my feet. "Go? Go where?"

The look he gave me was incredulous. "Go help of course. Jesus, Zoey."

"Help?" I shrieked. I was about to continue when alarms suddenly blared all around us. It was the emergency alarm. We'd had one drill since coming to Sanctuary. It meant one thing: danger. We were to go to the nearest room and lock ourselves in. "Ash, we need to get to a room. Hide. Not help."

"Hide? Why the hell would we hide?" Ash yelled, disbelieving, tugging my hand so I was pressed closer to him.

"He's right, Zoey," Liam agreed, and I shot a dark look in his direction. I didn't know if he genuinely agreed with Ash or was just agreeing to get on his good side, but either way, I was not a fan of it. "We need to go help."

I stared helplessly at both of them. "This is what Sanctuary has patrols for. This is what the guards are for. This is not what we're for!"

"We have experience in killing them," Ash pointed out. "And I'm tired of doing nothing. I'm tired of sitting around and going to freakin' school pretending that those monsters aren't out there, Zoey. I'm tired of pretending they aren't the reason that our friends and family are dead, and the reason we're covered in scars. I need this."

My heart was pounding in my chest. Every word rang true in my ears. These creatures were the cause of so much pain and they were the creations of one person orchestrating the entire thing. I needed it too. But fear was running through my veins like a current and it was hard to ignore.

Ash's hands grabbed my face firmly between them and he looked at me fiercely, his eyes burning. "I know you're scared. I know you'll never admit it, but I know you are. But you're the most badass fighter I know and we can do this together."

The whole exchange only took a few minutes but I felt like it had taken much longer. The alarms were ringing in my ears, making it nearly impossible to think. Liam was standing to the side, bouncing anxiously on the balls of his feet, looking down the corridor like he was ready to sprint at any moment.

"Let's go," I finally said. My voice was low and could barely be heard over the incessant alarms but Ash and Liam heard and immediately went running. I hesitated for a split second, and then ran after them.

I had never run up the corridors to the higher levels. Running in Sanctuary was mostly discouraged. It was a sign of chaos, disorganization and everything here was perfect. Even then, with the alarms, everyone was moving calmly and locking themselves in. The three of us were getting glares and irritated looks as we moved through the crowds, not really paying attention to who we ran into. I wasn't positive but I might have even knocked down a little kid. I winced but kept running.

The two of them stopped at level three and I looked confused for a moment. The Awakened were on level one...

"We need weapons," Ash explained, as if it were obvious. It *was* obvious. Apparently I had been ready to run into a crowd of Awakened without a weapon.

Level three was absolute chaos. Most of the time it was empty of anyone except patrols and guards and all the doors were tightly sealed. This was not true right now. For all their practice and drills, they looked a little ill prepared for what was happening just above us. We snuck in without a problem and grabbed weapons without anyone noticing.

The gun in my hand felt wrong. The last I had held was my dad's gun, the one he'd owned for years, the one he always had with him, whether he had been in uniform or not. This gun was similar but it didn't feel right. I swallowed hard, taking the extra ammunition Ash passed me and followed them up to level one.

If level three had been chaos, level one was literal hell. The three of us halted as we entered, horrified looks painted on all of our faces. They were everywhere, and even though we weren't outnumbered, it certainly looked like it. Those blue bodies stood out amongst the regular black uniforms. I hadn't seen this many Awakened since I had escaped New York City.

Liam and Ash barely hesitated. Both of them ran into the crowd, taking down Awakened like a pair of Spartans or something. I registered dimly that Ash hadn't known how to shoot a gun or even throw a *proper* punch a year ago and now he was out there, ducking under and around people, and landing bullets in several Awakened as he did so.

Something went whizzing past my ear and my heart stopped in my chest for just a moment. I didn't know what it was but I immediately ducked behind the nearest vehicle. I had left myself as an easy target for too long.

It had been so long since I had done this that I missed the first few Awakened that came into close proximity. I had never been that great at using a gun, despite the amount of lessons my dad had forced on me.

I was, however, good at fighting. My body was rusty and out of shape, but my muscles remembered the movements and I took down two Awakened fairly easily, sending them crashing to the ground before landing a bullet between their eyes. They stared unseeing at me, and I shuddered before turning my attention back to the fight.

It seemed to last forever. For every Awakened I killed, another appeared in its place. It was like they were coming out of the walls, the pipes, from under the floor beneath us. They were endless and I could feel the exhaustion take over me. I leaned against the car for a moment and immediately regretted it. My foot slipped in a pool of dark blood and I went crashing to the ground, landing hard on my elbow. The pain ricocheted up my arm and I cursed loudly, dropping the gun in the process.

"Zoey!"

Ash's voice rang out above the cacophony of noise but I couldn't react. My vision was blurred and I nearly passed out. I hadn't eaten and I was so tired. I hadn't slept properly in months and my muscles were screaming at me. I reached for the car, trying to hoist myself up when something came flying at me. I ducked but it was too late. The large cold body of an Awakened hit me and I screamed as it landed on top of me.

"Well, look what we have here." The raspy voice sent a shiver up my spine and I squirmed underneath the heavy weight pinning in place. The gun had slid underneath the car. I couldn't reach it and I couldn't breathe. I opened my mouth to scream, yell for help, but the weight on top of me was too heavy. The Awakened was a middle-aged man, heavy, and his meaty arm was braced against my neck. My head seemed to expand as the air left my lungs. I pushed at him, but he barely reacted. My hands were useless against him. He was just too damn strong. His mouth came closer to me as he ran his tongue slowly over the raised scar on my face. I recoiled and felt a few tears escape the corners of my eyes.

"Ash!" I managed to gasp. "Liam!"

"Someone already beat me here, didn't they?" He sounded amused and I hated it. I hated that they had conscience. I had always laughed at zombie movies and TV shows, so slow, so stupid. I would do anything for those now. The Awakened were smart and hearing them talk made me sick every single time. "That's okay. Now it's my turn to taste."

His teeth sank into the soft skin of my collarbone and the pain was excruciating. My vision went black for a moment; his teeth felt like needles piercing my skin and I could feel the flesh being torn from my body. I was losing myself. I didn't know what to do. I didn't know how to get myself out of this situation. I tried to yell but I could barely breathe. I was going to die. This was it. My fingers fumbled at his grip around my neck but they merely slipped in the blood that had pooled there.

Then, suddenly, the pain lifted and I heard howling above me. I was confused, momentarily distracted by the throbbing coming from my chest. He was clutching his face, blood pouring down his cheeks. My fingers were covered in blood and I realized that I had somehow managed to get him the eye. It was gruesome and my stomach rolled at the sight.

I took advantage of the situation and kneed him hard in the groin. He fell backwards and I scrambled away from him. I flipped onto my stomach and crawled closer to the car, my fingers reaching for the gun that had disappeared underneath. The gun slipped through my sticky fingers a few times before I got a hold of it. I rolled over just in time as he came at me. The shot sailed cleanly through his throat. His wails immediately ended and he crumpled to the ground.

I collapsed against the car, pressing my shaking hand to my forehead. A few silent sobs escaped my lips and I wiped my mouth with the back of my hand. There was no one in my corner for the moment but it wouldn't stay like that for long.

Get up, Zoey. Keep fighting. Don't give up.

I was startled to hear Dad's voice in my head and it nearly sent me over again. But it kept repeating itself, over and over again. Don't give up. Ash and Liam were out there. Kaya and Corbin and so many others were below. My hand slipped as I pulled myself up once more. I peeked out from behind the car and nearly fell back down in the shock.

Each and every remaining Awakened was frozen, standing perfectly straight and staring into nothingness. I had only ever seen them like this once before, in the confines of Sekhmet, when Razi had shown me that they were the product of her supposed genius. They were being controlled, and I wasn't sure what to do with them. Neither, it seemed, did anyone else. Everyone's guns were still raised, but no one moved.

It felt like ages, but it couldn't have been more than a few seconds before we started reaching for our guns. Every one of them snapped to attention and went sprinting, faster than I had ever seen them go. They were a sea of blue as they ran...away from Sanctuary. Shots rang out after them and several of them went down as they escaped. But they were incredibly fast and they disappeared, up the stairs and out of Sanctuary, taking out guards as they left.

No one looked particularly eager to go after them.

Except me.. I wanted to follow them back to Sekhmet, taking each and every one of them down, but the pain in my chest came rushing back and I nearly passed out. I couldn't see it but it was bleeding like crazy, running down my stomach. I knew it was too much. I felt lightheaded.

"Zoey. Jesus." Ash grabbed at me, keeping me from losing my balance and falling to the floor. "Is it possible for you to get through a fight without getting torn to pieces?" He was trying to joke but I could hear the stress in his voice. He was ripping his shirt and pressing it against me but I could barely register the feel of the stiff fabric against my collarbone.

"Where's the fun in that?" I mumbled.

"Is she okay?"

"Does she fuckin' look okay, Liam?" Ash barked at him. I waved my hand uselessly at the two of them, wishing they would just stop fighting already but I was too tired to even open my mouth.

"We have to get her out of here, to the infirmary."

I dimly remembered those words but they sounded faint, far away, and I slipped easily into unconsciousness.

CHAPTER ELEVEN

THE DREAM WAS different than any dream I had ever had before. It wasn't a nightmare, which was a nice change from the usual channel my brain tended to be on when my head hit the pillow. But it was definitely different, definitely weird.

I was in my mother's farmhouse in Nebraska. It looked exactly the same, the way I remembered it except it was before the chaos of the Awakened, before the United States became a nuclear wasteland. The TV was blaring from the living room and I could hear my mother's laughter. She didn't laugh much the last time I saw her.

She was talking to someone in the kitchen and she was happier than I'd ever heard her, whilst I was lounging on the couch in the living room, watching a baseball game on the TV. The details were fuzzy and I wasn't sure if I was watching my favorite team, the Mets, playing. I swore loudly at a bad play.

"Zoey! Language!"

I winced and shouted back. "I'm sorry!"

"Come on, its dinnertime. You and Ash get in here."

I suddenly noticed Ash was sitting next to me. He lounged in the corner of the couch, looking incredibly relaxed, an arm thrown casually along the armrest. His legs were propped up on the coffee table and I knew that if Mom saw him, she'd scold him. Nicely, of course, because she adored Ash. He caught me looking at him and stole a kiss before I could even process that he was there. He was not the Ash I knew now. His brow was free of worry and his skin was smooth and scar free.

"Come on, your mom made lasagna and I'm starving."

He helped me off the couch and I followed him into the dining room where my mom was setting a casserole dish of incredibly wonderful smelling lasagna in the middle of the table. She smiled as we entered and the smile I returned was easy. I can't remember the last time I had given her a genuine smile and it felt so natural to do it. I missed it.

I slid into a chair and Ash immediately slid into the one next to me. His hand reached out to squeeze my knee before he served himself a heavy portion of lasagna. Cheese dripped all over the dining room table but Mom barely noticed as she checked the clock and frowned.

"Hey guys! I'm home!"

Mom brightened up. "Right on time."

My heart pounded in my chest and I froze as I reached for the spatula. I knew that voice. I knew that voice better than I knew any other voice in the world. It was the voice I missed so much that it physically hurt.

Dad walked through the doorway, and seeing him in a police officer's uniform with that trademark grin on his face was like a punch to the gut. I stared at him in wonder, as he crossed the room and laid a kiss on my mom that had her bent backwards and giggling.

They both came up, laughing, and Dad turned to us. "Hey, champ." He nodded at Ash, who nodded back, his mouth full of blood.

My voice failed me and all I could do was stare at them, Dad's arm wrapped tightly around Mom's waist.

"Zoey? Zoey, what's wrong?"

I shook my head. Dad's mouth was moving but the words weren't coming from him; they weren't even in his voice.

"Zoey? Zoey?"

I jerked awake, a cold sweat trailing a small stream down my spine. My hand went to my forehead, where a pounding headache was threatening to burst through my skin. I looked around and saw Ash looking at me, concerned. "Ash?"

"I'm sorry, honey," he apologized, quickly, sitting closer to me. "You've just been out for a whole day and you were whimpering in your sleep. I was worried. I didn't mean to wake you." His hand was clutching mine, his thumb rubbing comforting circles across my skin

"It's okay," I said, my voice cracking. "I'm glad you woke me up."

He raised his eyebrow at me. "Bad dream?"

"Not bad, exactly," I answered, vaguely, trying to clear my mind of the weird dream. "I've been out for a day?"

He nodded. "They knocked you out. You were torn up, Z. Like usual." He shot me a wry look and I rolled my eyes. The movement sent a searing pain through my sinuses and I winced inwardly. "I had to fight to be able to stay with you."

I sighed. "Oh, I'm sure. Even though I was passed out for the most part."

"This is very true. On the other hand, we got the most alone time than we had the entire time we've been here…"

"Your sarcasm is not appreciated at this very moment," I told him, and he laughed. I lifted my hand to pull at my hospital gown but immediately dropped it. The pain was too much. "How bad is it?"

Ash stood up quickly, reaching for the collarbone of my hospital gown. God, even the damn hospital gown was black. What was wrong with a little bit of color in this place? Ash's fingers brushed against my chest lightly and I sucked in a breath at the tingles it sent through me. He winked at me and I shook my head. I immediately regretted the action, as it sent pain shooting through me.

He pulled the gown far enough to reveal a large white bandage covering most of the left side of my collarbone. He peeled back the tape carefully, and took a step back, letting me take in the damage.

"They injected you with...something," Ash explained. "Prevented you from any infection or anything. Apparently Sanctuary medicine is way more advanced than what we had."

I could barely see the damage. It was incredibly hard to look at your own collarbone, but what I could see didn't look pretty. There were a ton of stitches but they looked neat and clean and hopefully that meant it would heal much better than the scar on my face. The entire thing was a painting of black and blue and it made me sick just looking at it. "I guess I'm just glad to be alive."

"Not funny, Zoey," Ash said, dryly. "You lost a ton of blood. I've never seen you that pale, not even when that piece of shit Awakened cut up your face. I didn't think..."

"I'm fine," I cut in. I was about to continue when the door of my room slid open and Octavia walked in, looking...well, not exactly angry. She had the best poker face of anyone I had ever met in my entire life. But she definitely didn't look happy.

A nurse had followed her in, clipboard in hand, as she checked the monitors that surrounded me.

"Zoey." Just my name but it felt like a curse on her lips. She nodded at Ash in acknowledgment. "Mr. Matthews, I see you still haven't left Miss Valentine's side."

"I don't really plan to, Director," Ash said. The words rang sincere but he was goading her though she ignored the bait.

"Even if that means dragging both of yourselves into something you should have avoided at all costs?" Her voice was even but there was a thin veil of anger there. Ah. That was why she was here. I highly doubt every injured Sanctuary citizen got a personalized visit from the Director. She was pissed at us.

"You'd rather we hid with everyone else?" I tried to keep my voice even but trying was very different to succeeding. The disdain dripped from my tongue as I looked at her from my hospital bed.

"You are a citizen of Sanctuary, Zoey Valentine." Octavia's voice was angry. I had never seen her lose her cool this way, and yet her face still remained smooth. "You are not a solider."

"I won't keep hiding, Octavia." There's a hiss of outrage from the nurse and I resisted the urge to hit her over the head. It wasn't much of a resistance; I doubted I could even swat a fly away at that moment. Not that I had ever seen an actual fly in Sanctuary. "I'm tired of it. You guys might be content to just hide in a hole in the ground but I'm not doing it anymore."

There was a long pause and I wondered if I had overstepped. Scratch that. I knew I had overstepped. No one talked to the Director like this, not even Patrick, her second in command.

"What would you have us do?" Her voice was so calm. I didn't know anyone with that kind of patience. I definitely didn't have it and it drove me insane. I wanted to be able to tell what she was thinking but it was nearly impossible. I didn't know if she genuinely wanted to know what I would do in this situation, or if she was just humoring me. It could have been both.

"Fight."

A loud laugh filled the room and the three of us turned to the nurse, staring. She immediately paled and ducked her head, wrapping a blood pressure cuff tightly around my forearm.

Octavia's eyes narrowed on the nurse for a long moment, her lips pursed. The nurse pretended not to notice, but the tips of her ears were burning bright red as she studied my blood pressure before entering it on a chart.

Finally, Octavia looked away from the nurse and back over at Ash and myself. Ash had perched on the bed next to me, his hand resting gently against my blanket covered knee. "You say it like it's so simple."

I snorted and the movement jostled my body. The nurse glared at me but I ignored her. If she was going to laugh at my suggestion, I had no business giving her what she wanted. "I didn't say that it was simple."

"It's definitely *not* simple," Ash muttered under his breath, his fingers tracing the bandage over my collarbone.

"But come on, it has to be done! We can't just hide under this rock and pretend that the outside world doesn't exist, Octavia." The nurse gasped again but I didn't care. I respected Octavia's position in this establishment but I didn't think that she was so far above me that using her name was *that* taboo. "Maybe it won't happen now. Or in the next year. Or even the next five or ten years but it is going to happen. Sekhmet will reach us down here. They already have. Ignoring them, pretending they aren't there, its not working for you."

Octavia folded herself neatly into the chair that Ash had vacated. Her brow furrowed, and not for the first time, she looked so familiar. I couldn't place it. There was something about the wrinkles on her forehead as she thought and the curve of her full lips that jogged something in my memory. "They somehow got Liam to our entrance."

"Yes," I agreed.

"And have been dumping bodies of our patrols on our front doorstep like a taunt."

My stomach sunk at this but it was nothing but the truth. Too many innocent patrolmen and women had lost their lives, been torn to pieces and dropped on our front porch like a cat bringing home dead mice. "Yes."

Her voice shook as she continued. "They got into Sanctuary. How is it possible they managed to get in here with those...with those things?"

I sighed, relieved. I didn't like anything about this situation. People were dying. So many people were dying and there weren't a lot of us left, not after the US government bombed the crap out of their country. But Octavia was finally seeing it or, at the very least, was allowing herself to see it. Sanctuary wasn't perfect. Even if it were perfect, it wouldn't stay that way for long. People knew we were here and Sekhmet was coming. They'd been telling us that for months.

"We have to fight. We have to take them down. No one is safe with that institute still functioning. No one is safe with that crazy lady still alive," Ash insisted.

Octavia's eyes met Ash's and she studied him. The two of them didn't speak much, at least not to each other. Octavia always seemed to defer to me, and Ash usually ended up being with me, but they didn't have a lot of one-on-one interaction with each other. It was interesting to watch Octavia regard Ash with such respect. "You sound very much like my father when you say things like that."

Ash and I looked at each other and back at her. "Your father?" I asked, surprised.

She nodded, looking lost for a moment. We left her in her own thoughts for a few seconds before I made a huff of impatience. "Sorry. Yes, my father. Smart man. Great man. You've met him."

For some reason, the grouchy old man, Peter, in the laundry room was the first person to come to mind. It made no sense. Peter was paler than the moon and Octavia's skin was the color of milk chocolate...

"Bert," Ash immediately said. "You're Bert's daughter."

My eyes widened. Bert Washington was the man that had saved our lives when we had thought we would be at the hands of Sekhmet for all eternity. He was the man that took us in, fixed Ash when I thought he was going to die. He gave us food, and clothes. He brought us to Sanctuary. I remembered how he seemed to just have clothes that fit us and how that seemed to be a little too convenient. Now it all made sense. I had been wearing Octavia's clothes.

I had to admit, this bugged me out a little bit.

"I didn't know Bert had a daughter," I finally said, breaking the silence that had fallen in the room. The nurse finished her examination, though it seemed to have mostly consisted of eavesdropping on our conversation.

"He did. He does," Octavia explained. "He also had a son, my brother Marcus."

I had not met a Marcus in Sanctuary at all. This also explained where the clothes for Ash had come from. "Marcus?"

Octavia sighed. "He died when he was just barely eighteen years old." She didn't elaborate more than this and I knew that the two of us were way too intimidated by her to ask her to explain. "But he was always the active one, the one to *do* things. He would have been much better at this."

She always looked so careful, so calm and collected and it made her look much older than she was. Seeing her as she was right now with emotion on her face, talking about her brother, made her look younger. Instead of looking like an old, stressed out woman, she looked like the young forty-something she was.

It didn't last long. She shook her head, dismissing the thoughts going through her mind. "That's beside the point. My job is to keep everyone here safe. That is my main priority. I can't go tearing into a facility like that. We weren't built for war. We were built for sanctuary."

A flash of irritation went soaring through me. "It doesn't matter what you were built for. War came here whether you wanted it to or not. You can't ignore that."

Octavia stood up abruptly, smoothing her skirt out with her palms. "You've given me some things to think about," she replied, diplomatically. "However, I will not have my people running into battle, no matter their experience. Only trained soldiers are authorized for this. I will have your word that you will not repeat this incident."

I didn't say anything. Neither of us could or would promise that to her. I wasn't overly fond of the new marks that had added to the landscape of pain on my body, or the fact that I was attached to way too many monitors but I wasn't sorry for going up there. I had stopped a lot of Awakened. I had contributed and it felt good to finally do something for once.

"Very well." The anger crept back into Octavia's tone. She turned to leave but stopped just before passing through the doorway. "They left something behind. Sekhmet, I mean. They left something."

Ash and I stared at her, and then exchanged quick confused glances.

"They left us a girl," Octavia said, stonily. "A girl named Astrid."

CHAPTER TWELVE

THEY KEPT ME in the infirmary for two more days, though that seemed to be overkill. True, my injuries had been pretty damn severe but I was alive. I was fine. And I was going absolutely crazy in that room, especially since they only let Ash stay with me one day before making him return to his normal schedule. I didn't see him for the rest of my stay and I hadn't seen Liam at all.

I also hadn't seen Astrid.

Apparently they'd brought her into the infirmary, an improvement from when Liam was brought here. This place was huge though and every time I had the inkling to go searching for her, a nurse magically appeared and kept me in my room.

I was also told they hadn't yet informed Liam that she was here. I didn't know why. He had been losing sleep over her for weeks now and he deserved to know that she was here, and she wasn't in the clutches of Razi Cylon anymore. I knew I had to tackle the "why" of her appearance soon but not yet. Not until I could tell Liam that she was here.

I woke up the morning I was being let out and after being cleared, nearly sprinted down to the cafeteria. My walk was brisk – and admittedly painful – but I wasn't capable of running so it was the best I could do. I practically burst through the doors. A few heads turned but most people here had gotten used to my antics, or so it seemed, since they turned back to their food pretty quickly.

I spotted Corbin, Liam and Ash at our usual table. A smile stretched across my face and I headed over to them. My arms wrapped tightly around Ash from behind and felt his laugh rumble up and down his spine. "Hey, Z," he said. "Welcome back."

I planted a soft kiss on the side of his neck and, despite the cocky grin on his face, he shivered a little. I grinned back. My eyes met Liam's and I practically tripped in my hurry to get to him. He smiled, warmly, before catching me.

"I am so glad you're okay," he whispered to me.

A shaky laugh escaped my lips. "I'm always okay." I pulled back and looked over at Ash. He was trying. I could see it. But it was hard for him and I was about to make it harder on everyone. "Between the two of you, I'll always be okay." I hesitated, looking over at Ash. He immediately sat up straighter and nodded. "Liam, I have to tell your something."

He took a step back, holding me at arm's length. His hands tightened on my shoulders, as he looked down at me with concern. "What's wrong?"

"Nothing is...wrong. Just...they haven't told you yet and I knew you had to hear it from me, but Liam, Astrid is here."

The color drained from Liam's already pale face and his hands gripped my shoulders righter. I winced but he didn't seem to notice.

"Liam, she's here." His eyes were crazy and darting in all directions. I grabbed his hands and held them firmly in mine. "Look at me. She's here. Astrid is here."

"Astrid," he breathed.

I nodded. "Yes, honey. Astrid."

His eyes finally met mine and they turned from the deep ocean blue back to his normal pale ice blue eyes. He was focused on me and I breathed a sigh of relief.

"Do you want to see her?" I asked, squeezing his hands.

Liam nodded, looking a bit dazed, and Ash immediately stood up to join us. We walked out of the cafeteria and up through the halls to the infirmary. The staff looked shocked when the three of us entered but I held my head high and dragged Liam through, right to the room where everyone was crowded. I may not have known before but I knew now. Octavia exited the room just as we reached it. She looked startled to see us.

"She needs rest," was all she said.

"I'm sure she does," I agreed and Octavia looked taken aback. "But Liam also needs to see her. And you know that's true." I looked back up at him, staring in a daze at the door behind Octavia. "He's going to be no good to anyone until he sees that she's safe."

Octavia sighed, exasperated. She was getting awfully tired of me. "Very well." She stepped aside and the three of us pushed forward, opening the door and closing it behind us.

Astrid was perched on the bed. She was a tiny little thing, and she looked hardly older than thirteen, but I knew she was eighteen, from what Liam had told me about her. She had deep black hair that was tied in two messy braids, which only made her look younger, and large brown eyes. She was definitely of some Hispanic descent and I wondered where she had lived before being captured by Sekhmet. Her hands were resting lightly on her stomach. Her round stomach.

"Oh my god," I choked out. My eyes widened and my hand slipped out of Liam's grip. "You're…"

It wasn't obvious. It wasn't like she was tipping over from the weight or anything. But there was no mistaking it. She was pregnant, probably only a few months but she was definitely, completely, undeniably pregnant.

Astrid looked up, her braids whipping around as she regarded us. Her eyes took us in, confused at first, until they landed on Liam. The two of them stared at each other so long that I felt like I was intruding. I was about to tell Ash that we should leave when Astrid finally spoke. "They told me that you were here. I didn't know if I believed it. But here you are.

Liam didn't respond. He looked in shock, as if he was unsure of what to say or do.

"Don't trip over your words, Liam," Astrid said, dryly, shaking her head. She'd gotten over her initial shock. Her teeth were biting into her bottom lip but she was barely concealing a smile. She was happy to see Liam; that was clear. "You might overwhelm yourself."

I couldn't help it. I laughed. Astrid's eyes immediately shot to mine and I shut up, clamping my lips tightly together. Her left eyebrow rose at the sight of me and she studied me for a second. It had been so long since someone had done that but I didn't allow myself to squirm under her scrutiny.

"Well, shit, you're Zoey," she finally said.

"Um, yes," I answered, waving my hand awkwardly in the air. "That's me." My heart pounded in my chest as my eyes took in her pregnant belly again. That was almost me. It should have been me. I didn't know whether to be relieved that I had escaped that or upset that it had worked so successfully on Astrid.

Astrid looked back over at Liam. She crossed her legs, like a little kid sitting down for story time, and propped her chin up on her hand. "You didn't say she was so damn pretty, Liam."

Liam finally seemed to have woken up from his stupor. He crossed the room and sat gingerly on the edge of the bed. For a moment, it looked like he was going to reach for her but he pulled away before he touched her. I might have imagined it, but she looked disappointed. "That wasn't exactly significant when I was talking about her, Astrid."

"Oh, wasn't it?" she teased. Her small hand reached for him and it rested gently on his knee. He startled at the touch before relaxing into it.

"She's with me." Ash said, firmly, behind me, and I groaned.

"Jesus, Ash, she's kidding," I pointed out, and sure enough, Astrid had a huge smile on her face. She was already pretty but the smile was the winner. It lit up the entire room and even I was dazzled for a moment under its bright light.

"Wow, a lively room," Astrid remarked, looking back and forth between the three of us and I decided immediately that I liked her. She probably had given Liam a run for his money back in Sekhmet. It was evident by the look on his face that no matter how many times he had denied it to me, he was insanely in love with her.

I hesitated and then stepped closer. "So she succeeded?"

Astrid's fingers clenched on her stomach for a moment and she looked panicked, looking down. Her eyes rose and darted around. "Yeah, she succeeded." She looked at me carefully and my hands folded over my own stomach. Her eyes narrowed but there was no judgment in her expression. Not in the slightest. She was just observing.

"But, um, does that mean…" I looked at Liam and then back to her and she smirked.

"No. We didn't. Apparently after trying and failing to get the two of to…ahem, consummate your match at Sekhmet, she just forced the issue." The hand on Liam's knee moved up, closer to his thigh. "This is a product of in vitro fertilization."

Liam sucked in a breath, looking absolutely miserable. His eyes drank in every feature of Astrid, like he could never stop looking at her, but he looked guilty as well. "Are you okay?"

Astrid smiled at him, and it was small, sweet and reserved only for him. "Of course I am. I'm here with you." Her hand fluttered nervously on his thigh before she raised it and cupped his cheek.

His hand immediately went to hers and grasped it tightly, pressing it harder against his cheek. "And our baby?"

Our. He said *our.* Astrid looked relieved at his words and slumped over, looking tired for the first time in the conversation. "Oh, Liam," she whispered.

"Okay, that's our cue to leave," I whispered to Ash and I hustled him out of the door.

When we made it out of the infirmary and out into one of the empty corridors. I stopped and collapsed against the wall, sliding to the ground. My fingers were digging into my thighs, my knees pulled against my chest. "Oh, Ash. She's pregnant. She's going to have a baby."

"I know," he answered, sliding onto the floor next to me. He yanked on me hard, pulling me into his lap and pressed a hard kiss on my forehead. I hated that it took seeing that girl pregnant with Liam's baby for him to act like this with me again, but it felt so much safer in his arms. "I know."

"That was supposed to be me. I was the only who was supposed to be in that situation. I was the one who was supposed to have started the new master race, or whatever." I shook my head. "I got cocky or something. I thought...well, I escaped. I couldn't get pregnant and she couldn't have my baby if I had escaped. And her plan was ruined." I took a deep breath. "But she just found someone else. She. Just. Found. Someone. Else. And Astrid didn't even get a chance because of the hell I caused."

"It's not your fault, Zoey," Ash reassured me, but his arms reaching around to bring me in closer. "I know this is probably wrong, but I'm glad it's not you. Especially with Liam."

I rolled my eyes. "You're impossible."

"It's what makes you love me so much," he replied, easily.

"Maybe. Something like that," I answered back. There was a long pause and I enjoyed the sound of Ash's heartbeat through his thin shirt. My fingers were wrapped in the fabric and I inhaled. I missed this. I missed the easy way he used to be, even when the world was falling apart. He always made me smile; he never failed to make me laugh.

"It's okay that it's not you," he whispered in my ear, his fingers playing with the ends of my hair.

"That's why I feel so guilty," I groaned into his chest. "I'm so glad that it's not me. I saw her stomach, Ash, and it made me so sick. I never even knew if I wanted kids before all this happened. I knew I didn't want them at nineteen. Now? I don't think I'm going to be popping them out any time soon." My hand ran absentmindedly over the small birth control implant in my arm. "It's just...she's so tiny!"

Ash laughed, my head bouncing on his chest as he did so. "She's only a year younger than us." I opened my mouth and he continued. "I know what you mean though. She looks like a kid herself. But you have to admit, she looked pretty well taken care of in there."

I raised my head off his chest and met those deep blue eyes that drove me crazy in all the good and bad ways. My eyebrows rose on my forehead. "So you saw it too?"

It was his turn to roll his eyes. "Anyone with eyes could see the way the two of them looked at each other. I don't think Razi would have had to wait that long to get them to actually make a baby."

"You're impossible," I repeated. "Does that mean you'll finally get off my case? And Liam's?"

Ash opened his mouth and then closed it, looking sheepish. "I'm sorry."

I smirked up at him. "You're what? Can you repeat that again?"

He shoved me playfully but his expression remained serious. "Really though Z, I am sorry. I was acting like an ass. Sometimes I just think..." He sucked in a gulp of air and let it out slowly. It blew a few strands of hair into my face and I pushed them away, looking up at him. "Sometimes I think...what if you and I aren't actually supposed to work?

What if we only ended up together because we were all each other had? What if someone else changed what we had because they were actually better?"

I pulled away, my mouth dropping open. "Jesus, Ash."

He looked down at me in shock. "That's not what I meant…"

I cut him off. "Ash, I love you. And you know that. And you know that this is how I've felt since before all this shit happened. I'm not with you because you were my only option. I'm with you because it doesn't matter how many other options I have. I only want you. I can't believe you would think otherwise."

"Z, you know that's not what I was saying." Ash pleaded with me.

"Don't call me that. And besides, Liam? Liam was my better choice? If that were true, I would have stayed in Sekhmet with him, instead of breaking out and risking my life to save yours." I pushed myself off of him and glared down at him. "But if you think there might be someone better than me in this stupid place, then go find her. I won't have you staying with me because I'm your only option."

I spun on my heel and went stomping away, the anger roaring in my ears, drowning out Ash's cries of my name.

He caught up to me easily, his hand reaching out to grab my arm. He spun me around and the movement sent the both of us off balance. My back collided with the hard wall, made worse when Ash landed against me. I was so full of anger with him but his warmth always felt good against me.

"Get off," I said, sharply.

Ash shook his head, his eyes boring into mine. I raised my right fist, to punch him or something but he dodged me quickly and grabbed my arm. His other hand came up and next thing I knew, both of my arms were pinned above my head. I aimed to kick him in the groin but he shifted his weight and leaned more against me. "Stop fighting me, Zoey. You don't get to be mad at me."

I stopped struggling and looked up at him. "Are you kidding me?"

"No, I'm not kidding you," Ash barked out sharply. "You wanted to know what was wrong. You wanted to know why I was acting like a total douche and here I am, trying to explain it to you and you just walk away from me. You don't listen to me. You don't talk to me and you don't listen to me."

"That is not true…" I started to say but he cut him off.

"Is it true, Zoey. You don't talk to me. You disappear and you spend all this time with Liam and you talk to him and you listen to him and what am I supposed to think? I'm supposed to be the one you come to and you don't."

I opened my mouth and then closed it again. Ash's entire body was pressed against mine, making it incredibly hard to concentrate. "Ash…it's not that…it's not that I don't want to come to you. I love you. But Liam has become a best friend to me. And he understands. He was there with me, in that place. He knows what it was like. He knew what it was like to be so terrified."

Ash's mouth came crashing down on me before I had the chance to react. I was shocked, unable to move, before his tongue probed at my lips and I opened myself to him. Our kisses were fast and feverish and desperate and there was a reminder in the back of my mind that we were fighting, but he felt so good and it had been too long since he had kissed me like this. A moan caught in the back of my throat and he groaned, his hands pressing my arms tighter against the wall. We kissed again and again before he pulled himself away.

"Ash?" I asked, confused. My head was spinning and my lips felt bruised. My heart was racing in my chest and I wanted to pull him back onto me, to feel him against me once more.

"Sorry," he whispered. His forehead pressed hard against mine and his breathing was quick and fast. "I got carried away."

There was a long bout of silence before he spoke again. "You just...you forget. God, Zoey, you forget that I was there too. And I didn't have anyone to keep me going. I was locked in a five by five cell, and I saw no one. I didn't know what they were going to do with me and I had no idea if you were okay. I spent most of my days staring at the wall, wondering if it was the day I was going to die. I was terrified in that place. I have nightmares too. I know exactly what it felt like to be in there, and it kills me that you can't come to me when you're scared or you're anxious or you've had a bad dream, but you'll go to *him.*"

Ash took a deep breath and dropped his arms. My own arms stayed glued to the wall for a moment as I stared at him. "Ash...why didn't you ever say anything?"

His fiery gaze turned on me and I shrunk into the wall. "Zoey, I've tried! I've tried to get you to talk to me. I've told you, I'm here, I'm here, I'm here, and all you saw was a jealous boyfriend. And yeah, I was jealous, not because I thought you and Liam had something going on. I know better than that. No, I was jealous because the girl I love, the girl I'm with, couldn't even come to me, not even when she knows how much I understand how scared she is."

A flush of shame went through me. I wasn't happy with Ash Matthews. I wasn't happy with him or Liam right now to be perfectly honest. But I couldn't deny that he was saying things that made complete sense. It was another testament to how much Ash had grown up in the last year since the Awakened had struck. Last year, I would not have given him the credit of having a valid point in an argument. Then again, we had never really argued, just bickered. The Ash of last year would have just thrown water balloons full of Jell-O at me, instead of standing in front of me explaining things rationally.

"Ash, I'm sorry," I finally said, quietly.

He sighed loudly, sounding impatient but the lines on his face had smoothed out and now, he simply looked tired. "I know, Zoey." There were mere inches between us and it felt like so much more. I had never been afraid of reaching for him, not in the last four or five months that we had been "official" but this was the first time we'd ever really fought and I was afraid to even look at him. I studied the tile on the floor.

Ash reached for me first, his hand coming up around my neck. I collided into his chest, and clung onto him. "I know you are," he repeated, his voice much softer. More understanding. I felt like I was shrinking smaller and smaller. If I could, I would just melt into the wall behind me.

His fingers ran patterns on my skin, sending goosebumps rippling across me. Normally I'd be a little embarrassed. "Don't disappear on me, Zoey. Not now." I felt his lips brush the top of my head and I pressed myself tighter into him.

"I'm not going anywhere," I promised.

"Good. You're the only person I have left, Zoey. You're it. You're the only person that I have left in this world. I don't know what I would do if you were gone too."

I swallowed hard, biting back the tears that had been threatening since I had escaped the hospital room with Liam and Astrid's reunion. The pain from the losses we had experienced over the past year had dulled some, but they never went away. Ash's parents. My parents. Our friends. Our families. Everyone.

"The world is a shitty place right now and relationships are hard enough. Let's not make this harder than it has to be, okay?"

I nodded. "You're right."

"And don't you forget that," he joked weakly as I smiled sadly against his chest. "I love you, Zoey."

Hearing those words sent a wave of relief through me, though all the negative feelings were still battling in my chest. But out of everything else going on in Sanctuary, there was one thing I was absolutely sure of and that was I loved him too. And so I showed him.

CHAPTER THIRTEEN

THE NEXT DAY, Octavia called another assembly meeting down in the amphitheater room. To say that the looks on the faces of the Sanctuary citizens were nothing but shock would be a complete understatement. It had been just a couple of weeks since Octavia had assured us all that this would not happen again, that the problem would be taken care of, and they had taken her at her every word. Seeing the grim faced Director in front of us, clearly about to deliver bad news, wiped the confidence off the board.

"Citizens of Sanctuary, it is with regret that I bring us all together as one again so soon. Just a few weeks ago, we sat here and mourned the loss of a few of our best patrol and I promised you that action would be taken to prevent this from happening again."

Octavia took a deep breath. The lines on her face were deeper and there were more than a few strands of grey streaking amongst her dark hair. In just the past few weeks, she looked as if she had aged another ten years. "I have not kept that promise. We have continued to suffer tragic losses. Each life lost has hit us all. We are a family here. We live to protect and survive together and an outside source has threatened our peace. I am, of course, talking about Sekhmet Industries."

A hush settled over the room. There were roughly about 3000 residents in Sanctuary. It looked like a large number in the room, but when compared to the population that had once existed across the country, it just seemed sad. It was even sadder when you considered that a fair chunk of the people had lived here their entire lives.

"There are people here that would have me arm up against Sekhmet, to take them down." Octavia didn't even glance in my direction but the slight was there just the same. "I will not do that. I will not ask what little humanity we have left to sacrifice their lives against this corporation. We do not have the numbers. We do not have that sort of training here. We would lose."

"Loving the enthusiasm, Octavia," Ash whispered under his breath. "Your optimism is uplifting as hell."

I stifled a giggle.

"We are hanging by a thread here. There are so little of us left and I could never ask any of you to leave the safety of this place to fight the unknown. No one could ask you to do that."

This time her eyes met mine. My lips curled up in a smile and she immediately looked away.

"However, measures must be taken. Bodies have littered our front doors for far too long. And now there has been an attack. Several more of our military have died. Our first floor has been destroyed. This is unacceptable. While I do not condone this facility going on the offensive, I do understand that we must be more adequately prepared to defend ourselves."

I raised my eyebrow, and turned my head slightly to look at Ash. There was an expression of surprise and curiosity on his face that I was sure was matched on my own.

There was more than one whisper in the crowd. Several people were shifting in their seats, looking around to see how others were reacting. There was a younger woman next to me, probably late twenties, chewing on her tongue. I fought the urge to pop her in the back of her head.

"I would like to make it clear that what I am about to say is not mandatory. No one will be forced to do anything that they do not wish to participate in. This will all be purely voluntary." She took another deep breath before continuing. "For years, we have supplied our military and our patrols with only trained professionals. We have either had Sanctuary citizens go through the proper training or they've been provided to us from outside sources, like the Army or the Marines. Under the circumstances, we are now changing this policy."

I couldn't help it. I sat up straighter, more in tune to the speech than I had been before. Sure, Octavia wasn't suggesting that we storm the gates of Sekhmet and take them down, which would have been the ideal situation, but she was willing to do something and this, to me, was huge.

"We will be providing military training for anyone who wishes to learn. This will include weapons training, various hand-to-hand combat and other similar skills. As I said, everything will be on a voluntary basis and it will not cement your participation in any possible future attack. This is merely if you wish to learn more skills in order to protect yourself more efficiently."

"That being said, we will be taking those that volunteer, and are proficient in these training sessions for patrols. It is a sad thing for me to say that our numbers have dwindled immensely and we are desperate for help. I cannot stress it enough though; this is on a voluntary basis only."

Everyone had been very quiet during her announcement. There had been creaks, as people shifted in their seats, and a few whispers, but it was nothing compared to the outbreak of noise that had erupted at the sound of these words. People were shouting and yelling, looking horrified at the idea. Despite the fact that Octavia had made it clear more than once, that it would be volunteers only, the citizens of Sanctuary were, well, they were freaking out.

"This is supposed to be a safe place!"

"I don't *want* to learn to fight!"

"This isn't what I came here for!"

Octavia's lips had thinned even more so; they nearly disappeared into her face. "I know that many of you will have questions as we make these changes over the next few days. I encourage you all to share those with me and we will work together to create an even safer place than we have been for the past sixty years."

She nodded once, and disappeared off the stage nearly running into Patrick in her haste to escape. For the first time not everyone left at once in a calm and uniform matter. People lingered, talking loudly to each other from across the room. Change was not something that came often to Sanctuary and it looked like most people were fairly resistant to it.

"Well, it's something," Ash admitted, stretching his arms above his head.

"Why doesn't it feel like enough?" I said, leaning forward. My chin was cupped in my right hand as I looked at Ash.

"Because it isn't," Liam cut in, from where he sat behind us. "But you know they aren't going to do anything else. We have to take what little we can get. Maybe this means we can fight."

"I really want to fight," Ash said, wistfully, and he exchanged knowing looks with Liam. The two of them had been getting along much better since the appearance of Astrid. They weren't exactly best friends yet but I wasn't the only person who had noticed an obvious truce between the two of them.

I didn't think I was the only one grateful for it. Even Kaya looked happy that the two of them weren't bickering during meals.

Ash and I on the other hand, were struggling to get back to where we once were. The talk we'd had had been necessary and overdue, and even though it had been way more emotional than either of us were used to, I was so glad it had happened. But now there was a tension between us, one that I was seriously desperate to get rid of.

"Um. Zoey?"

Astrid had been hanging on the outskirts of the conversation. She had spent a couple days in the hospital wing but it was determined that she, and her baby, were quite safe and she was released. She was staying in her own room, which was rare in Sanctuary, but no one really felt comfortable rooming with her. That didn't' really stop Liam from spending most of his time in there, but it wasn't an official thing. He definitely was not afraid of breaking the rules. No one said anything to the two of them and I started to think that maybe rule breaking wasn't far out of reach for me and Ash.

Now Astrid stood outside the circle, looking nervous. She had spent a fair amount of time with the five of us – me, Ash, Liam, Kaya and Corbin – and I had learned that the last word used to describe her was shy. There was a baby that she hadn't wanted growing below her navel and she was in a place that was unfamiliar to her. Despite that, she was funny and teasing, especially when Liam was around. Seeing her look nervous, her hands folded protectively over the small bump of her stomach, made me wary.

"What's up?" I answered, trying to sound breezy.

Astrid swallowed hard, her fingers clenching tight for a moment. She looked at Liam, who nodded encouragingly. She took a deep breath and smiled. Just like it had the first time I'd seen it, it dazzled me. Even looking uncertain, her smile had magical powers. "Can I talk to you for a moment? Alone?"

An icy dread filled my veins and my brain went immediately into flight mode. I felt the coolness of Ash's fingers on my back, finding the short space between my shirt and pants. He didn't have to say anything; I knew exactly from the slight touch that he was showing me that he was there if I needed him. I had been dreading this ever since Astrid had appeared on our doorstep. I didn't want to talk to her alone. I caught her staring at me often and I usually found an excuse to disappear. Talking to her alone would only bring me face to face with the one thing that had consumed me since I had seen her in that hospital wing.

Guilt. Overwhelming guilt.

I nodded, afraid to open my mouth. I was afraid I wouldn't be able to stop apologizing, for what, I wasn't sure, and even then, it wouldn't be enough. She was the one with a baby in her belly.

We walked away from the rest of the group. Liam and Ash watched us as we disappeared out of sight. Neither of us said anything as we wandered the corridors and I wondered who would speak first.

"Sorry," Astrid finally spoke up and I jumped, startled. I wiped my sweaty palms on my pants. "I'm not really sure where we're going. I keep getting lost here."

"It's easy to get lost here," I admitted, my voice cracking. "You'll figure it out."

She nodded, looking unconvinced. I saw the way her eyes took in everything as we walked, as if trying to memorize every detail. I admired her for that. I had done the same thing.

"What did you want to talk about?" I asked her, as we took a left and ended up in the central spiral walkway.

Astrid squirmed a little bit. "Is there anywhere we could go that would be more…private? I keep feeling like everyone is staring at me."

Sure enough, several eyes followed us as we walked past. Their gazes lingered, zoning in on Astrid's stomach. She was hardly showing but she was tiny and what little weight she had gained was obvious. She was so small, several inches shorter than me, and I wasn't exactly a giant.

"That'll stop too," I cut in, wryly. "That takes a little longer, though." The corner of her mouth lifted in a smile. "I think I know where to go."

She followed me as I made my way up the spiral. Most people slowed as we passed, staring. I had gotten used to the stares and pretty much ignored them now and I was impressed when Astrid held her head high, ignoring them as we made our way further upward. The only sign of her noticing was the slight pink tinge in her dark cheeks.

We reached one of the upper levels and I pushed my way through a door. Astrid blinked in surprise as sunlight came streaming in. There was a distinct smell of manure and grass and...

"Are those real cows?" Astrid said, her voice echoing loudly in the room.

I laughed. "Yeah, of course."

She shrugged, embarrassed. "I mean, would fake cows really be surprising at this point?" I had to agree with her on that. "So what exactly is this?"

"It's an indoor pasture. Sanctuary has to get food from somewhere. This level always contains crops and other livestock. They can't exactly keep it aboveground since this place is supposed to be secret and all that, so they created this level. The ceiling is specially designed. It feels like sunlight but it's all synthetic." I climbed up on one of the fences, perching there. "No one ever really comes up here unless there's work to be done."

Astrid came up to the fence next to me. She crossed her arms and leaned forward, her chin balanced on her folded arms. "I haven't seen cows in so long. They sometimes grazed on the hills back home."

"And that's...?" I asked.

"California," she supplied. "I lived in Fullerton." I raised my eyebrow at her and she smiled, her eyes still on the cows in front of us. "Near Disneyland. Everyone knows Disneyland."

I nodded. I had been there once a few years ago with my mom and Caspar.

"My abuela had a couple cows roaming around her house in Mexico too. They weren't her cows; they had just wandered by one day and she fed them and they never went away. She always complained about them but she loved those stupid things." Astrid's voice was soft, and she didn't say much after that. The two of us sat there for a few minutes, staring at the cows uninterested in us as they munched on hay.

"I'm really sorry," I finally blurt out after the long silence.

Astrid pushed herself up off the fence and turned to look at me. Her brow was furrowed. "You're sorry?"

I swallowed hard, my hands gripped the fence tightly. "Of course. I am sorry about…about everything."

"Zoey, did you think I was going to yell at you or something?"

My ponytail whacked me in the face as I whirled around to look at her. I swatted it away, impatiently. There was a smirk on Astrid's face and amusement in her voice. "Um," I hesitated. "Sort of?"

She laughed, hoisting herself up on the fence next to me. I reached for her but pulled back immediately when she glared at me. "I'm pregnant, Zoey, not broken. I can sit on a fence. And I'm not mad at you. I'm definitely not going to yell at you. That's what I wanted to talk to you about. You've been looking at me like a kicked puppy all week."

I flushed, caught. "I didn't mean to."

"I know that. But you have been anyway." She paused as one of the cows came ambling curiously in our directions. He – or she, really I had no idea what the difference was – stopped a few feet away from us. "But I was tired of you looking at me that way. There's no reason for it. It's not your fault."

I sighed, watching as our curious friend moved closer to us. He stared at us with his large black eyes before dropping his head and munching at the hay that lay below us. "What does it feel like it is?"

"Would you rather be in this position?" Astrid said, pointing to her protruding stomach. My lips pressed tightly together and I fought hard to keep my dinner from making a return trip. I shook my head. "Exactly. And I wouldn't wish that on you either, Zoey. You got out."

"So did you…" I said, softly, trailing off.

She shook her head, her long braids swaying. "I don't know why I'm here Zoey, it makes no sense. That bitch is crazy. I don't know what she was like before your escape but according to Liam, she just got worse afterwards. I guess getting shot in the throat does that to a girl."

I shuddered. I couldn't imagine Razi Cylon any worse than I had already known.

"I'm pregnant, Zoey. That's it. Period. I couldn't fight her on that and there was no way for me to escape. Not like you did. Don't feel bad for me, shit happens. Feeling guilty over who is and isn't pregnant is just a waste of time and energy. There's just no point."

I squirmed uncomfortable. "After the initial shock of seeing you pregnant, I was relieved. I was so relieved and that felt terrible. All I could think was…it's not me. That makes me a horrible person.

"Not at all. I would have felt the exact same way." She laughed a little when our cow friend lifted his head and head butted her knee. There was some hesitation when she spoke again. "Don't get me wrong. She still wants you, Zoey. She was constantly comparing me to you."

"Oh god."

"It's okay," she joked. "Liam constantly assured me that you weren't really as great as Razi made you out to be." She winked at me and I laughed. "But I did honestly feel like I was just going to fail, that I was going to disappoint her in some way and she would just get rid of me. It helped so much that

Liam was the one in there with me. He had a way of keeping me calm. He made me feel safe."

I smiled, in spite of myself. "Yeah, he has that kind of effect on people, doesn't he?"

Astrid looked at me, sharply. "You and Liam…"

"Are friends," I finished for her. "Period. We had a brief moment of…well, it was nothing. Nothing important. Nothing that you have to worry about." Astrid flushed and ducked her head. "Come on, I'm not stupid. I can see it."

Astrid laughed lightly. "Yeah, it's probably pretty obvious on my part. But hey, when you're eighteen years old, everyone you know is dead and you get captured by some crazy doctor who wants nothing more than to get you pregnant with a sexy and amazing guy like Liam…well, can you blame me?"

"Nope, not at all," I said. "If it weren't for Ash, I would probably be in the same boat. But I've been crazy about Ash since I was a kid so there was no competition. Not for me, anyway."

"Yeah, you can see that," Astrid whispered, wistfully. "I don't think Liam feels quite the same way."

I looked at her incredulously. "Oh, honey. You are so very wrong. He's been a bundle of anxiety ever since he appeared here without you. If you hadn't made your own appearance, I think there's nothing that could have stopped him from leaving this place and going to get you."

She rolled her eyes, sighing. "Which would have been stupid." She hesitated, biting her lip, looking uncertain. "It's because of the baby. It's because he's a genuinely good guy."

"You know the doctors could…the could…well, the baby…" I stumbled over the words, unsure of how to word it.

"No," Astrid cut in firmly. "No matter the circumstances, I am keeping this baby."

I let that sink in for a moment before replying. "Don't get me wrong, I totally respect that. But…Razi isn't going to stop until she gets her hands on that baby."

"I know," she whispered, one of her hands going to her stomach. "I know that. Which makes me wonder why the hell I'm here and not with her. She's planning something and I'm terrified." She looked up at me, her brown eyes wide. "That bitch seriously needs to be taken down."

"You're preaching to the choir, honey," was my wry reply. "But you heard the speech in there. They're not going to do anything about it. They think they're safe in this little hidey hole."

Astrid let out a frustrated groan. "Then I think it's best that we prepare ourselves as much as possible."

I looked at her appraisingly. I liked her. She was so different from Madison and incredibly different from Kaya but I already liked her. There was something about her that reminded me so much of Liam, and it showed why they bonded so quickly. She was a survivor just like him. "Agreed."

Astrid smiled at me before turning back to the cows. "Good. Because I have no idea what Razi Cylon is going to serve us, but I want to be ready for it when it comes."

CHAPTER FOURTEEN

TRAINING BEGAN ALMOST immediately. I had to give credit to Octavia and her team. She may not have wanted to launch an attack on Sekhmet – an action I would have supported – but she backed up her promise to further prepare the place for an attack and the evidence came quick. There were sign ups in the dining hall at breakfast the next day. Liam and Ash were amongst the first sign up, with me right behind them. Astrid signed up as well, despite Liam insisting that she stay out of it. She threw him a withering look and signed her name with a flourish. The two that surprised me the most were Corbin and Kaya.

Kaya had marched over to the list and signed up with a fierce look on her face. The pen pressed so hard to the page that it poked a hole through it. She was the first Sanctuary born citizen to sign up and a few others lingered near the list after she walked away. The rest of us followed her as she walked away, filling her breakfast tray and taking a seat at our regular table.

"Kaya?" I asked, curiously, sliding onto the bench next to her. She dipped her spoon in her oatmeal calmly, barely registering that the rest of us were staring at her. "Kaya, do you know what that list was for, right?"

"Of course I know what I signed up for." Kaya's voice was even as she replied. Her eyes met Corbin's and a flush filled her cheeks. "I don't know if you guys remember, but my brother died. He. Died. And he died to protect this place. I don't really plan on sitting around and letting others do the same if I can learn to protect myself."

The rest of looked at each other, sheepish looks on our faces. I knew they, like me, often forgot how strong Kaya could be. She was quiet and shy, sure, but she was resilient and her brother's death had rocked her hard. Even with Corbin sitting next to her, she looked like she was fighting to sit up straight. Her eyes looked less red than the last time I had looked, but I had heard her crying quietly in her sleep the night before and I felt helpless. Learning to shoot a gun, or how to take someone down with a well-placed kick would be good for her.

"Sorry, I don't mean to be harsh," Kaya spoke up, putting her spoon down. She sighed and her eyes met mine. "I just…I get stuck looking at you, all the time, Zoey." I looked at her curiously and she sounded embarrassed as she continued. "You're a fighter. I've heard that you can shoot a gun and you know how to fight. And I think, if she can be covered in scars like that, and she knows how to take care of herself…what on earth would the Awakened do to me if I came face to face with them?"

A blush rushed through the raised scar on my face but I had to admit, she had a point. Kaya was not equipped to deal with anything outside of these walls. I had spent years being forced into various lessons by the overprotective Chief Frank Valentine and even then, I had been utterly unprepared for what the Awakened would do to me. The evidence was all over my body, not just in the ugly scar pulling across my face. No matter how hard I fought, I had still lost and bore the marks of those losses. I was lucky to walk away from these situations with my life. Kaya may not be as lucky.

"Well, I think it's a great idea," Corbin spoke up. Ash, Liam and I exchanged amused looks as Corbin reached for Kaya's hand. There hadn't been a book in sight the past few days and the two of them had stayed glued to each other's sides. Astrid hadn't known any different but seeing Corbin out from behind the cover of a book was a rare sight and it was no secret why. Kaya.

"Thank you," Kaya said, softening.

It turned out, unsurprisingly, that Kaya was god awful at everything we did in training.

But it didn't matter. She showed up every single day. She ran and fought and she tried again and again and again. I would find her in the hallway outside our room, practicing kicks and punches. She would stay late after classes and shoot at targets for hours. Her hands were covered in sores and blisters and they were constantly popping. She was plastered with bandages and you could constantly see the blood through the sheer material.

No one worked harder than Kaya. Even though she was starting at a disadvantage compared to the rest of us, with absolutely no experience at all, she didn't let that get her down. She was still timid, shy and unsure outside of those classrooms but as soon as we hit the mats, she was focused and determined. She practiced every punch and every kick until her skin was broken and bleeding, until her muscles screamed and she hobbled up to bed.

After everything that had happened, it was amazing to watch. She never once opened her mouth to complain. Occasionally her mouth would draw tight in a straight line or a flash of pain would ripple through her forehead, but she never cried, she never complained, she never made a peep. No one else said a word. No one else felt right complaining, not when she worked so damn hard.

Kaya had turned out to be a fighter.

And even I had to admit that I was damn proud of her.

***

"TRAINEE VALENTINE!"

The loud voice of the combat instructor interrupted my thoughts. Ash and Liam were standing a few feet away from me, talking under their breaths. Things had kept getting better between Ash and I, and I had to admit my skin was on fire every time I was near him. It had been a while since we'd had a good make out session and I was totally feeling the neglect. Ash's eyes caught mine and a grin spread out across his face. He winked at me, sending a shiver up my spine, and returned to his conversation with Liam as if he hadn't just sent me spinning.

I was so relieved that they got along so much better now but it always made me nervous when they spent time together like that. I knew how much trouble each one of them was capable of and the idea of them teaming up together was both scary and exciting.

"Valentine! Look alive!"

Our instructor was standing over me, looking less than pleased. I tore my gaze away from Ash and Liam and looked up at him. He reminded me of my dad; tall, built and determined. He took no crap in this room. It always sent a pain through my heart to think of my dad, the way he had taught me to throw a punch and how he never hesitated to flip me onto my ass, just because he could.

"Yes, sir?" I asked, wiping my palms on my pants. We were given different outfits for training and it felt so good to get out of the black uniforms of Sanctuary. These clothes were stretchy, and tighter fitting than our usual clothes but they were comfortable and even though they were gray, it felt like I was wearing a bright color compared to the dull black I'd been used to for the past few months.

"Matthews over here tells me you have quite a bit of experience with hand to hand fighting. I've yet to see any of this in the class. Care to share why you kept this vital piece of information a secret?"

I tossed an impatient look over at Ash, who merely grinned wider in response. "I took some classes back in New York. I wouldn't say I'm experienced."

"Liar," Ash teased.

I made a face and turned my attention back to the instructor, who was looking at me impatiently. He was much older than my dad was, but he was tall and broad and he had a no nonsense look on his face that was so familiar that I was torn between laughing and bursting into tears. I shook my head, clearing my thoughts. "Was there something I could assist you with, sir?"

"Step forward, onto the mats." I followed his instruction, aware of all the eyes on me. I took a deep breath, trying to picture the small martial arts studios I had trained in back in New York. It was just another day. Just another class. The instructor paced around me, studying me and I fought the urge to wince. I knew I was out of shape and I knew that most of the muscle I had built up had disappeared. I was nothing but a walking stick figure. Even a few months of decent food at Sanctuary hadn't brought me back to what I used to be.

"Matthews, you ever fight this girl before?"

"Sir, I try not to get on her bad side. That tends to work out better for me," Ash joked and everyone laughed. There was a quirk at the corner of the instructor's mouth and I resisted the urge to roll my eyes. Ash had a way of charming everyone, even hard combat instructors.

"Well, the two of you are obviously comfortable with each other, so why don't you show us what you guys know?"

Ash's grin faded for a moment and I nearly laughed. Last time the two of us had sparred, I'd flipped him back on his back. Hard. I didn't know if I was still capable of doing it as quickly as I had last time, but I knew I was still stronger and quicker than him.

I faced him and we stared at each other, circling. I waited for him to make the first move. Ash always made the first one. He was the quarterback. He called the plays. He was all about action.

Sure enough, a moment later, he was lunging for me. I dodged his punch and he went flying past me. I nearly giggled at the sight and lifted my leg to send a kick to his gut. To my surprise, he blocked it and I had to step back to regain my balance.

"Ooh, Zoey, didn't expect that one, did you?" Kaya's voice was full of laughter and even though it was incredibly distracting, it felt nice to hear her laugh.

The distraction from Kaya was enough. Ash threw another punch and as I went to go dodge, his leg connected with mine and I went sprawling to the ground, landing with a thump on the hard mat. The fight had lasted less than 30 seconds and somehow, crazily enough, my boyfriend had managed to land me on my ass.

Ash leaned over me, an earsplitting grin on his face. It was a gloating smile and I glared at him, even as he helped me to my fight. "Shut up," I said, rubbing the sore spot just above my butt.

"You know, they told me that you were some kind of badass fighter, Miss Zoey, but after that, I don't think I believe them."

My eyes grew wide and I turned around, unsure if I'd heard that familiar voice correctly. When my eyes met his, I didn't pause. I ran across the room and threw myself into his arms. We had never shown that kind of affection to each other but I would never feel anything less than love and gratitude to the man who had saved my life, who had saved Ash's life. "Bert," I said, hugging him. "What on earth are you doing here?"

He lowered me to the ground. "Seems like there's a lot of noise going on over here. A lot more Awakened around than there was before. I decided I'd come take a look and see what is going on."

I raised an eyebrow at him and his brow furrowed. He tried to pretend that he was a grumpy old man with nothing to say but I knew better. "And your daughter?"

He sighed. "Yeah, I can't expect that she'll be that happy to see me."

She wasn't. I had never seen Octavia struggle to keep her composure before. It seemed, no matter what position of power you held, you always felt a little underwhelmed when you were around your dad. Bert didn't speak much, which wasn't unusual for him, but he didn't seem entirely pleased at the way things were going in Sanctuary. Dead bodies, missing patrols and a lack of action weren't exactly congratulatory. She kept wringing her hands out and biting her lip. I felt almost bad for her, but it also felt sort of nice to see her nervous and anxious. She was too confident about her way of running things and that was frustrating.

Seeing her look less than confident around her dad? I had to admit it put me in a good mood.

My day was even better when Kaya came up to Ash and I just as we were finishing dinner that night. She ducked in between, startling us both.

"Sorry," she said, wincing. "I didn't mean to scare you. I just wanted to let you know that I'm going to stay in Corbin's room tonight." The two of us stared at her blankly and she shook her head, rolling her eyes. "Meaning that we would like to be alone." Her face flushed.

"Um, that's not exactly allowed, Kaya…" I said.

"I won't tell if you won't," she cut in, tossing me a knowing look.

Ash stared at her, his brows furrowed. "What the heck? Where the hell am I supposed to go?"

Kaya paused for a beat, waiting. Then, like a light bulb, it lit up for both of us. We turned to each other and I couldn't help the grin that spread across my face.

We were going to have the room all to ourselves tonight, for the first time in months. It felt like a gift. I knew that Kaya was only doing it so she and Corbin could have some alone time together, but it didn't feel like that. It felt like she had handed me the best present in the world and it wasn't even my birthday.

I leapt up and threw my arms around her. "You just might be the coolest person that I've ever met."

She staggered a little under my unexpected hug but just laughed. "Get out of here, idiots."

CHAPTER FIFTEEN

THE PROSPECT OF spending alone time with Ash after so long was the best gift that I could have ever been given.

We practically raced from the cafeteria, through the corridors and back to my room. We were finally getting the chance to spend some time together, just the two of us, outside of broom closets and dark corners.

The two of us stared at each other uneasily. I perched nervously on my bed, suddenly very aware that we were very much alone and that no one was planning on disturbing us tonight. The idea both thrilled and scared me. It wasn't like Ash and I hadn't had sex before but it had been awhile and I could feel the nerves coming on.

Ash crossed the room and sat on the bed next to me and I could feel the heat coming off him in waves. There were mere inches between us but they didn't matter. It felt like he was pressed up against me and he hadn't even touched me. "Zoey, are you okay?" he asked, a concerned look on his face.

I nodded, my head bobbing up and down. I was sure I looked ridiculous. I stopped abruptly and flushed. "Oh god, why am I so nervous right now?"

He laughed, scooting closer to me on the bed. "We don't have to do anything that you don't want to."

I raised my eyebrow at him and he smirked. My fingers lifted, wanting to touch the corner of his mouth where it turned up. There was something about that smirk that sent a wave of desire through my body. "That is not the problem."

"Then what is the problem?" he asked. His fingers were reaching for me, playing with the ends of my hair. It was barely there, so gentle, but it felt like he had touched me with a lightning rod. I responded to his touch, leaning closer to him.

"You make me nervous," I admitted, my lips hovering near his.

"Nervous?" Ash asked, incredulously. His lips were tracing light kisses on the sensitive spot below my ear and I shivered in anticipation. "I'm your boyfriend. Why would I make you nervous?"

"It's a good kind of nervous," I managed to whisper as his head dipped lower. His fingers played at the hem of my shirt before lifting it and pulling it over my head. The air was cool on my skin but his hands left a burning trail. I could feel his smile as his tongue darted out at the pulse of my neck.

"Good," he whispered back. His hand came up to grab me gently by the back of the neck as he pulled me into him.

When he kissed me again, it was deeper, slower, so different than when he'd kissed me frantically in the corridors just a few days ago. They were deliberate and I felt them all through my body. His fingers were tracing my skin, leaving goosebumps in their wake. I shivered. My breath escaped in gasps every time he pulled away, like I could never get enough air, not while his lips were pressed to mine. He pulled away, his hand wrapped tightly around the back of my neck and his eyes met mine. There was so much love in his expression, as if he could never get tired of looking at me. It filled me with warmth. No one looked at me like he did. No one else ever would. I reached for him, stroking his cheeks, feeling the soft stubble against the roughness of my palms.

My thumb grazed his bottom lip and he closed his eyes briefly, letting out a low groan that I felt all the way into my belly. I pulled him into me, needing his taste again. The kisses grew deeper and deeper. His hands were everywhere, spread across my back, lost in my hair, fingers digging into my shoulders as he pulled me closer to him. Everything that had been pent up between us over the past few months was pouring out now into each and every kiss. Every kiss screamed, I love you, I love you, I love you.

My hands pulled at his shirt and I yanked it over his head, tossing it in the general direction of Kaya's bed. Ash's skin was hot against mine, and pleasure rippled through me as my hands felt the hard muscles of his chest and the dips and rivets of his abs. I had missed this so much; it felt so good to touch him again. I sighed, content, and Ash let out a low chuckle.

"Don't laugh at me," I said, scattering kisses along his jawline.

A groan rumbled through his chest and the smile on my face grew into a full-blown grin. It never grew old, knowing that I was the one who could make him feel this way. I scooted backwards, lying on the bed, pulling him on top of me.

"Never," Ash replied. He was breathing heavily, and his hands were dipping into the waistband of my pants. I gasped, lifting my hips, encouraging his exploration. "Why are you still wearing these?"

I leaned forward to whisper in his ear. "I like it much better when you take them off."

Ash shivered but propped himself up, making it easier for him to snap the button open and start sliding the pants down my legs. It felt stupid to care but having smooth, unshaved legs were not a priority in Sanctuary and I was suddenly very aware of the hair that covered my legs. I started to lean away but Ash's hand gripped me tight around the back of my knee. He pulled my leg up and around his waist and a wave of pleasure went shooting through me as he pressed himself into me.

"Ash." His name was barely a whisper, desperate and needy, and I pulled him tighter against me, as his hips rocked forward again. "Ash."

"Do you like that, baby?" he asked.

I nodded, my face hidden in the crook of his shoulder. There was not much between us and yet it was too much. "I love it."

"You're so beautiful." Ash's voice was low and his words were coming out in gasps but each rang true. "You are so beautiful and you are so perfect. So freakin' beautiful."

"Stop," I said, playfully. "I'm not that beautiful."

Ash paused, and his eyes bore into mine. He reached for me, my face held firmly between his two hands. "Do you not own a mirror? Do I need to buy you one? Seriously. Just look in the mirror. You're the most beautiful girl I've ever seen."

The words felt just like a kiss or his fingers against me. They sent ripples through my body, and I closed my eyes briefly for a moment, overwhelmed by everything that I was feeling at that moment. "Ash…"

"Scout's honor."

I couldn't help; a small giggle escaped my lips. "You were never a Boy Scout, Ash," I replied, my nails digging into his back as his fingers dipped below the waistband of my undies.

"Shut up," he said, but there was a smile on his face. "You're perfect, okay? Even with everything about you that isn't perfect, you're still perfect. I love you. I love you so much."

A grin spread across my own face. "That never gets old, you know."

"Good," he replied, firmly. His fingers were making excellent progress on the clasp of my bra and his tongue was dipping into my cleavage. It was incredibly distracting and I found it hard to focus on words, especially when his fingers found my sensitive spot below. A moan escaped my lips and Ash groaned. "I could listen to you make noises like that forever." He brushed up against me again and I moaned again, louder this time. "Yes, that. Jesus, Zoey."

Part of me wanted to be embarrassed at the loss of control that I felt when I laid underneath his lips and his touch, but this was Ash. This was the boy I had known since I was nine years old. This was the boy that drove me crazy, dumped glitter in my locker and threw water balloons at me, but it was also the boy who saved my life again and again. Being embarrassed in front of him just felt silly. If there was anyone in this world that I could feel completely comfortable with, open and honest, it was Ash.

There weren't many words after that, just murmurs, gasps and moans, as his lips traced a searing line from my collarbone, all the way down between my legs. There was no time to protest and I got lost in the sensations that he was creating.

Before I could completely lose my head, he was back, his lips on mine. Each article of clothing was removed carefully, with just enough touching to drive each other crazy. Each tough, each graze, every kiss, was like a shock of lightning to my system. I lost where our bodies separated, where I ended and he began. We began to blur together, and when our bodies joined, a sigh escaped from the back of my throat and I pressed my lips tight against his shoulder and rode the wave until I crashed.

I woke suddenly in the dark sometime later, clutching the blanket wrapped around me tightly in my fingers. I reached out frantically in the dark, reaching for Ash, but all I found was empty space around me. "Ash?"

He walked out of the bathroom. He had pulled his pants back on but had left his shirt off. My heart was still beating a drum in my chest but I felt calm at the sight of my boyfriend coming toward me.

"Hey, hey, hey. What's wrong, Z?" Ash's voice was calm and soothing as he climbed into bed, lifting the blanket so that it covered the both of us. "Did you have a bad dream?"

I nodded, pulling the covers up and squirming closer to him. I liked having the solid presence of him behind me, knowing that all I had to do was lean back and know that he was there.

"Do you want to talk about it?" He asked, his fingers smoothing back my back and placing a soft kiss on the back of my neck.

"I don't even remember the details," I whispered back to him. "It's all a blur now. But I know I was alone and I was scared."

Ash's arms snaked around my waist, pulling me tighter against him and his lips were hard against the back of my head. "You don't have to be scared anymore, Zoey. You don't. Everything is going to be okay."

His hand was lying gently against my hipbone and I reached up, lacing my fingers through his. "And how do you know that?"

"Because we're together, Zoey," came his confident reply. "And nothing bad can happen as long as we're together."

CHAPTER SIXTEEN

"DOES IT FEEL weird to be out in the sunlight again?" Liam asked, looking around. "Because it is definitely weird for me." He was poised and ready, a gun clutched in his hands but he also looked relaxed. He looked more secure that I had ever seen him before. The breeze passed through his long strands of blonde hair and I smiled.

"Yes, definitely," Ash answered. "I can't believe they even let us out here. Do you think killing a couple Awakened gave us the privilege to do that? Aren't we lucky?"

I laughed. "I think Octavia knows she's running low on patrols and she knows that we can hold our own. She had no choice other than to let us out here." They looked at me and I shrugged. "Hey, I'm not complaining. This sun feels damn good. And the air! God I'm so tired of recycled air. Sanctuary feels like a damn airplane all the time."

"We could leave, you know?" Liam pointed out. "It's not like we're being forced to go back. It's not like we have to stay. The four of us could leave."

"Where on earth would we go? Who would take care of Astrid and the baby?" I asked, my arms wide, indicating the forest around us. "This was supposed to be the end goal, wasn't it? Sanctuary was supposed to just be it."

"That's not entirely true…" Liam muttered under his breath. Ash and I both spun around to look at him and he sighed. Loudly. The two of us stayed silent, staring at him, waiting for him to say something.

"What are you talking about?" Ash finally spoke up. "Weren't you the one that was all for Sanctuary? We didn't even now this place existed until we met you. Now you're saying there are other options?" Ash didn't even sound mad, just tired.

Liam sat down on an overturned log, rummaging around in his pack for a water canteen. It was still very early in the day, but the sun was beating down on us pretty hard. I didn't know it could get this warm in Colorado; I had always pictured snow-covered mountains. You could see mountains in the distance but they looked dark, gray and worn. Like pretty much everything else around us.

"Months ago, before I was captured by Sekhmet, my parents and I met a group of people on the way here. They cornered me while I was in the woods hunting."

"They cornered you? No way," I said, in a teasing voice and Ash smirked. "Sorry, continue."

"Anyway, as I was saying," Liam continued, looking unconcerned about my obnoxious interruption. "We ran into a group of people, surviving on the outside. They have a whole thing set up. We stayed with them for a while. They had…well they had something special set up. It was the way I expected Sanctuary to be, on the outside. Not buried below ground. They called themselves Hoover."

I fiddled with the safety on my gun, feeling a little anxious. "Why didn't you tell anyone about this before? About this Hoover?"

He shrugged in response. "Because…because it didn't seem like it mattered. We ended up in Sanctuary, which had been the whole point in the first place, right? And my mom ended up being here so that's the important part."

The three of us fell in companionable silence as we patrolled. There wasn't much going on, which I took as a good thing. It may have caused incredible boredom, but I liked it when it was silent. It was bizarre not to hear much at all, but our patrol leaders warned us not to expect the normal noises one was accustomed to hearing in the woods. Either the animals had died off or completely abandoned them. But the silence, besides the occasional crinkle of leaves, was welcomed. I would welcome it any time over the raspy breathing of an Awakened.

This became a normal part of our routine. We spent a lot of time training and a lot of time patrolling. The three of us ended up on patrol together almost every single time. We spent time getting to know each other better, Ash and Liam weren't exactly best friends but they had called an uneasy truce and under the sun, things were just easy.

For the first time since we'd arrived at Sanctuary, I felt free.

The situation was serious though and I knew that. I knew this was only possible because of the bodies that kept turning up on our doorstep but I was grateful to be outside. It felt better, healthier, in more ways than one.

Ash spent more time in my room, even though it was against the rules. I kept waiting for someone to yell at us but no one did. Kaya either just smiled at us and fell asleep in her own bed without comment, disappeared into her family quarters or snuck off to Corbin's room.

He woke me up one early morning, with a kiss pressed gently against my bare shoulder. I smiled at him, remembering the night before. We had spent quite a bit of time wrapped around each other and my body flushed, remembering how it all felt.

"Where are you going?" I whispered to him.

"Guard duty," he whispered back. I started to reach for my clothes but he shook his head. "No, stay in bed. I didn't mean to wake you."

"The bed isn't the same without you here," I grumbled and he laughed quietly. He pressed another soft kiss on my forehead and disappeared out of the room. I tried to stay awake but we had stayed up most of the night and I fell into a deep sleep before I knew it.

The hours of the day passed by so quickly that it was hard to keep track of time. It was so much busier now that we had added all this training to our schedules. By the end of the day, I was exhausted and collapsed into bed. Kaya had disappeared to Corbin's room for the night, which meant that it wouldn't be long before Ash joined me in here. I felt a jolt of anticipation shoot through my stomach and I smiled. I loved having nights alone with him in here.

I struggled staying awake, waiting for him. I tried to read a book but my skin was on fire in anticipation of his return, and it was so hard to concentrate. I tossed the book aside, determined to count all the slates in the ceiling to keep myself awake until he came back.

I must have fallen asleep because the next thing I knew, I was being startled awake by a loud pounding on the door. I rolled out of bed, my heart beating wildly in my chest. There was low talking on the other side of the door but I couldn't tell who it was. I stood still, waiting, until the pounding resumed.

"Who is there?" I asked, shakily. I realized I was still alone in the room. Where on earth was Ash?

"Zoey." I sagged in relief. It was Liam. "You need to come out here. We're wanted in Octavia's office."

Panic quickly filled my lungs and I sunk to the ground. "No," I whispered. My mind was racing and I tried so hard to remember if I had seen Ash since he had left this room in the morning. It was all a blur. I couldn't remember what had happened today or the day before.

"Zoey, please, open the door."

I managed to pull myself into a standing position and I slid the compartment door open. Liam and Astrid stood there, both of them clad in gray pajamas. They both looked just as worried as I felt. Liam looked past me and his shoulders sagged when he saw that Ash was not behind me. My panic and worry grew worse.

"Come on," he said, simply. One of his hands was already linked with Astrid's as he reached for me with the other, and I took his hand gratefully.

Each step to Octavia's office felt wrong. It felt like a huge effort to put one foot in front of the other. Liam and Astrid were whispering to each other next to me but it might as well have been in a foreign language. I focused on moving. It was going to be okay. Everything was fine.

Octavia and Patrick were waiting in her office. Both of them were in normal clothes, like it wasn't the early hours of the morning. It amazed me that the two of them always looked so well put together. They were like robots or something. There was no emotion on either of their faces, even though I knew they were about to give me bad news.

"Sit," Octavia said, softly. Astrid sat, looking exhausted. There were deep bags under her eyes and I knew she wasn't getting much sleep. I knew how that went.

I stayed standing, staring at her. "What is it?"

"Zoey, please…"

"No," I cut her off, flinching at the way my voice broke with that one simple word. "Just tell me."

"Ash…" The world went black for a moment and I almost didn't catch the rest of her sentence. "Ash was captured."

The words hadn't quite processed and I looked over at Astrid and Liam. They both looked shocked. Astrid was

137

looking at me, frantically, but it still hadn't registered. Ash wasn't dead. He wasn't dead. He was alive. But he was…

"Captured?" Liam echoed. His voice was loud and both Octavia and Patrick looked uneasy. "What do you mean?"

"He didn't return from guard duty so we sent out a patrol to look for him. The patrol searched for hours but they came up with nothing. We were beginning to fear the worst," Patrick explained, but his voice didn't match his words. He might as well have been reading the morning weather report.

"And?" Astrid cut in.

"We couldn't do much more. We looked for Mr. Matthews but there wasn't even a trace of him. He was just gone. Then we received this note. Two other guards were with him and the note was…pinned to them," Octavia explained, her face pale. I knew without her having to say it out loud that the note had been staked to the dead bodies, just like the ones before. I shook the horrifying thought out of my head and looked at the small white square in Octavia's hand. It looked like it was once clean and crisp, but being nailed to a dead body had left it dirty and bloody. She held it toward me but I just stared.

Instead, Liam reached for it and read it aloud. "Darling Zoey, Come and get him." He flashed the card in my direction and I saw the Sekhmet epitaph right below the neatly written message. He looked up at Octavia. "We need to go get him."

"Absolutely not," she spoke up, immediately. "I am truly sorry for these awful circumstances…"

"Awful circumstances?" Liam yelled. "One of your citizens was kidnapped! This is not an awful circumstance. This bitch has been killing left and right and now she's swooped in and taken one of our own, and you just say absolutely not?"

Octavia's eyes blazed. Her hands were clasped tightly in front of her, so tight that the tips of her fingers were white. "I am truly sorry. What has happened to Ash…but he is one boy. We've lost so many. I'm not launching an attack against that place for one boy."

Liam growled in frustration and looked over at me but my world was spinning. I could hear them talking but none of it made sense. Ash was gone. He was at Sekhmet. After everything we had been through and after everything we had done to survive, he had ended up back at that place.

It was hard to breathe. The walls were closing in on me. The voices around me sounded garbled, like we were underwater. I vaguely heard my name being called but I had forgotten how to speak. My mouth opened but the words wouldn't form.

"Zoey, I forbid you from taking action against Sekhmet. I know that you must be feeling a great deal right now but I won't have my citizens running away and getting themselves killed. He is gone. I am sorry. But you need to stay here."

I looked up at her, and even though there were so many mixed emotions burning through me, I couldn't bring myself to do anything else besides nod. She looked at me surprised.

"I mean it," she said. She looked at the three of us. "Each life lost here in Sanctuary is mourned. I do not take Ash's kidnapping lightly. But I can't risk the lives of everyone who still lives here. I will have your word."

"You're a coward." I took a deep breath, surprised at how empty I felt. My voice was soft when I continued. "But I promise, I won't go after him." The memory of Ash's lips on my shoulders that very morning felt like it had happened just minutes ago.

He couldn't be gone. He couldn't.

I left the office without a word to anyone else. I hadn't been dismissed but I didn't care.

I had to get out of there.

CHAPTER SEVENTEEN

I WAS SURPRISINGLY calm when I left Octavia's office. Her disbelieving face followed me as I left. I felt numb. The news that Ash had been missing, kidnapped by Razi and her band of evil geniuses was the worst thing I could possibly imagine but my entire body was a flood of ice.

"Zoey, are you okay?" Astrid's voice was low and concerned. Her small hand wrapped around my wrist but I barely felt it.

"I'm completely fine," I answered. My voice sounded far away, like an echo in the bottom of a swimming pool. There was a long moment of silence and I looked up at Liam and Astrid. They were both staring at me warily, as if waiting for something to happen. Like I was suddenly going to do the chicken dance or explode. Both felt like equally logical options. "What?"

"You can't be fine. There's no way you're fine," Liam said, disbelieving. He started to reach for me but I stepped back, out of his reach. "Zoey, come on."

"I just…I want to go to bed. I want to be alone," I said, calmly. They started to speak but I didn't wait to hear what they had to say. I spun around and took off, my feet carrying me away from Octavia's office, down the corridors and back into my room.

Kaya wasn't there and I was immediately grateful for that. I wasn't lying when I said I needed to be alone. I had felt numb while sitting in the office, listening to Octavia tell me that my boyfriend had gone missing while on patrol. The emotions had built up like a dam when I read the note, and when she told me that they couldn't...no, they *wouldn't* do anything to get him back. But now, alone in my room, it felt like the dam was about to break. Tears pricked the corner of my eyes and I climbed onto my bed, pulling my knees up to my chest.

The walls felt like they were closing in on me. Ash was gone. Ash was not here. Just last night, we were in this bed, our limbs tangled together, whispering to each other. Just a few days ago, he had told me he would love me forever. It was just hours ago that I had kissed him and told him to be careful. And now he was gone. He was gone and my mind couldn't comprehend that. The tears started flowing down my cheeks, silent but strong. I choked on my sobs.

It felt hopeless. Like there was nothing I could do. Ash Matthews was only one person in Sanctuary and Octavia and the rest didn't care that he was gone. They didn't care that my walls were coming down and that he may be only one person, but he was my one person.

I cried for hours. In the back of my mind, I questioned why I had been left alone for so long but I didn't care. I couldn't stop crying. The tears kept coming as I imagined what was happening to him, what Razi Cylon was doing to him. I pictured the worst. I pictured him locked up in that room again. I pictured bruises. I pictured Awakened feeding on him. I couldn't stop shaking and I cried until I felt like I had been drained dry. There was nothing left for me to let out.

I lay on my side for a while, staring at the wall. Back at home, my walls were wood and I would stare for hours, trying to make pictures out of all the colors and variations in the grain. The walls here were perfectly white, the paint so even it felt like staring into a void. All the sadness and the fear that had been boiling in my veins since Octavia had handed me that note was barely there anymore. They were a simmer, overtaken by the overwhelming anger.

Ash was in Sekhmet. He was there, trapped, being subjected to god knows what, and it was my fault. No one could ever tell me differently. It was there in the note. Razi didn't want Ash; she never had. She wanted me and she had taken him to get to me.

It burned me up. I had been out on patrol before. Why hadn't she taken me then? Why did she take Ash? Why not me?

The realization hit me like a bowling ball to my stomach. She wanted me to come on my own. It was a test. Just another test, like everything else she had done before.

I sat up abruptly. Octavia had said she wouldn't send anyone. She had expressly forbidden me to do anything about this. But she wasn't the law. She wasn't in charge, not really. This wasn't a prison – I didn't have to stay here. And I wasn't going to. I was going to leave. I was going to go get Ash back. Even if I had to trade myself for him, I would do it. He didn't deserve to be there, not for me.

The decision came quickly. I climbed off my bed and nearly pitched to the side. My head was throbbing and my eyes were red and puffy from all the crying I had just done. I knew I should stay, regroup and rest, but now that I had my mind set on this, I didn't want to waste any time. There were things that I had to do. I needed supplies and a weapon, but none of that would be available right now. There were two hours before curfew and the entire place would be lit up and monitored.

I had to wait until everyone went to sleep.

Kaya returned about an hour later and I pretended to be asleep. I curled myself up in a ball, facing the wall, and forced myself to breathe as evenly as I could.

"Zoey?" Kaya whispered, carefully. I heard her come closer to my bed. She whispered my name one more time before I saw her shadow on the wall pivot, and get smaller as she walked away from me.

I could hear her moving around our room, quietly changing into pajamas and brushing her teeth in our small bathroom before the lights went off and her bed creaked as she climbed into it. I stayed there, with the blankets pulled up to my chin, my heart beating a drum solo in my chest, as I impatiently waited for Kaya to fall asleep. It felt like ages before her snores filled the room.

I tossed the blankets aside and climbed out of bed as quietly as I could. Kaya was a deep sleeper and didn't flinch as I crossed the room to the bathroom. I splashed water on my face, before tying my hair back. I glanced at my reflection for a moment and winced. I looked like a nightmare but it didn't matter.

I tiptoed my way back to our room and squatted down next to my bed. There were packs stored under each bed, with two pairs of clothing, underwear, socks and a small supply of food. It was an emergency kit in case anything happened in Sanctuary, and most days I forgot that it was there. I had only remembered it while waiting for Kaya to return. There wasn't nearly enough food in there, but it was a start. I would still have to raid the kitchens and somehow find my way into the weapons storage.

The door of our room slid open with loud swishing noise and I paused, looking over my shoulder at Kaya. The light from the hallway hit her bed and she fidgeted for a moment before sighing and snuggling closer to her pillow. I sighed in relief, and pressed the wall for the door to slide close again.

Sanctuary was sort of creepy at night when there was no one else awake. There were a few lights here and there, but most were dimmed or turned off completely. Sanctuary was all about conservation and I had never been so grateful for it until now. I was also insanely grateful for the dark uniform we were forced to wear. I had grown so tired of wearing black but at night when I was trying to sneak out, it was a huge advantage.

It felt like hours had passed when I finally made it into the kitchen. It was large and intimidating in the daytime, even with dozens of people in there working and even more so now that it was empty. No one would be in here until the early hours of dawn to prepare breakfast. For now, it was silent. I crossed the room to the large industrial fridges that were embedded in the far walls to the right. I huffed as I opened a heavy door, a blast of cold air hitting me as it squeaked open. My eyes darted around, as if someone was going to jump out of the shadows merely because the door made noise as it opened. The nearest person was at least two floors away.

There wasn't much inside the fridge that I felt like I could take with me. I grabbed a lumpy block of cheese and some bread and then scooted out to the pantry, to find more sustainable food. I wasn't sure exactly how far Sekhmet was from Sanctuary but the last thing I needed to worry about was having spoiled food with me. There was some jerky and some packaged dried nuts and crackers all in clean white boxes with a simple Venn diagram symbol printed on them. The Sanctuary logo was on everything, subtle but a reminder of where we were. I tucked them into my pack and snuck my way out of the kitchens, back into the cafeteria.

I was halfway across the room when I heard it, the unmistakable noise of shoes scuffing against the linoleum of the cafeteria floor. I froze, franticly looking around in the dark for the source of the noise. There were shadows cast all over the floor from the dim lights that were spaced out on the wall. I was afraid to move. I didn't think I'd get in too much trouble for being out of bed this late, but I knew I would get in trouble for taking things from the kitchens. Every resource here was precious.

I didn't know how long I stood there, waiting to hear the noise again, but I finally convinced myself that I must have imagined it. I continued, my steps slower and more careful than before. My heart pounded in my chest. If this was what sneaking into the kitchens was like, I didn't know how on earth I was going to get into the weapons rooms.

That's when my name echoed across the empty room, barely more than a whisper. I whirled around, and spotted him almost immediately. Now that he was not lurking in the shadows, he was easy to see. Liam. "I *knew* I heard someone in here!"

Liam ignored me. "What the hell are you doing?"

I opened my mouth to answer and then closed it.

"You heard Octavia. You heard exactly what she said about going after Ash. She completely forbade you from doing anything about it and you sat there and promised that you wouldn't." Liam's voice was even, his hands tucked in his pockets as he studied me. He was a good ten feet away and showed no sign of wanting to close the distance.

"Now I was sitting there in bed, worried about you. Because you came out of that office looking like you'd seen a ghost. And I've seen you go through a lot, Zoey Valentine. And I've never seen you look like that. And so I couldn't sleep. All I could think about was what you were going through."

"Liam…"

He continued, acting like he hadn't heard his name. "So I found myself getting out of bed, even though it's not allowed." He rolled his eyes. "And what do I see when I come to your room? A tiny shadow, sneaking away to the kitchens."

A flush filled my face and I was glad that he couldn't see me in the darkness of the cafeteria.

"What are you doing, Zoey?"

"You already know what I'm doing," I shot out, hating the impatience I was hearing in his voice. "So why even bother asking?"

Liam regarded me carefully. "I had always taken you as a survivor, Zoey. This is a suicide mission and you know it."

The word suicide brought a lump to my throat. The smart part of my brain knew that, knew that he was right and that leaving Sanctuary and heading to Sekhmet was just asking to die but... "I can't leave him there, Liam. I can't do that."

"He wouldn't want you to do this for him. You know that right?"

My lips pressed tightly together. I would not cry. I would not cry. I would not cry. "Yeah, well I don't really care what he wants right now. Because I want him here. With me."

"This is exactly what she wants you to do, Zoey." Liam's voice rose, bouncing off the walls in the empty room and my eyes darted to the entrance. A guard could come by at any moment. "You know this is why she took him."

"So? What are you trying to say, Liam? That I should just leave Ash there because this is what she wants? Then it's my fault. That makes it my fault that he is there."

"No." Liam crossed the room and was in front of me. He grabbed my arms, shaking me a few times. "It is not your fault, Zoey. Not at all. Don't you ever think that!" He took a deep breath. "You just can't go back. That's what she wants. She wants you."

"I don't care!" Despite my previous concern about being heard, my voice came out as a shriek and I almost didn't recognize it as my own. I felt out of control, hysterical and that was not the mindset that I needed to be in if I wanted to make my way across Colorado and into the most dangerous place in the country.

"Zoey!"

"No." I interrupted. "I'm going. I've decided. You can try and stop me but we both know that I have no problem throwing your ass on the ground."

My heart was racing and my breathing was coming out heavy. Everything felt loud as the silence hung between us and I wondered if I would actually have to fight Liam to get out of here. Every moment wasted here was a moment that Ash could be...no. I didn't want to think about it. I needed to focus. I needed to leave. I needed to get to him.

Liam sighed, letting out a frustrated groan, pacing around. His fingers raked through his hair and he looked over at me. The look on his face was nearly unreadable; I couldn't tell if he found me impressive or crazy. I watched him as he paced, making incoherent noises. Finally, his hands fell to his side and he sighed again. "All right. What's the plan?"

My jaw dropped in surprise. "Excuse me?"

Liam's jaw was straight and his lips firm and thin. "You heard me, Zoey. If you're going to do this, fine. I obviously can't stop you. But you must be out of your damn mind if you think I'm not coming with you."

CHAPTER EIGHTEEN

"NO," WAS MY immediate answer. "No way. You're not coming. Come on, Liam…"

"Come on, Zoey." There was a smile on his face, though I could see even in the dark that it was strained. "Don't act like this is surprising. I'm not going to let you do this by yourself."

I let out another frustrated shriek, this one much quieter than the previous one. I had the sudden urge to stamp my foot or punch him in the face. "God, you just said that it was a suicide mission. Why the hell would you sign up for that?"

Liam shrugged one shoulder. "Maybe I'm crazy too."

"What about Astrid? What about the baby?"

He faltered, his face going pale. He swallowed hard before responding. "Let's face it, Zoey. None of us are safe with Sekhmet out there. We aren't. No body is, especially you and Astrid and my baby."

I shuddered. He had a point and my heart squeezed in my chest, thinking of Ash in there. "You're talking about taking down an entire evil corporation, just the two of us, Liam. I just want to get Ash back."

"Who knows, Zoey, maybe we can accomplish both."

It was my turn to consider him. His face was set and I knew how stubborn he could be. We were too much alike, the two of us, and I knew now that he decided there would be no changing his mind. "Fine."

A smile flashed across his face. "Let's do this then." He held out his hand to me and I looked at it, questioningly. "Give me the pack. I'll carry it."

I frowned. "You know, I'm perfectly capable of carrying it."

"I didn't say you weren't," he replied, easily. "Just hand it over."

I sighed, again, handing it over. I didn't want to waste time arguing. Well, anymore time than we already had. "Can we go now?"

There was a smirk at the corner of Liam's mouth. "Yes, ma'am." He pulled the pack over his broad shoulders, adjusting it so it didn't cut off his circulation. "What was the next step of this plan?"

It was hard to tell if he was being condescending and I shot a dark look in his direction. His face was clear though. "Well, we can't exactly go without weapons and I honestly couldn't figure out to get in there."

The two of us made our way out of the cafeteria, our shoes making no noise on the floor beneath us. The spiral walkway was abandoned, but the two of us stayed close to the wall, away from the light beaming in from the top dome. There wasn't much light but the moon was bright enough to cast shadows everywhere, and we hid in those as much as we could.

Liam's voice was barely more than a whisper as we made our way to the weapons arsenal. "There are guards rotating throughout the day and night, which means they come and go, picking up weapons. We just need to sneak in while someone is going in or out."

"You make it sound so much easier than it is actually going to be," I hissed back. We finally made it to the right floor, both of us pressing tighter against the wall. There was no one in sight yet but that didn't mean someone wouldn't sneak up on us. I bounced back and forth nervously from one foot to the other before Liam's hand landed on my wrist and I stopped.

Several people came in and out of the weapons' room. No one guarded the room; there was no need to. The guards merely swiped their wristbands against a keypad. I knew that neither Liam's nor mine would work; we weren't cleared for guard duty this late at night. There was also no way to sneak in after someone. The door slid open and closed in an instant.

"Shit, shit, shit..." I whispered, starting to bounce again.

"Shh," Liam said, his eyes wide. "We'll just have to be careful."

"Careful?" I mouthed hysterically, fighting the urge to whack him upside the head. "That door opens and closes within seconds, Liam. We're fast but we aren't that fast."

Liam's gaze slid back to the door to the weapons' vault. "We'll figure it out." He didn't sound that convincing.

I resisted the urge to roll my eyes.

We waited for what felt like ages, hidden in a dark alcove. A few people came and went, about every fifteen minutes or so. I was about ready to just give up and figure out the weapons situation later when Liam sucked in a sharp breath.

His grip on my wrist tightened. A guard, someone I hadn't seen before, had exited the room, and was heading in our direction. We were hidden in the shadows but it wouldn't be long before he ran into us. "Zoey, can you..." He made some indecipherable hand movements.

"What are you doing?" I whispered, frantically, as each footstep brought the guard closer to us. Getting caught anywhere in Sanctuary would be bad on its own but being caught near the weapons would be...well, I wasn't sure but I knew I didn't want to find out.

The man staggered closer to us and I glanced around, still unable to decipher the absurd sign language that Liam was doing. Then it hit me, just as the guard stepped into the shadows where we were hiding. My arms darted out and in a few quick movements; the guard hit the ground with a soft thump. Liam moved forward, grabbing him under the armpits and dragging him further into our dark alcove.

"Jeez, I forget how fast you can be sometimes," Liam said, looking down at the unconscious body.

I shot him a dark look. "Let's just go." Liam smirked at me. "Get his wristband. We're going to need that to get into the weapons vault."

Liam nodded, twisting the wristband back and forth until he was able to slip it off the guard's wrist. He held it tightly in his hands as both of us approached the door. I tried to act normal, like I belonged here, but my heart was pounding in my chest as the pad flashed green and the doors slid open. The two of us stepped in and immediately went in separate directions.

During patrols, we used the same weapons, the sort of weapons that shot fast and accurately and were meant for one thing: killing. These were the kind of weapon that soldiers used and they had always felt unfamiliar in my hands, though I knew the perks to having them when several Awakened were heading your way.

However, this place was stocked with nearly every kind of weapon imaginable, and during practices we were allowed to use whatever we were comfortable with. I knew exactly where I wanted to go. The small weapons — the sort of handguns that I had grown accustomed to using — were tucked in the back corner. I felt a pang at the loss of my father's gun but shook it off. These weapons were just as good.

I grabbed a handgun off the shelf, making sure to grab a holster and plenty of ammunition. With the gun strapped carefully around my waist, I clutched the ammunition boxes tightly in one hand as I hurried back to Liam. He had a rifle strapped across his back, looking more at ease than I felt. He held out his hands for my ammunition and I passed them to him so he could tuck them into the pack.

We left the vault quickly. I felt both more and less confident with the gun strapped around my waist. The weight felt familiar and comforting, knowing that I had something to keep me protected outside of Sanctuary. But I needed to get out of Sanctuary first, before they caught me with an unauthorized weapon.

"So what's the plan now?" Liam asked, as we made our way quickly down the hallway. We barely spared a glance for the guard, still passed out in the shadows. I regretted having to knock him out but we had his wristband now and it would help us get out of Sanctuary.

"We can't go up. There are guards everywhere posted outside. They'll catch us in an instant. We have to go to back entrance. There are less patrols there and plenty of forest to hide our way down," I said, quickly. Liam nodded and indicated that I should lead the way. I took a deep breath, squaring my shoulders and started the descent down the spiral.

We didn't make it far. We were darting down the lower corridors when someone stepped out of the shadows and stopped our progress. My hand reached for my gun automatically and I immediately regretted the action. The people at Sanctuary didn't want to hurt me and I didn't want to hurt them either. I blinked a few times in the dim light and stepped back when I realized who it was.

"What on earth are you doing here?" I nearly shrieked. Liam shushed me but I barely noticed him. I could hardly believe it. "Caspar..."

My stepfather looked exhausted and there were a couple of books tucked underneath his arm. "Where are you going, Zoey?"

I looked over at Liam who had an impatient look on his face which I knew mirrored my own. Ash had been gone almost a full day now and I was tired of the interruptions. I just wanted everyone to get out of my way and let me leave. This was becoming a problem.

"I asked you first," I finally said, straightening up and loosening my grip on the gun, letting it sit in its holster.

He studied me before replying. "I was up late, in the library. I don't sleep much these days." He sighed and I could see the dark circles underneath his eyes. I had never noticed them before and I wondered if I had ever really paid attention. I tended to avoid eye contact with him as much as possible. "I was leaving when I saw the two of you sneaking your way up the spiral. I waited to see what you were doing and I knew you were in trouble when you reappeared with weapons."

Caspar's eyes lingered at the handgun on my side and the rifle strapped over Liam's shoulder. If he wanted me to feel shame, he was going to be disappointed. I had never seen much use for having a gun in the real world, in the normal world that I had grown up in. But these days I felt better with one at my side.

"Get out of the way." Liam's voice was firm as he took a step forward, shielding me from my stepfather. I nearly laughed. Caspar couldn't do anything to hurt me. I would knock him over before he even had a chance to wonder what had happened. Liam's face was a mask of calmness but I could see the tension in his hands as he opened and closed them in tight fists. He was as impatient as I was.

"You can't leave, Zoey." Caspar looked at me as if there wasn't six feet four inches of strength and muscle standing between us. "I can't let you leave."

This time I laughed. "*Let* me leave, Caspar? We've already had this discussion. You're not my father. You have no say in what I do."

Caspar's eyes were wide and desperate as he looked back and forth between the two of us. "Zoey, please," he pleaded with me, his voice rising a few octaves. Liam and I both glanced over our shoulders. "You are safe here. You can't leave. You're all I have left of her. You're the only thing that's left. And she would kill me if I let her baby leave the one place where she was safe."

A lump formed in the back of my throat at the mention of my mother. The last time I had seen her, she'd been pale and bleeding. Her eyes unseeing as she succumbed to her wounds. "Stop it. Stop using her to guilt me. It's not going to work. I'm leaving. He already tried to stop me." I indicated toward Liam, who shook his head. "If my best friend didn't succeed, what on earth makes you think you will?"

There was a long bout of silence between the three of us as Caspar took in my words. "You'd really be willing to risk it all, just for a boy?"

I moved so fast that neither Liam nor Caspar had any time to react and stop me. I pushed past Liam, my hands landing on Caspar's chest. I shoved him hard, sending him spiraling. My arm came up to his neck and despite the height difference between us, I had him pinned in an instant right up against the wall.

"Jesus, Zoey…" Liam said, racing over to us. His hand came up to my elbow and I shot him a dirty look. He stepped back, his hands held up in surrender, his brow furrowed.

I looked back at Caspar whose eyes were wide in shock. He'd never seen me fight before and I knew I didn't look like much. It felt good to get my hands on him. I had hated him for such a huge part of my life and it felt good. "Don't you dare talk about Ash like that. He's not just a boy."

"Zoey…"

"I'm so sick of everyone telling me what to do. I'm so sick of everyone telling me that he isn't important. He is *everything* to me. He's been the only constant in my life since this world went to complete and utter shit and you want me to just leave him there." I could hear my voice rising and I wasn't surprised when tears sprung to the corners of my eyes. "I would do *anything* for him."

Liam reached for me and this time, I didn't push him away. The fight started to leave me and I sagged a little, loosening my grip on Caspar. "You don't understand. I can't leave him there. I can't just leave him…" I swallowed hard, blinking back the tears. Ash didn't need my tears. He needed my fight. "You gave up on my mother, Caspar. Just because you didn't go after her doesn't mean you should keep me from going after Ash."

His eyes met mine and I saw the guilt written all over his face.

"You didn't know if she was safe. You didn't even know if she was alive. You just *hoped*, but you didn't do anything about it. You just accepted it. And you loved her, Caspar."

"I still do," he replied softly, his eyes closing.

My lips pressed tightly together. The truth in his words rang in my head and for the first time, they didn't feel like a knife in the back. "Exactly. I love Ash. I love him so much and I can't do what you did. I don't know if he's safe or if he's hurt. I don't know anything except I can't just sit here and wait. Can't you understand that? Don't you wish you could have done it differently? Wouldn't you have gone for her?" My voice was urgent and pleading. We had wasted too much time in here. It wouldn't take long before they noticed the missing weapons we had stolen and we needed to get the hell out of Sanctuary.

After what felt like an eternity, Caspar's eyes opened and he nodded. I lifted my arm and he fell to the floor, looking completely defeated. I felt a moment of regret at the rough way I'd handled him but there was no use in dwelling on it now. I offered him a hand and he took it, letting me hoist him up. I opened my mouth to say something but I had nothing. There was nothing more that I could say to this man. I didn't hate him anymore; I couldn't. But I also would never love him. I offered a small smile and turned my back on him, following Liam down the corridor.

We were near the end when I heard Caspar's voice call out after us. "What about your mother?"

Tears threatened to spill again but when I spoke, my voice was clear. "You know, I think she'd approve. She loved Ash too."

CHAPTER NINETEEN

THERE WERE TWO guards at the back entrance to Sanctuary. These were two more than I had expected but I had to hand it to Octavia. She was definitely beefing up security. It hadn't exactly stopped Sekhmet from killing the two men patrolling with Ash and it hadn't stopped them from kidnapping him so I didn't feel too bad about the fact that I most likely was going to have to knock these two unconscious.

The back entrance of Sanctuary was hidden behind the cliff dwellings that made Mesa Verde National Park famous. They were built literally into the cliff, yards above the ground, and they provided cover for Liam and I as we squeezed our way out finding ourselves nearly face to face with the guards. They were young and I recognized them from some of our training classes. I nearly sagged in relief. They were newbies then, not nearly as trained as some of the guards that had been here since before I'd even been born.

I glanced around, wondering if there was a way that we could get around them without them noticing. It would be nice to leave as few unconscious people behind as possible. I still felt bad for the guy we left stuffed into the dark corner on the weapons level. Liam's eyes met mine and we had a silent conversation. He indicated in a direction and I saw that, if we were quiet, we could possibly sneak past the two of them, but only if we were absolutely silent. It was dark, with very little light from the moon which was hidden behind the clouds.

We crept across the dirt floor, taking each step carefully. It was a slow and agonizing pace. Each step took time, as we made sure the ground was clear and that neither of the guards were facing us as we moved. We were crouched over and my poor legs were starting to feel it.

We came to a big break in between dwellings, and we both stopped to rest for a moment. I pressed my forehead against the hard wall keeping me shielded from sight and tried to control my breathing. I was exerting myself more than I had in months and it was even harder to do so without getting caught. My heart was pounding in my chest, so loud that I was sure it was echoing in the almost silent night.

Liam nudged me. The guards were walking in the opposite direction. Now was our chance. He took off, crouched low, his steps careful and quick as he crossed the space until he could duck behind another wall. I watched him with keen eyes, noting where his feet landed. He peeked out from his hiding spot and waved me forward.

I darted forward, and immediately lost control of my feet. I tripped, sprawling flat out in the dirt. I heard Liam swear under his breath and froze. I was terrified to move. I couldn't tell yet if I was caught. I pressed myself further into the dirt, wishing the ground would just open up and swallow me whole. I took a chance and lifted my head slightly, locking eyes with Liam.

Now, he mouthed. I scrambled forward, afraid to stand up. The dirt was rough on my skin, especially after falling, but I pushed forward and crawled my way to Liam's hiding spot. I practically collapsed in his arms as he hugged me fiercely but there was no time for that. We had to keep moving.

The two of us crept along. We were reaching the path that would lead us away from the dwellings and away from

Sanctuary. It had been months since I had made my way up here but I knew Liam and I couldn't take the obvious hiking path, the one that was in plain sight. The way Ash and I had arrived had been much harder, more strenuous but it kept out us out of sight. This was the way that Liam and I had to go down. The only obstacle was getting past without being noticed.

Luck was on our side. The further we got to our intended path, the further the guards were moving in the opposite direction. I had never been much of a believer, but at that moment, I was convinced someone was watching over us. It was almost too easy, it was making me nervous. That is, until I thought of everything else I had to get past to get to Ash. This was just the beginning.

We kept pushing, unable to see much in the dark. I had stuffed a flashlight in the bottom of the pack but neither one of us made the move to bring it out. We were still too close to Sanctuary. I didn't think there would be a punishment for leaving Sanctuary; no one was forced to stay there. However, I'm sure there would be a huge punishment for taking weapons and I wasn't willing to take the chance.

Instead we pressed on, stumbling over branches and rocks. I was not normally a clumsy person but I found myself tripping over literally everything in the dark. I wanted to cry out in frustration but I kept my mouth shut. I was already so exhausted and I remembered that neither one of us had gotten any sleep. I wanted to stop and rest but I knew we were still too close. We had to keep going.

The sky was beginning to pale, showing definite signs of morning when we finally reached the old campgrounds. The place was a disaster. There had definitely been people here when the Awakened hit. There were abandoned tents everywhere and I was afraid to look too closely, afraid to see if there were any bodies left behind. Surely the Awakened would have devoured them. Did they leave anything behind? How long did it take for a body to decompose? This was not the sort of information I had at my fingertips and I didn't really want to know now. We walked through the picnic area, toward the main building.

When we reached it, Liam reached for the knob and we were both surprised when it turned under his palm. It was dark inside, and nothing happened when I flipped the switch. I had expected this. Most places didn't have power anymore. Sanctuary and Sekhmet had their own, and a few other places had small generators but other than that, the bombs had knocked out all power, possibly forever.

The inside of the main building was a mess as well. There was a small store, a check in desk and not much else. Liam looted around a bit before finding a couple of blankets and laid them out between two of the aisles, away from the windows and front door.

"Lay down. Rest." His voice seemed loud after the silence that we'd kept between us over the past few hours.

"We should take shifts," I pointed out, shaking my head, even as my body begged me otherwise. "You should rest."

Liam gave me a funny look. "Jesus, Zoey, you're falling asleep while standing up. Lay down. I'll take the first watch."

I hesitated for a moment, wringing my hands out.

"What's wrong?"

"I don't think I can sleep," I admitted. "And I'm sort of afraid of what's going to happen if I do."

Liam's shoulders sagged and he stepped forward, reaching for me. I stiffened a little at the contact before sinking into him. There would never be that sort of relationship between the two of us, but there was such an overwhelming amount of love and comfort and affection there instead.. Liam was my best friend. He had to be to go on this crazy, insane mission with me.

"You're no good to Ash if you are exhausted and delirious. This isn't going to take a matter of hours, Zoey. It's going to take time. It'll probably take us days to make our way there. You need to sleep. You have to be at your very best to get him back. You want to get him back, don't you?"

I pulled way from him and glared, ignoring the amused look on his face. "Of course I want him back. That's why we doing this, right?"

His voice was gentle when he spoke again. "Okay then. Rest. You need it. We both do. But you've been through a lot in the past twenty-four hours. You need it more than me so can you just listen to me for once in your life and rest?"

I stuck my tongue out at him and moved to sit down on the pile of blankets. My muscles screamed in protest and I groaned as I stretched out. I was already disgusting, covered in dirt and grime and who knows what else but it hardly mattered. The blankets were covered in a thick layer of dust. I fought sleep for a while before I gave in and everything went dark. The last thing I remembered before sleeping was the soft pink and orange in the sky as the sun began to rise.

Blood.

There was blood everywhere. It seeped out of every crack, every crevice. The more pressure I put on the wound, the more it poured out. It wasn't even red; it was only the darkest, deepest shade of burgundy, almost black, and it was thick and warm and I wanted it off. I wanted to scrub myself over and over again until my skin was pink and raw. I never wanted to see this blood again.

Ash's eyes were so dark. There was no trace of the beautiful blue that I had grown to know over the years. He was staring off into the distance. No matter how many times I tried to catch his gaze with mine, he stared off at something unknown. He was unfocused and his breathing was labored. Each breath that he took was an effort, a shot of pain shooting across his pale features. He was dying. He was dying and there was nothing that I could do about it.

"None of this would have happened if you would have just stayed with me." The voice that spoke was cold and unsympathetic.

"You would have killed him anyway," I told Razi Cylon. My eyes never left Ash. If this was going to be his last moments, if this was the last time I would ever see him breathing, I would not look away. I would waste not one of those seconds on her.

"Maybe. Maybe not."

Ash's hands rose, shaking in panic. His breathing came out sharper, quicker and I could feel my heart sink in my chest. This was it. I had nothing left. I had nothing to help him and all I could do was grab his trembling fingers and hold on while he took his last breaths.

"I love you, Ash Matthews. I love you."

***

"YOU HAVE GOT to be kidding me."

Liam's voice was loud in the silence of the small store and it startled me out of my sleep. The sun was shining in, bright, and it had been so long since I had woken up to the sunlight. I blinked a few times, trying to clear my vision, wondering why Liam had called out when we were trying to hide. My hand reached for my gun, but I was slow, sluggish, and I realized how right Liam was. I was pretty much useless without any decent rest.

"What's going on?" I said, rubbing my eyes. I blinked a few more times and then my eyes widened, my jaw dropping. I disentangled myself from the blankets that had wrapped around my legs and stood up. "Wait...what the hell?"

"I swear, it's like neither of you have seen a pregnant girl before," Astrid joked. The two of us stared at her for a long moment, neither of us responding. "Wow, tough crowd here."

"What are you doing here, Astrid?" I asked carefully, since it seemed that Liam was incapable of saying anything at the moment. His mouth was open and it made him look a little bit like a fish. I resisted the sudden urge to laugh and focused on Astrid. She was dressed in normal clothes, not a Sanctuary uniform, with a pack slung across her shoulders. "How on earth did you get out of there?"

Astrid rolled her eyes. "You guys snuck out in the middle of the night. They're going crazy looking for you. They're so focused on looking for you that they didn't even notice that I had left. When we get back, we need to file a formal complaint to Octavia because, seriously, it should not have been that easy for me to leave…"

I shook my head. "Okay…" I said, slowly, taking it in. "But that doesn't really explain what on earth you are doing here."

She shrugged. "I assume you're going to go get Ash. So I'm coming too."

This, it seemed, finally woke Liam out of his stupor. He shook his head and nearly sprinted over to Astrid, even though she was barely ten feet away from us. His hand grabbed her bicep roughly and he pulled her toward him. "No. No way." His voice was so firm and settled that for a moment, he reminded me of my dad when I told him I wanted to go to a midnight showing of the Rocky Horror Picture Show.

"Liam…" Astrid started to protest.

"No. No, no, no, no, no. No way. Astrid. Come on. You're not going. If I have to drag you all the way back up to Sanctuary myself, I'll do it. You are not coming with us. You're crazy." Liam's voice was strained, like he was barely able to control himself. His entire body was shaking; I had never seen him so angry before. "You realize this whole thing is basically a suicide mission, right?"

"And yet you're still going," Astrid grumbled, trying and failing to yank her arm out of Liam's grip.

"That's different. I'm not…" He was unable to finish his sentence.

"What? Short? Female? Mexican?" Astrid's voice was dripping with sarcasm. "I'm not an invalid, Liam. I'm

163

pregnant and I'm barely pregnant. And if you recall, it's her fault. So if you think you can leave me behind while you go taking down the enemy, you have another thing coming, honey."

There was a silence between the two of them while I fought really hard not to laugh. The more time that I spent around Astrid, the more that I really liked her. She had a stubborn look on her face that made her look even younger, I knew that Liam would always have a hard time with her and I was glad. Liam needed someone to keep him on his toes.

"I just want you to be safe, Astrid. Is that so much to ask?" Liam finally said, softly. He was looking down at her like she was the most important thing in the world and she was returning that look. I suddenly felt like I was intruding on a moment that I definitely should not have been a part of.

"I'm safer when I'm with you." Astrid's hand fluttered anxiously at her abdomen. She looked down at it, biting her lip, before looking back up. "She did this to me, Liam, and even though the two of us are going to do this, I'm still angry. I'm angry and I'm scared. This is not our baby and you know that. While that bitch is still alive, he or she belongs to her. And I'm not okay with that. So if you guys are going, I'm going too."

Liam growled, frustrated, running his free hand through his hair. I had seen him do that way too much in the past few months and knew it as his nervous tic. He only ran his hand through his hair when he was frustrated.

"Look," I said, cutting in. the two of them turned to me in surprise and I realized they had forgotten that I was there. I rolled my eyes, annoyed. "I get where you're coming from, Astrid. You're angry and you have every damn right to be. But you know she wants that baby and you know..." I trailed off, as it finally connected.

"Zoey?"

"She knew. She knew we would be back," I said, my voice low. "She's playing games. She's been testing us. That's what she does." The two of them looked at me confused and my next words came out impatiently. "Razi Cylon. She let the two of you go. Just handed you to Sanctuary without an explanation. Why would she do that?" I swallowed hard. "She knew that we would all be back. She knew that I would come for Ash, and she knew that you would come with me."

"Zoey..."

I shook my head. "You can't come, Astrid. You can't just willingly walk back in there and hand it to her. That's exactly what she wants. That's exactly what she's expecting. Sanctuary might not be the safest place in the world but at least it's not walking into freakin' Sekhmet."

Astrid yanked her hand out of Liam's grip now that he seemed distracted and she stumbled, catching herself before she could tumble to the ground. Her arms folded tightly across her chest. "I don't care, Zoey. I don't. I have every right to be there as the two of you. You know that. I'm three months pregnant. I'm capable of coming with you. I'm capable of a lot more than you think I am." She threw a scathing look in Liam's direction.

"I do think you're capable!" Liam protested faintly.

"You don't though. I see the way you look at me, Liam. Like you're ready for me to just crumble to pieces, even though you know I'm not. I was a mess in that place, Jesus, but could you blame me? Then I see the way you look at Zoey..." Astrid looked over at me and I flushed. "You look at her like she's constantly impressing you and it drives me insane. I'm strong too! It might be in a different way than Zoey. I may not be able to shoot a gun and I may not be able to flip a guy onto his back but I'm strong too. So let me come with you."

The two of us were looking at her flabbergasted. She was breathing heavily, frustration and anger rolling off her in waves. Her face was bright red and her eyes were darting to Liam in panic, waiting for his response.

Liam was staring at her. Even if you didn't know him as well as I did, you could see that he was looking at her the way she thought he looked at me. He was drinking her up, like he could never get enough of her and it was both beautiful and painful to look at it because Ash looked at me like that. I needed him to look at me like that. I needed him back here with me.

"Why are you so frustrating?" Liam finally said, his voice a low growl. "Why do you have to be so damn stubborn and frustrating?"

Astrid's face was even redder than before but her voice was firm and demanding when she spoke. "Well, you're just going to have to get used to it because I love you and I'm not going anywhere so you just...you just have to get used to it."

My fists clenched tightly. She had said it; she had said those three words and she had said them with so much defiance. She was standing there, her small face set and determined, waiting for him to say something and Liam's face was just shocked and pale. There were no words coming out. I was starting to get worried and I could see the doubt in Astrid's eyes.

Then Liam moved suddenly, closing the distance between the two of them in a matter of seconds. His hands went to her hips, lifting her easily, and her legs instinctively wrapped around his waist. Their mouths collided and the kiss was fast and feverish and I could feel the emotion even from where I was standing. My face was a wave of embarrassment but I was happy for them. They clung to each other, and when I heard Astrid emit a tiny moan, I cleared my throat, loudly. The two of them broke apart, looking sheepish.

"Sorry, Zoey," Liam said, not taking his eyes off of Astrid. I didn't say anything. I doubted they would have even heard me if I had.

"That was unexpected," Astrid said, softly, looking a little bit dazed. "It's not often a girl gets pregnant and then gets the kiss the father."

Liam laughed softly, using his fingers to push her hair behind her ears. He didn't look angry anymore; he actually looked more relaxed than I had ever seen him. "Always with the jokes," he said, shaking his head. He pressed a kiss to her forehead. "I love you too, you little monster." He laughed again, sounding out of breath. "God, that's fucking crazy but it's true. I love you too."

Astrid smiled and it lit everything up. I felt a shoot of pain go through me. Ash, I wanted Ash. I needed him. He was gone and he'd been gone for over 24 hours and I didn't even know if he was still alive, but I had to believe. I had to believe that she was keeping him alive, making sure that we made it back to her. We had to go. I couldn't keep her waiting.

My voice shook when I spoke next. "Not that I'm not super happy for the two of you because, duh, you love each other and anyone with eyes could see that, but I have someone who I love that isn't here and I need… I need…" I broke off, unable to finish.

Liam and Astrid both frowned, looking concerned, and Liam put Astrid back down. Astrid came over to me, wrapping me up in a hug. I squeaked in surprised before closing my eyes and pressing tighter into her. She was smaller than me but softer, and hugging her felt like the right thing to do.

"We're going to get him back, Zoey," Liam assured me, coming to stand next to us. "We won't leave him in that place."

I squeezed my eyes shut tighter as if the action would prevent the moisture from pooling in the corners. I was so tired of crying. I was so tired. "Can we go, please? I can't stand knowing that the longer the longer we take, the longer Ash is there…"

"Of course. I'm sorry, Zoey, this is my fault," Astrid said, squeezing me tighter before letting me go and looking at me straight in the eyes, her hands still gripping my shoulders.

I shook my head. "No. It's not. I'm so insanely happy for you guys. But it makes me miss him more and I don't know what she's doing to him, whether she's hurting him or…" I couldn't say the words. Killing him. She might be killing him right at that moment and I couldn't think of that because she wouldn't. She wouldn't do that, not while she thought there was a chance that I would be coming to get him.

"We're going to go. We're going to go right now," Liam said, reaching for our pack and grabbing his rifle off the shelf where he had stored it. He slung it over his shoulder and then looked over at Astrid, hesitating. "There's really no way I can convince you to stay behind."

Astrid shot him a look and he sighed. "You don't even have a weapon…" he grumbled under his breath, but Astrid remained firm. "All right. Fine. Let's go then."

CHAPTER TWENTY

I WAS EXTREMELY dirty.

I had been spoiled the past few months at Sanctuary, even the month prior to that at Sekhmet. I had been given access to clean water, which meant that I got to be clean. Being back in the woods again, traipsing over abandoned highways, and sleeping in the dirt had given me a thick layer of grime that I was not overly fond of. Not only was I exhausted, my muscles screaming with each step that I took, I felt disgusting. Everything about this felt wrong, hopeless, and we had barely left.

It had been two days since we left Sanctuary. We only had a vague idea of where Sekhmet was. Liam and Astrid had no memory whatsoever of the journey from one to the other, and I had come there from Bert's place. I hardly remembered my own escape from Sekhmet to Bert's house. I had been too preoccupied keeping my hands on Ash's bleeding wound.

I was also hungry. I had only packed enough provisions to last myself a decent amount of time and between the three of us, especially the pregnant girl who was hungry all the time, the supplies had diminished fairly quickly. Liam was a good hunter, had been so since he was a kid, or so he had told me, but there wasn't much to hunt. Ever since the Awakened had appeared last year, the animals had disappeared.

But with exhaustion and hunger came another obstacle: irritability. The three of us had settled into a tense silence, barely speaking to one another except to debate on which direction to head. The two of them kept turning to me. To be fair, I was the only one that had any memory of leaving Sekhmet, and this was my crazy mission. But I had no answers and I knew it.

I was about ready to lose my mind when we ran into some luck. The area in which we were travelling was starting to look familiar, and I guided us in an actual direction, feeling, for the first time, that I actually knew where I was going. The two of them grumbled behind me as we picked our way through broken and abandoned cars on the highway. My feet were aching, and I didn't want to walk anymore. I was so done with walking. Each step felt like pins and needles and it didn't help that the shoes I was wearing were soft, meant for walking around the halls of Sanctuary, not hiking across Colorado.

Just as I was about ready to give up, crawl into one of the cars and pass out for as long as my body wanted to, I spotted it. There was a turn off the highway that I knew I recognized and I started running. I heard faint protests behind me as I took off sprinting. Everything in my body was protesting but I knew where I was.

The house appeared sooner than I had expected and I felt a crushing wave of relief flood through me. I hadn't seen it in months and had only spent a few days there, but it had felt like a temporary home. It was where I had finally been safe. It had been where Bert had saved Ash's life. It reminded me that not all was lost. There was still hope.

I stopped in front of the house, waiting for Liam and Astrid to catch up. They were both out of breath. Astrid was particularly red in the face and I felt bad. Every hard moment that we'd had, climbing over rocks, or even just a straight shot down the highway for miles in the hot sun, sent a shock of guilt through me. She tired much quicker than Liam and I but she never complained, not when she fell, not when she was scratched up, not even when a sunburn bloomed all over her shoulders.

"What is this?" Astrid asked through heavy breathing. She was looking up at the house in curiosity.

"This is Bert's house," I explained, unable to keep the excitement and relief out of my voice.

Recognition flashed on Astrid's face. She knew who Bert was and she knew what he meant to me and Ash. She knew this had been our safe haven. "Do you think he'll mind if we break in?"

I laughed. "Yeah, I don't think he'll care. Now that he's at Sanctuary, this place isn't being used. And even though I doubt he'd be completely okay with the fact that we are on this rescue trip, I think he'd be glad to know we found this place."

Liam shrugged. "Either way, it's easier to ask for forgiveness than permission, right?"

"Considering he's not even here…" I trailed off. I sighed, and started making my way up the steps. "Come on."

It turned out we didn't need to do much breaking in. Astrid shoved past both of us, bending over the lock. She dug through our pack until she came up with the first aid kit and she removed a needle out of it. She studied it for a moment before inserting it into the lock. After a few moments, it clicked and the door swung open when she turned it. She smiled triumphantly and swept out her hand, inviting us in.

I was impressed. "Now where on earth did you learn to that?" I asked, moving past her to take refuge inside the house. She smiled but didn't answer.

It was dark inside and none of the light switches did anything when flipped. I remembered that Bert had his own generator and I figured he probably shut it down now that he wasn't staying here. It was late in the day and there was some light drifting through some of the windows. We rummaged through the drawers in the kitchen before we found a flashlight and even a couple of candles. We had a box of matches in the pack. We would be okay.

"Zoey!" Liam called from the bathroom. "We have running water. It's freezing as hell but its here."

I sagged. "It's probably so wrong but all I really want right now is to be clean."

He came out of the bathroom and raised his eyebrow at me.

A sigh escaped my lips and I plopped myself down on the sofa, which nearly collapsed underneath me. "I know. Perspective."

He reached forward and squeezed my shoulder tightly. "Go take a shower. And get some rest. You deserve both. We are going to get Ash, Zoey. But don't feel bad for feeling anything. Don't feel bad for wanting to be clean or for wanting to sleep."

I swallowed hard and nodded, pushing myself off the couch, which was an ordeal in itself. Liam offered his hand to me and yanked me up. I smiled at him gratefully and headed down the hallway to the bathroom.

After I had showered, which felt good even with the cold water hitting my skin, I wrapped myself in a towel and let myself into the room that I had stayed in last time I was here. The memories hit me like a heavy brick to the chest. Last time I'd been in this room I'd been with Ash. It was the same room that he had told me he loved me. It was the room where everything had changed. I took a deep breath, trying hard to clear my thoughts and crossed the room to the dressers, looking for something clean to wear.

It may still have been weird to wear Octavia's old clothes, but I figured she owed me. I made a face as I yanked out a shirt and pants. Clean clothes were clean clothes, no matter who they used to belong to.

I climbed up into the bed, yanking the covers down, loving the softness that brushed against my bare skin. The blankets at Sanctuary had been for utility, not comfort, and there were many nights where I missed my big fluffy comforter back in New York. Not that it existed anymore. It was probably nothing more than ashes.

I didn't want to think about that though. All I wanted to do was sleep. Sleep was the only thing I could think about. There was a slight rumble in my stomach. I hadn't eaten anything substantial in days but my stomach was also churning, full of worry for Ash and terror for the three of us, taking on this entire place to get him back.

I wasn't sure when I fell asleep, lost in my thoughts about Ash, but when I awoke it was dark and I blinked a few times in confusion, unsure of where I was for a moment. I had awoken suddenly, like I had heard a noise or something. I squeezed my eyes shut, wanting to stay in that bed. Then I heard it, the noise again, a whisper in the darkness. It was my name.

"Zoey. Zoey, wake up."

I bolted up, reaching for my gun before remembering that I'd left it in its holster in the bathroom. I swore under my breath; I was usually never this careless. I had grown accustomed to not carrying a weapon around with me at all times. I looked around and saw Astrid standing in the doorway. She was gripping the doorway, tightly, her eyes wide in anxiety. She looked smaller, clad only in a large t-shirt that hit her right above the knees.

"What's going on?" I whispered to her, pushing the blankets off of my legs and sliding out of bed.

"There are people outside," she whispered back, chewing the end of her braid nervously.

My heart stopped in my chest and I looked at her, in shock. "What? Who? How many?"

She shook her head. "It was hard to see, but I didn't recognize them and I couldn't tell what they were wearing. There's only three, maybe four, but I don't know for sure."

I nodded, feeling the adrenaline running like currents in my veins. I pushed past her, tiptoeing to the bathroom across the hall, grabbing my gun. I already felt better having it in my hands. "Go wake up Liam. Quietly." I wondered for a moment why she hadn't woken him up first. Surely they had shared the same bed last night.

Astrid must have read my mind. "I couldn't sleep. I haven't really been sleeping well since…" she trailed off, but she didn't need to finish. I knew exactly what she meant. "I didn't want to disturb Liam so I was on the couch and that's when I heard them. I was on my way to his room but then they sounded like they were closer to the house so I ducked into your room."

I nodded. "Go wake him up. I'm going to go check it out." She nodded a few times in response and stopped chewing her braid, letting it fall back over her shoulder. She disappeared.

I turned to the front of the house, suddenly very glad that it was dark – that we had no access to lights, and therefore, had none on to attract attention. I crept down the hallway, wincing at every noise I made. Every creak seemed to echo in the silence and I understood why Astrid had been terrified to take the few extra steps to the room where she and Liam had set themselves up.

The curtains were closed in the front room, and I was immediately grateful. I crept closer, and stopped when voices floated through the walls and into the house. Whoever they were, they were unconcerned about keeping their voices down and I realized they probably thought the house was unoccupied. This was a good sign and worked in our advantage. Either they would move on, unaware that we were here, or we'd be way more prepared for them than they would be for us.

I moved even closer to the window, wishing that the curtains weren't so dark so that I could see through. I took another deep breath, my trembling fingers reaching for the edge of the fabric and pulling it aside just enough so that I could peek through with one eye.

I could see three dark shapes, all of them fairly tall. They were dressed in dark clothes, not that it would have mattered much. The only light present was from the moon and it barely allowed enough light for me to see them. It let me see enough though.

All three of them carried weapons.

I let the curtain fall back in place and stepped back. The best thing for these strangers was to walk away, to not come anywhere near the house and to move on, but I didn't know what the likelihood of that was. If they were just people traveling through, they might not want to pass up the opportunity to scavenge for whatever this house had to offer. We had locked the door behind us when we came in, but locks weren't going to stop anyone. Not these days.

Liam came up from behind me, his hand at my waist in warning. I jumped and glanced over my shoulder at him. His rifle was clutched tightly in his hands, locked and loaded. He was ready. Astrid was a few feet behind him, looking nervous, but set. She had a knife in her hand. I was confused at where she could have possibly gotten it, but when it glistened in the light, I saw it looked like a cooking knife and I realized she had probably stolen it from the kitchen. This girl never failed to impress me.

Liam moved forward, his steps careful as he reached for the curtain, pulling it aside slightly. His brow furrowed as he studied the people outside who continued to talk amongst each other. Their voices carried but I couldn't tell what they were saying. Liam pushed the curtain further aside, looking confused, and I glanced back at Astrid, who looked as dismayed as I felt.

"Oh my god," Liam said, and I flinched at the volume. He was speaking normally, as if we weren't trying to hide from three armed strangers right outside our door. "Kris. Erik."

He moved past me, toward the door and I looked at him in shock, when he flung the door open and went sprinting down the front steps.

Astrid and I both looked at each other in shock and went sprinting after him.

CHAPTER TWENTY-ONE

THE THREE STRANGERS had immediately drawn their weapons and they had them pointed at us. My gun was in my hands, pointed at them. Astrid appeared at my side, her knife clutched tightly in her small hand. She looked fierce and ready, and I was glad to have her by my side. The only person who didn't have their weapon ready was Liam. He was staring at the trio, his eyes wide with shock.

Now that we were closer, I could see them better. They were young, much younger than I had expected. They could not have been more than a year or two older than me, and they looked hard and tough but not an immediate danger, despite the three guns pointed in my face. There were two guys and one girl, and they were looking back and forth between the three of us. Their glances passed over Astrid and me easily but they all paused, their faces paling, when they landed on Liam.

The girl spoke first. "No way. Liam?"

"Kris?" he asked, hesitantly. He was staring at the girl as if he wasn't quite sure what he was seeing.

The girl's face broke out in a huge grin, startling me enough that I dropped my gun, slightly. The guy to her right was smiling as well. They exchanged looks and then approached Liam in unison. I raised my gun again and nearly dropped it when the two of them embraced Liam and...he embraced them right back.

"Oh..." Astrid said, softly. "They're from Hoover."

Comprehension flitted through my brain and I lowered my gun completely. "Well, shit."

The two strangers stepped back from Liam, who was grinning widely. The third moved forward to clap Liam on the back, though they didn't look nearly as chummy as the first two. All four of them turned to Astrid and me and the girl's eyebrows rose, her grin widening. I suddenly remembered that I was wearing no bra, and that Astrid was only wearing an overlarge t-shirt.

"You have quite a situation going on here, don't you, Liam?" Amusement colored the girl's voice.

Liam rolled his eyes. "Guys, this is Kris, Erik and Nathan. They're from that group I told you about, Hoover. This is Zoey and Astrid."

Erik's smile grew wider and knowing. "Oh, so this is Zoey..."

Astrid groaned but there was a smile on her face. "Always Zoey, isn't it?" She nudged me playfully, her hand reaching for Liam's. I shook my head, my eyes meeting Kris's. She was looking at me, sympathetically, and I wanted to tell her, no, no it wasn't like that but it would bring up Ash and I wasn't ready for that.

"What happened, man? You disappeared and then your mom decided to leave us for Sanctuary. We all thought you were dead," Nathan spoke up. His voice was low and soft, unexpected for someone as large as him.

Liam shook his head. "Still alive, last time I checked." He gave a brief rundown of his time spent at Sekhmet and how he had ended up at Sanctuary. He left out a lot of details, sticking to the important stuff, but he definitely left out the point about Astrid being pregnant. She looked over at me and I shrugged, knowing that Liam would have his reasons.

"This is all fine and dandy but anyway, we can go inside this house of yours?" Kris asked, looking over her shoulder. "I really don't like just hanging around. You never know what's hanging out in the dark."

"Yeah, of course," I said, quickly. "Come in."

The six of us made our way back into the house. I fumbled around for the candles that I found earlier and lit a few, placing them on the table in the dining room. We gathered around it, though no one made a move to sit down. Everyone seemed to be weighing each other up, unsure of what to do.

"What are you guys doing out here, by yourselves?" Liam finally asked, ending the uncomfortable silence.

"Scouting. There have been more Awakened in the last couple months, more so than usual and Greg has been reluctant to keep moving. You never know when you're going to run into a group and we just don't have the numbers to take them on," Erik explained, sounding tired. "A few at a time, sure. But the numbers we've seen have been overwhelming. So Greg usually sends out a small team before we move on."

Liam nodded. "You guys are awfully close to Sanctuary."

Kris shrugged. "We figured that place was safe. We don't much agree with hiding in a hole in the ground but we can't deny that they have the numbers, so we've been thinking of trying to settle nearby for the time being. Awakened don't get over that way much."

I snorted and all eyes turned to me. "You're a little out of the loop. Awakened have been attacking quite often lately."

Kris's eyes grew wide and she looked over to Liam for confirmation. When he made a face, she swore. "What the hell?"

Astrid, Liam and I exchanged looks and I sighed. "So here's the thing…" I proceeded to tell the three of them about Sekhmet, about the creation of the Awakened, about Razi's purpose, about my escape, everything except Astrid's pregnancy and Ash's current kidnapped state.

Kris whistled, looking slightly overwhelmed. "Well then." Her eyes met Liam's and then she glanced back at the two of us. She was tall, looming over both of us. Astrid was tiny but I had always thought I was a good size. Everything about Kris was large. She was tall, broad shoulders, long limbs, but it all combined for a beautiful Amazonian look. Her blonde hair was short, chopped unevenly, and there was a tint of some faded color at the ends.

She noticed me looking and smirked. "You've gotten yourself into some trouble, Liam." She indicated toward the two of us and I rolled my eyes. "Last time you were with us, you were with your parents. Now you have two pretty girls with you."

Astrid was studying Kris, carefully, and Liam looked uncomfortable. I started to laugh. Everyone looked at me in surprise. I was pretty sure that every girl here had kissed Liam and it was funny to me that even in this mess, there could still be this kind of awkwardness. My laugh grew louder and suddenly, before I knew it, before I could even prevent it, I had burst into hysterical tears. I covered my eyes with my hands, my heels digging in tight, as the tears spilled down my cheeks.

There was a sudden movement and Astrid's arms were around me. The crying only lasted a minute or two. I was starting to think that my tear supply was going to completely run out.

"Sorry," I said, my voice thick, when I managed to clear the tears from my eyes. I saw no judgment on their faces. Nathan, Erik and Kris were looking at me with one defining feature on their face: understanding. Even though they didn't know the actual reason why I was crying, they still understood. They had seen bad things too.

Nathan pulled his eyes away from me and looked over at Liam. "If you made it to Sanctuary, then why are you out here? Unless you were looking for us…"

Liam shook his head. "The plan was to stay at Sanctuary, because Astrid…well, because it just seemed like the safest option. I had considered leaving Sanctuary to come back to Hoover but…yeah, circumstances. We're actually on our way to Sekhmet…"

The three of them recoiled and their voices overlapped in protest.

"You're crazy…"

"What on earth are you thinking?"

"Didn't know you had a death wish, Liam…"

"We have to," Liam said, firmly. He looked over at me and a small smile passed over his features before he turned back to them. "They took one of our own. We're going to get him back."

There was a long pause as the three of them took this piece of information in. Finally, Erik sighed. "You should come back with us to Hoover."

"No!" I protested, loudly. "I'm sure it's safe. I've heard a lot about you guys, actually. But I can't go there. I need to get to Sekhmet. I need to save Ash."

Kris raised her eyebrows, looking unsurprised, but I ignored her. I knew what she was probably thinking but I didn't care. Ash was more than just my boyfriend. Ash was my family, the integral part of the small family that I had left.

"I know," Erik said and Kris shot a surprised look at him. "But you're not going to do it by yourselves, not just the three of you, especially since that one is pregnant."

Astrid jumped as if physically shocked and her hands went protectively over her stomach. "How did you know?"

"Isn't it obvious?" He looked around and we all just stared at him. His face flushed a little. "My sisters were always getting pregnant. I had about a thousand nieces and nephews. I guess

I just know how to tell. You have a little weight in your stomach, and only your stomach." He sighed. "And it's not like people are eating that well nowadays. It was a guess, mostly."

The three of them looked at Liam but his face was set and they all hastily looked away.

"The point is, you need help. You can't do it on your own," Erik said, his face still bright red. He avoided looking at both Liam and Astrid and focused on me instead. "So I think you guys should come back with us to Hoover."

Liam cleared his throat, his brow furrowed. "I don't know that we're going to get any help at Hoover..." he trailed off, looking unsure.

Erik scratched the back of his head, studying all three of us. We looked positively spoiled next to them. We had all taken showers recently, had clean clothes and had been eating pretty well at Sanctuary. They looked well fed, but worn, tired, and dirty. They had lived hard the past year. "I don't know that Greg will do anything. But I think it's worth a try. And I'd hate to just let you guys break into Sekhmet – which is insane – without at least trying to get you help."

I considered that for a moment, shocked. Ash had been a member of the community at Sanctuary, a place sworn to protect its inhabitants and they had done nothing to prevent all the deaths that had occurred and they refused to lift a finger to get Ash back. Then there were these people, who I didn't know at all, willing to help us out. A smile broke out across my face. "Well, let's go then."

It took us no time at all to gather us back up again. We changed back into normal clothes, grabbed another pack from one of Bert's closets. We took a few things from his house. Bert hadn't said anything about returning but I didn't want to take anything that he may need in the future. Nathan, Erik and Kris wandered around the house, looking around with varying degrees of emotions on their faces. I wondered when they had last seen a bed or any of that and I realized again how spoiled we were at Sanctuary.

When we finally set out, the sun had risen and there was a heat beating down on us. I was grateful to be out of the black Sanctuary uniform. It had been so long since I'd been able to wear a pair of shorts, and the ones I'd pulled from the drawers had been soft and worn in. I tried my best not to think of Octavia wearing them before me.

Liam and the Hoover kids talked back and forth for the entire trek to where Hoover was currently camping. Astrid and I stayed behind, trying to keep up as they climbed over rocks and fallen logs and led us through a few streams, one of which was up to my thighs, and nearly to Astrid's waist. We stayed quiet as they talked about people neither of us had heard of. Liam looked more animated than I had ever seen him, reminding me of the Liam I met in the woods so many months ago, before the events at Sekhmet and Sanctuary had changed us all.

It didn't take us long to get Hoover. Kris explained that they were scouting ahead, looking for another safe place for them to camp when they had run across the house. It was in the middle of nowhere, and looked intact, unlike a lot of other houses they'd run into and they'd debated breaking in before we had run out to meet them.

We passed Hoover's sentries first. Kris whistled, a series of short and long sounds that were answered in return before we could proceed forward. There were two older men, both who nodded at the three returning scouts. Their eyes went wide when they spotted the rest of us but they let us through without comment.

I knew we had reached Hoover; there were voices right away, several all at once, all talking in hushed tones, like a low buzz. I spotted one tent followed by another and another and then there was a whole sea of tents. There were big ones and small ones. There were people everywhere. It was probably only close to roughly about fifty people but it seemed like more.

They were spread out, all doing different things. There was a huge bonfire in the middle, where something large was tied up, emitting an incredible smell. People were milling about, bent over various tasks, like washing and mending clothes, tending to the children – *children* – that were running around and things like that.

It looked like a community. A real actual live community of people living together. They weren't just surviving. They were living. Several people sat in the openings of tents, conversing. People said hello as they passed each other. My eyes were wide as I took it all in. It felt real and alive. No one was avoiding eye contact or whispering. Despite the situation, despite everything that had gone on, they looked...happy. Taken care of. They were alive and aware of it and they were living those moments.

Erik caught the awed look on my face and smiled. "Welcome to Hoover, Zoey."

CHAPTER TWENTY-TWO

BACK WHEN I lived in New York City, I used to make fun of tourists. You could always spot them right away. Their eyes would be wide and their jaws would be dragging along the dirty sidewalks. They'd be wearing the most ridiculous clothing as if trying to call attention to the fact that they weren't from there. They took pictures of *everything*, and smiled way more than the average New Yorker did. They were the ones scratching their heads over the subway maps. They were the ones that overreacted, squealing and acting like they had never seen something that was relatively normal.

I suddenly knew exactly how they felt.

The stares followed us as Kris, Nathan and Erik led us through the camp and I stared right back. There was no hostility in the way they stared. In fact, I felt like their stares mirrored mine: curiosity. Everyone there looked tired and worn, like the three I'd already met, but they looked clean and taken care of and all around relatively unharmed. One older woman's eyes lingered on my face for a moment and I knew that despite the fact that I was in clean clothes, I looked worse than the rest. My body was marked with scars, my face especially, and I wondered what they thought when they saw that.

It took us forever to make our way through the makeshift camp. Several people came up to Kris, Nathan and Erik, greeting them on their return. Several more stopped Liam, embracing him and welcoming him back. Most had assumed he was dead and were ecstatic to see him alive and well, while they offered Astrid and me cautious but kind smiles. I hovered on the outskirts, feeling out of place, shy, something I had never had much experience with in the past.

We finally came to pause in front of a particular tent. It wasn't special in any way. It was larger than some of the others but there ones definitely larger than this. The flap was open and I could see someone in there but before I could look closer, Kris stepped in front of me.

"We should probably go first," Kris said, pointing to herself and Liam. "Not that you aren't welcome, because that's not it. But..." she hesitated. "But I'm not sure how Greg is going to feel about a bunch of Sanctuary kids coming to us for help about something like this."

"You mean he won't want to help us?" I shot out, feeling the apprehension fill my throat. I had no idea how close we were to Sekhmet but I knew that every moment that I spent not on my way there was another moment where Razi Cylon could have been doing something terrible to Ash. Now I was afraid I had come here for help that I wouldn't get.

"That's not it," Nathan spoke up. He rubbed his forehead. "Greg is in charge here and it's not like it's a dictatorship or anything. Its just...so many people found each other and didn't know what to do next. Most people felt pretty lost and helpless. Greg saved a lot of lives."

"He's one of the kindest people I've ever met," Kris said, her voice soft. She brushed her hair out of her face and it was the first time that her face was clear of amusement. This, it seemed, was the actual Kris, the one that didn't hide behind sarcasm and jokes. I knew that kind of strategy all too well. "He runs a tight ship here, but we've survived months because of it. That's all he wants, for everyone in hoover to be safe and to be happy. He'll want to help. That's just who he is. The problem is if we are actually able to help."

I nodded and looked over at Astrid, who shrugged. She looked exhausted, sweat and dirt smeared across her forehead. She was close to collapsing. My eyes met Liam's and I saw he was worried too.

"Astrid, you…" Liam paused, his brow furrowed. "You and Zoey should rest. This might take a while and I don't want you waiting outside this tent."

"That was a nice save," Astrid smirked, but she didn't argue. She looked up at Nathan. "All right, big guy, lead the way."

Nathan blushed, looking startled to be addressed directly. He was so much quieter than both Kris and Erik. "Oh, right. Follow me."

The three of us left Liam, Kris and Erik behind. I glanced back briefly, my eyes locking with Liam's once more before he ducked into the tent and disappeared from view.

Nathan led us through the camp. There was no direct path so we weaved through the tents and people, making our way to some unknown destination. People waved to Nathan as we passed them. He introduced us to some but there were so many and the names and faces began to blur, especially since I was so exhausted.

We finally made it to our destination. There was a delicious smell coming from a massive pot. I wondered for a moment how they managed to transport that thing around; it was huge. It reminded me of a witch's cauldron. There was an older man serving something into bowls to a short line of people. He smiled as we approached.

"I heard there were newbies in camp but no one told me that they were pretty ones," he said, immediately pouring two bowls and handing them to us. It looked like some sort of stew, thick and emitting the kind of scent that made my stomach rumble pleasantly.

Nathan rolled his eyes. "Don't ever listen to Jeff, okay? He's a charmer this one; next thing you'll know, you'll be chopping up onions and carrots for days."

I laughed, lifting the bowl to my lips and tipping it back. It was delicious and I immediately took another huge gulp, not caring that it was too hot to be consumed so quickly.

"Now, don't you go scaring off the help, Nate," Jeff said, scolding him with the ladle. His voice was firm but there was amusement in his eyes. There were wrinkles in the corners around his eyes, like he smiled often. He looked over at us. "Besides, everyone pitches in around here."

"Where do you get all of this?" Astrid asked, studying her stew. There were chunks of meat, and several different vegetables, all smothered in thick gravy.

"We hunt, mostly," Nathan explained, accepting his own bowl of stew. He grabbed a couple of spoons from a bucket placed nearby and handed one to me. "That's deer that's in the stew. The rest we scavenge. We hit abandoned grocery stores to see what's left. Most stuff is canned; it's the only stuff that lasts. Occasionally we run across crops and we take what we can from there. We could plant our own but we're always on the move so we take what we can carry."

He led us away, weaving through the tents again. He stopped in front of a small one, a red and gray tent that looked a little worse for wear. There were dark stains on one side that looked like blood but easily could have been something else. Nathan took a seat on the ground, folding his legs, and dug into the stew. Astrid and I glanced at each other before joining him.

We sat in companionable silence a while, each of us munching on our own portion. I took this opportunity to take a look around. There was so much to the community. There weren't a lot of people but it was large and intricate. There were people everywhere and they had so much. There was a makeshift kitchen area, tucked behind where we'd gotten the stew, where people were already preparing for some future meal. There were people washing laundry in large plastic bins. There was a large tent guarded by three men, where people came in and out. I eventually realized it was their weapons arsenal. It was impressive but there was something about it that bothered me.

"You said you're always on the move, but you guys seem to have a lot of stuff for people on the move. How on earth do you guys manage that?"

Nathan sighed. He finished the last few bites of his stew before putting the bowl aside and leaning back on his palms. "We try to stay in one spot for as long as possible. We've been here for about three weeks, but the Awakened have increased in this area and we've shot more than we've been comfortable with. We carry a lot. We have a few large wagons. We attract attention. It's a large group and we can't exactly skip through the woods anymore. That's why they send us out to scope out the area before we move on. We make it work."

It was an incredibly flawed system but as I looked around, I realized how much it worked. These people were surviving. They were living. Despite everything that was going on around us, they looked happy. Nathan's tent flap was pinned open and I saw a sleeping bag and a modest amount of person items. There was a picture tucked in a wooden frame, with a crack across the glass. Nathan was sandwiched between two older people who looked like they could be his parents.

I looked away, taking a deep breath. I didn't even have a photo of myself with my parents anymore. Everything in New York had been blown to pieces and I hadn't thought to bring anything with me from Constance, though it probably would have been confiscated when Sekhmet kidnapped me. I sighed. I missed them. I missed Ash. Ash would like it here. I knew he would.

We sat there for a couple hours. There was a flurry of anxiety in the pit of my stomach and I could tell by the way Astrid constantly chewed on her thumbnail that she felt the same. Nathan kept us pretty distracted though. He told us more about Hoover, the way it was run and the way they kept it going. Greg had been a professor back home and Nathan was one of his students. Nathan had been with Hoover since the beginning.

"It's just continued to grow. Greg has created something amazing," Nathan told us.

Several people ambled by as the hours passed. Some stopped to talk and Nate introduced us. People looked at us with open interest, sometimes staring a little too long, but no one looked at us at all with hostility. They asked us about ourselves, where we had lived, who we had lost. Everyone was sympathetic and unafraid to talk about the tragedies that had occurred. Astrid and I fumbled awkwardly through these conversations with encouragement from Nathan.

I was lying back, letting the sun soak into my skin with my eyes closed, when I felt something land on my hand. It was wet and familiar but it startled me. I jerked back, my eyes flying open. I was face to face with a Labrador. He was small, and a little mangy looking, but he looked happy. His tail wagged behind him, and he licked my hand again.

"You guys have a dog?" I asked, my voice strangled.

Nathan looked over and smiled. He seemed to have not noticed the dog's arrival but he didn't seem surprised. "He wandered into our camp one day. I have no idea how he got past all the sentries we have, but he came in, looking like a skeleton. So, of course, we fed him and he never went away."

The dog sat next to me, panting heavily. I caught the distinct scent of wet dog and dog breath. It sent a wave of nostalgia through me and I remembered my own dog, Bandit, who I'd been forced to leave behind when the Awakened attacked New York City. "Does he have a name?"

Nathan shook his head. "Nobody could agree on one. Of course. So he's just Dog. He answers to it so there's that."

Dog lay down at my feet and I felt another wave of emotion pass through me. I reached for him, patting him on the head and his eyes closed. I took a deep breath and scratched him behind his ears. I really missed Bandit. He was just another reason that I hated Razi Cylon and everything she had done. I had lost too much.

"He likes you," Astrid smiled, as the dog scooted closer to me.

It was getting late into the afternoon when Liam returned, this time only with Erik, who smiled at me. "Kris is on sentry duty," Liam asked, when I looked around curiously. "She already missed a great chunk of it talking to Greg."

"So?" I asked, my fingers gripping my knees tightly. The three of us were poised, waiting for Liam or Erik to say something.

Erik shrugged and Liam sighed, running a hand through his hair. "He didn't say he wouldn't help. So there's that."

"But he didn't say he would help, did he?" Astrid said, sharply, her brown eyes focused on him.

"You have to see his point of view, Astrid. He isn't as well stocked as Sanctuary, nor are his people trained for that sort of thing. When they said they wouldn't do anything to help Ash, they were being weak. Greg isn't like that. He is focused on the well-being and survival of a few dozen people. They come first. And that's what he's doing."

"So he's not going to help," I said. My hands reached for my hair, loose around my shoulders. I pulled it up into a tight ponytail, if only to give my shaking hands something to do.

"I didn't say that," Liam said, sitting down on the ground next to us. Erik made his goodbyes before disappearing through the tents. "We discussed it for a long time. A long time. I'm sorry we were gone so long. You guys were probably worried."

"Nah," Astrid and I chorused and Liam smiled reluctantly.

"Anyway, we talked for ages. We went in circles. It's not that Greg doesn't want to help. His immediate response is to help. At this point, he's just unsure of what he can do so he doesn't want to promise us anything. I'll give him that. He hates to break promises so he makes very few. He said he'd think about it, see what he can do and then make a decision from there."

The anxiety that had been simmering in my stomach was starting to boil. The hairs on my arms stood up and the panic rose in my throat. There was wetness at the corners of my eyes and I wiped it away angrily. I was tired of reacting to every situation, every moment, every answer with tears. I was past that. "I don't have time for a maybe, Liam. I don't have time for him to think about it. Ash is gone *now*."

"I get it, Zoey," he said, sounding impatient. "Don't shoot the messenger."

I sighed, my fists clenched tightly. "The longer it takes…"

"I get it," he repeated. "But let's face it. If Razi wants to keep Ash alive until you get there, which is likely her plan, then it doesn't matter how long it takes." He must have seen the mutinous look on my face because he continued. "We're obviously going to get there as quickly as we can but if we have to wait in order to get more help, I think it'll be worth it."

"He's right, Zoey," Astrid spoke up, softly, pulling her knees closer to her chest and hugging them tightly. I noticed that she did that a lot when she was feeling nervous or anxious. She sort of pulled herself into a smaller compact ball, as if by doing this, she could keep herself safe from everything else. I wondered if she realized that she wouldn't be able to do that for much longer. "We just have to hope that Greg has a way to help us and we can continue on."

"Besides," Nathan spoke up, hiding his yawning mouth behind his palm. "Either this is Ash guy is alive or dead, right?

If he's alive, I doubt she's going to kill him now. She's obviously keeping him alive for a reason. And if he's dead, it doesn't matter how quickly you get there. He's already dead."

Liam shot Nathan a sharp look but it was too late. My heart had already sunk in my chest, landing with a splat in my stomach, taking up residence right next to the boiling vat of anxiety that was already housed there. Nathan looked around and then his words seemed to catch up with him. He flushed and looked uncomfortable, suddenly unsure of what to do with his hands.

"Shit, that's not...Zoey..." Nathan said, stumbling over his words.

I stood up, brushing my hands on my dirty pants. "He's not dead," I said, firmly. "He's not."

CHAPTER TWENTY-THREE

WE STAYED AT Hoover for two days before Greg came to a decision. It was agony waiting for him to do something but I tried to stay patient. This was the longest I had been apart from Ash since we had escaped from Sekhmet and I wasn't a huge fan of it, not when I had no idea if he was alive or dead, not when I felt like I had the means to find out. When I was stuck at Sekhmet, separated from Ash, I'd had no choice but to accept that there was not much I could do.

Being here, in the middle of the woods, with a ton of other survivors, made me feel much stronger. I didn't have my weapon but I knew I could get it back, no problem, if I made the decision to leave. No one kept weapons on their person at Hoover and when Liam handed over his rifle with no fuss, I had known that I should do the same.

It seemed sort of illogical to me, to keep the weapons in one central location. It wasn't as if Hoover was protected by walls. But they had patrols surrounding the camp at all times and they were confident that this would keep Awakened from getting too close if worst came to worst.

I tried not to think about Greg and Ash, though that was easier said than done. I threw myself into helping wherever I could. I helped chop vegetables and prepare meals. I did laundry and mended clothes and laughed good naturedly when the others made fun of me for my uneven stitches. Everyone was welcoming and always looking for more helpers.

Astrid was a fascination to everyone though. It had been so long since anyone had shown up pregnant after the Awakened and all the older ladies clucked around her, making sure that she rested enough and had enough to eat. Astrid said it reminded her of her grandmother and seven aunts back home. They all were mother hens, both caring and intruding at the same time. She took it with grace, though, and despite her complaining, she seemed happy to be taken care of.

I loved everything about Hoover. It was everything I had expected when Ash and I had arrived at Sanctuary. It was so organized, and everything worked together. There was a place for everyone. There were people of all ages, some of them who knew each other, some who didn't, some who were the remnants of family, but they were all accepted and they all got along. There were disputes, Erik had explained to me, but everything was handled well.

I loved how friendly everyone was. I loved how everyone worked together. I loved the tents, of all sizes, scattered around. I loved how people sat and talked about all sorts of things with each other, books and movies and the good times before all of this. It was so refreshing to see people talking about it, not hiding away, and not pretending like it didn't exist. They repeated the same stories. They told us where they came from, how they had ended up here, who they had lost.

I wanted to stay here. I had every plan after rescuing Ash of returning to the Sanctuary, mostly because I hadn't really known where else to go. I knew that Liam had spoken of Hoover before but I didn't take it seriously, not until it was right in front of my face. It was beautiful. It was everything that I wanted. As soon as we found Ash and brought him back, I wanted to be with them. Wherever they went, I would be there. I finally felt like I had found a home.

I was getting impatient though. I had seen Greg from a distance a handful of times. The guy kept himself incredibly busy. He worked just as hard as everyone else, sometimes even harder. He washed clothes and prepared food, all sorts of things. He solved conflicts between several people and listened to everyone who came to him. Even though I was impatient for him to make a decision, I had to admit that he impressed me. He was a much more welcoming presence than Octavia had been. We made eye contact a few times and he would smile before moving along.

At first I thought he was ignoring me. He seemed to be making time for everyone in the camp, and his smile seemed condescending, since he always walked away from me. When I pointed it out to Erik, he thought about it and reasoned that he wasn't ignoring me, but only giving me a patient smile, letting me know that he didn't have an answer for me yet.

"Wake up, Zoey, wake up!" Astrid's singsong voice came through the thin fabric of the tent. I groaned. My eyes opened for a quick second and when I saw that it was still that gloomy gray of morning, I groaned again and shut my eyes, turning away from the door.

"Go away, Astrid," I grumbled, yanking the sleeping bag over my head.

"I guess I *could* go away, but Liam just came to tell me that Greg would like to see us so…" Astrid trailed off but I was already up, kicking the sleeping bag off my bare legs. It was the third morning that we had spent in Hoover and I was impatient to go get Ash. There was a part of me that hated to leave, and wanted to stay in the safety of this camp, but this place meant nothing if I could not share it with Ash.

I threw on a pair of shorts and stuffed my feet into my boots. I ran a hand through my hair. I felt like I was going to a job interview and, despite my excitement and impatience, I was suddenly full of nerves.

Astrid and Liam were waiting outside my tent, looking just as nervous as me. Astrid's thumb was back in her mouth and Liam was pacing back and forth, kicking up dirt in the process. They both looked up as I exited and smiled. I returned the smile as best I could.

"You ready to do this?" Liam asked.

I shrugged and the nodded. "Yes? I think so?"

He raised his eyebrow at me and I shook my head, taking a deep breath. "Yes," I said, quickly. "Of course, I'm ready." Ash was counting on me to be ready.

The three of us picked our way through the camp. There were very few people awake; it was too early for most of the residents. There were sentries on duty and a few people preparing for breakfast but most of the camp was quiet. The early morning air was chilly and I wrapped my arms around myself, keeping my head down.

We reached Greg's tent within minutes. Kris was already waiting there for us. She smiled at us all, and it was her smile, more than my two companions, that calmed me a little. Her smile was confident, unwavering, and not nervous like the ones plastered on the faces of my friends. She lifted the flap of the tent, indicating that we should step inside.

Greg was sitting inside, bent over a large leather bound book. He was scrawling quickly. He smiled at us as we entered but continued to write for a few moments. This was the first time I had been up and close with Greg and I had the opportunity to study him. He was much younger than I thought, even from the distance glances I'd had, only in his late thirties, maybe early forties. He had sandy brown hair that looked as if he'd stuck his fingers in a light socket. His face was tanned and tired, wrinkles crinkling at the corners of his eyes and mouth. He looked steady though, despite the fact that he was tired.

"Sorry about that," he said, finally, tucking the book to the side. He looked up at the four of us. "Sit down, sit down. I'd rather not stare up at you. It's pretty uncomfortable."

The four of us took a seat in front of him. I shifted uncomfortably on the ground, afraid to make eye contact with Greg. He didn't look like much but he also put out an air of leadership and authority and, unlike with Octavia, it was incredibly intimidating.

"Astrid. Zoey. It is so nice to finally officially meet the both of you. I'm sorry it has taken this long," he said, sincerely, extending his hand to the both of us. I shook his head. "I've heard much about the both of you."

Astrid and I exchanged looks and both looked over at Liam. He shook his head, a small smile at the corner of his lips. "All good, of course," Liam assured us.

I rolled my eyes, ready to dispel some of the tension that had filled the small tent. I looked over at Greg, who was studying me carefully. My face flushed under the scrutiny, and I resisted the urge to let my hair fall in my face.

"You know, most people would think you're on a fool's errand, " Greg eventually said to me. I opened my mouth to protest but he cut me off before I could. "I'm not saying that I think that, but most people would."

I opened my mouth and then closed it again.

"I think anyone who doesn't understand what Zoey is doing hasn't loved someone the way she loves Ash," Astrid spoke up. "I think many of us would go on a fool's errand to save the people we care about, or so we'd like to think. Zoey actually has the guts to do it."

Greg smiled at Astrid, appraisingly, and turned back to me. "I agree, Astrid. Which is why, even though it took me some time, I have agreed to help. I'm afraid I don't have a lot of help. We are a community of survivors, of family, not soldiers. I don't have what you need to storm into that facility."

"I know," I cut in quickly. "I would never ask you to do that."

Greg held up his hand. "And I know this. I know that you hadn't even planned on coming to us for help. I also know that it was the suggestion of Erik for you guys to come here in the first place. This is why I want to help you."

"How can you provide help?" Liam asked, his brow furrowed.

"I can't ask anyone to go with you. That's not what I'm about. I welcomed every single member of Hoover in here as part of a family and you don't send your family to something like this. However, I can ask if anyone would like to voluntarily go with you."

I sat up straight, my eyes wide. "And did anyone volunteer?"

He nodded. "As a matter of fact, yes. You have four people who would like to go with you."

Liam whirled around, his eyes landing on Kris. "You," he said, accusingly.

Kris smiled, revealing a dimple in her left cheek that I hadn't noticed before. "Me," she replied, cheerfully. "Come on, did you really think I'd let you go storming the castle without me?"

"You know you might die, right?" Liam asked, his voice sharp. "This isn't exactly a trip to Disneyland."

Her smiled disappeared, replaced by a scowl. "I know that, Liam. But I'm coming along. So is Erik. So is Nathan. We're doing this, with you. We care about you and you care about them." Her eyes drifted over to where Astrid and I sat. "So we care about you. It's not rocket science."

Liam looked over at Greg, who shrugged, still smiling. "I cannot stop them from going, Liam. You asked for help and your friends are ready to provide that."

"You said four people," I pointed out. "Kris, Erik and Nathan only make three. Who is the fourth person?"

Liam frowned. I could see that he was trying to figure out who else in this place would volunteer for such a crazy mission.

"Ah, yes," Greg said, clapping his hands together, indicating toward Kris. Something passed between them quickly and Kris ducked out of the tent. "This is what took three days to come up with. I knew I had something...or rather, someone, that could help you but it was a matter of speaking to him about it. He was reluctant at first to share his help, understandably so, but in the end, I think his acquaintance with Mr. Garrity and Ms. Valentine is what convinced him in the end."

I leaned back, surprised. "Me?" I squeaked. "With me? But I don't know anyone in Hoover. I mean, I didn't until a few days ago."

"I think you'd be surprised, Miss Valentine," was his only reply. His eyes lifted toward the entrance to his tent and he nodded.

I looked over my shoulder, barely registering the person standing in the doorway. Then I spun around, my legs scraping against the rough dirt floor. My mouth dropped open and my heart slammed in my chest. I didn't know him well but I owed him for eternity for saving my life when I thought all hope was lost. The last time I had seen him was after I had punched him in the face, trying to make my escape.

But he was dead. I had heard the gunshot.

A smile spread across his handsome face, which didn't quite match the anxiety in his eyes. Liam drew in a sharp breath behind me, but no one else reacted. No one else knew who he was. "Hello, Zoey," he said, his voice even. He looked past me. "Hello, Liam."

"Tommy," Liam said, dumbfounded.

"You're supposed to be dead," I replied, unable to come up with anything else to say.

Tommy winced but his smile didn't fade. "I probably should be," he admitted. "But I'm not. So there's that."

"That's all fine and dandy," Astrid cut in impatiently. "But who the hell are you?"

Tommy opened his mouth to reply but I replied first. "Tommy used to work for Sekhmet. He helped me escape, but he was…" I paused. I had heard it with my own ears. Razi had taunted me with his death herself. "He was shot. He was dead. You were shot! How on earth are you not dead?"

"It's not a very exciting story," Tommy admitted, shrugging. "I'm lucky."

Liam and I exchanged looks before turning back to him. "Explain," Liam said.

Tommy's shoulders sagged for a moment and there was a faraway look in his eyes, as if reliving something in his own mind. He stepped away from the opening of the tent, closer to us, and took a seat right next to Tommy I couldn't help it. I reached for him, poking him on the thigh. He glared at me. "Really? Poking me? I'm real."

"You can't blame me for checking," I shrugged. "Or you're a new version of an Awakened." The dread of it filled my throat and I looked at him, as if waiting for blue skin or deep black eyes to spring up out of nowhere.

Tommy shook his head. "Don't be ridiculous." He sighed, fidgeting slightly. His eyes met Greg's and Greg nodded, encouragingly. I reached for him again, this time, sliding my hand into his. His palm was warm and comforting and he smiled at me. "I should be dead. I really should. I should be dead or I should be an Awakened. There are no other options, not in Sekhmet."

"What do you mean?" I whispered. "If she decides to kill you, she just brings you back as an Awakened?"

"Bingo," Tommy praised me. "Razi Cylon doesn't hesitate to kill anyone that steps out of line. There is no room for mistakes in her world. I made a mistake. I helped you escape.

So she shot me. It knocked me unconscious. Just the blow from it alone…" He shuddered, remembering. "I have never felt anything like that before, and I would rather not feel it again."

"They left me in the room as they went to go chase after you. They thought I was dead. I thought I was dead. I was bleeding everywhere, in and out of consciousness before I finally just passed out. The next thing I knew I was in the middle of the woods."

"What the hell?" Liam interrupted, his eyebrows raised.

"Right. I was confused. One, I didn't know how on earth I could still be alive. I was in so much pain. I could barely register what was going on. Two, I didn't understand how I had ended up there. Unless…" he paused and then shrugged. "I'm just guessing at this point but I figure they thought I was dead, and didn't bother to check. Why they didn't try to make me an Awakened, I'm not sure."

"I do not that since you escaped, Razi hasn't been at her best. She's making mistakes left and right. She's not nearly as composed as she was before. No one knows why she does anything she does nowadays. Letting the two of you" Tommy indicated to Liam and Astrid, who looked surprised at being addressed, "go was something she would have never done before, no matter what game she's currently playing. She's dangerous right now, even more so than before."

"Wait." I held up my hand to stop him. "How do you know all this?"

A quick smile flashed across his face before he continued. "I have my ways. Anyway, there I was in the woods. I wasn't dead but I was well on my way there. I had no idea where I was. I had no idea where to go. I had no idea if I could even move. I'm sorry to say that I basically gave up," Tommy admitted. He looked sheepish. "It embarrasses me to say that in front of you, of all people, Zoey. You would have never just laid there in the middle of the woods and just let it happen. You wouldn't have given up."

I blushed. "You guys always give me way too much damn credit. You were shot! You were bleeding out!"

"Yeah, well, either way, I was done. Until these guys found me. They were scouting in the area, had heard some things about Sekhmet and wanted to stay as clear as possible from the place. Instead, they found me. They brought me back to Hoover and somehow, they saved my life. I've been here ever since."

"That is..." I fumbled for the right words.

"Crazy. Unbelievable. Insane. Lucky as hell. Trust me, I've thought them all." Tommy let out a loud breath and it filled the stunned tent. Kris and Greg had already heard the story, I assumed, but the rest of us were still letting it soak in. we were still reacting to it all.

Finally, after a while, I turned and looked at Tommy. His eyes met mine, patient, waiting for me to catch up. "So, you volunteered to help us? To go back there? Are you insane?"

"I'm no crazier than you are," he pointed out. "Besides, I know that place. I spent a long time working there. I can help you get in and I can hopefully get you back out."

"But why?" I asked. "Why the hell would you want to do that?"

Tommy thought about it for a moment before replying. "Because I hate that place, Zoey. It stood for something amazing in the beginning. Because Razi Cylon had beautiful visions in the beginning, you know? She wanted to help people. Somewhere along the line, she fucked up and I watched as it fell to pieces and I watched as she orchestrated millions of deaths. I'm over it. I'm tired of it. It's why I got you the hell out of that place. It's why I'm glad I'm not there either. And..." he trailed off. "And I didn't help you get Ash out. Somehow you got him out anyway, but I didn't help. So this is my way of making it up to you."

"You don't have to make anything up to me," I mumbled, under my breath. I looked up and saw everyone staring at me. I sighed. "Not that I don't appreciate your help. It's actually…probably the best news I've gotten in a really long time."

"I think I have a way to get us in, with little to no detection at all, and get Ash out. It's going to be hard as hell but I think it's possible," Tommy explained. "And with a small group like this, it'll work even better."

I sat up straighter. Finally, after what felt like forever, something solid was being set and we were making actual plans to save Ash. This wasn't just me leaving Sanctuary in the middle of the night with my friends following me on a whim. Tommy knew Sekhmet. He knew how to get us in. This was starting to feel real. It was starting to feel like we could actually succeed.

Tommy started fidgeting again, and I resisted the urge to put my hand on his knee to stop him. "There's more to it."

"What do you mean, there's more to it?" I asked, slowly. "More than just storming into a well-guarded, top-secret, death trap of a facility? There's *more* than that?"

Tommy cleared his throat, looking nervous. "Look, Zoey. I can get us into Sekhmet. We can get Ash back. It won't be easy. It's going to take a lot of work, a lot of stealth and a lot of luck too. But I think we can do it."

He took another deep breath before plowing on. "But if we are going to do it, I think we should accomplish more than just rescuing Ash. Not that we shouldn't rescue Ash," he assured me, hastily, but I waved my hand, impatiently, urging him to continue. "I'm just saying, if we sneak in, we should do more. We should have a larger mission."

"Wait, are you saying…" My brain was moving slowly, my thoughts crawling at a snail's pace. I understood what he was saying, but it hadn't quite caught up with me yet.

"I'm saying that I know how to take down the Awakened, Zoey. I know how to shut down Sekhmet for good."

CHAPTER TWENTY-FOUR

I LAUGHED. THE noise of it bounced off the vinyl of the tent and reverberated back to us. Everyone was staring at Tommy and my laugh faded.

"You're kidding, right?" I finally said. "There's no way. Tommy, come on."

"I'm not kidding," Tommy said, his face clear and firm. "The one thing that Razi always tends to do wrong is that she trusts her employees, completely. She keeps nothing from anyone. Well, when you kill anyone that disobeys you, you don't really have to worry about your secrets getting out. She didn't really count on me surviving."

"Everything about the Awakened is down to control. She showed you just a small portion of what goes into controlling them. It's all about controlling the neurons in the brain to react the way we want them to."

"This is all very science-y to me," I told him. "What are you trying to say? Cut to the chase, Tommy."

"Every single person who has been made into an Awakened has their own unique chip installed just below their brain. This manipulates the brain, sending signals that we specifically set. This is what causes them to migrate to certain areas, to attack or be docile. Everything they do is controlled, even if it doesn't feel like it. We never targeted specific groups, not after sending them into the large cities, but without that chip in their neck, without the control that Sekhmet has over them, they're dead bodies. Period."

I stared at the ground, my brows furrowed as I concentrated. "This is information that we already knew though…"

"To an extent you did," Tommy pointed out. "But what you don't know is how exactly it's controlled. The chip lies dormant in the back of their necks until we send out a signal. Most chips aren't dormant because we have a constant signal feeding out to them, keeping them active and hungry. Everything is controlled by computer and satellite signals, Zoey. Its tangible."

Liam shifted next to me and I looked over at him. Clarity spread across his features. He had reached the end of Tommy's thoughts before I had. I turned back to Tommy. "So everything is controlled…"

"By a program. One simple computer program designed by one of Razi's minions. And its only installed on one computer in the entire facility," Tommy said.

The realization hit me and I staggered back. "We could take down the entire Awakened force? But how?"

"If you shut down the program, completely, basically destroying it, you kill everyone Awakened out there. This doesn't make them dormant. This kills them. Period. You won't be able to use those chips again. They basically burn up. Shutting down the program would basically take down most of Razi's force."

I shook my head trying to clear it of the overwhelming possibility of stopping the Awakened. These stupid things had only existed for a little over a year now, but it had felt like an eternity. It was hard to remember that there was a time when they didn't exist, when they weren't the threat around every corner.

"So you want us to get into Sekhmet and not only save Ash, but also, somehow, take this program down?" I asked carefully as if speaking to a child.

Tommy nodded but before he could continue, Liam spoke up. "Taking out the Awakened isn't exactly taking out Sekhmet."

"True," Tommy conceded. "But you were just trying to get Ash out. This is simple, small, something that she won't be expecting. She'll be prepared for a full attack, but not this. It may not take down the entire operation but she's going to be crippled, big time, if the Awakened aren't functional anymore. They're terrifying and they're everywhere. She has the control because she has them. She'll be scrambling and maybe then, it'll leave an opening for someone to come in and take it down, for real."

I let this sink in. It was unknown how many Awakened were out there. I had taken a fair few of them out myself but it was nothing compared to the large number that existed. Shutting them down may not completely shut down Sekhmet but it would give whoever was left a better chance at survival. Hoover wouldn't have to be on the move all the time. They could settle, and create their own community without having to constantly change locations.

"You don't even know if this is possible, Tommy. It's a wonderful idea. But there's nothing that guarantees we can actually accomplish that" I scoffed, my arms folded tightly across my face. "It's a lot of what if's."

"It's no different than you storming in to rescue Ash, except now you have four more people going with you. Not only that, you have someone who worked there for years. I know that place like the back of my hand. You have an insider." He sighed. "Besides, I know how to take down the program."

There was a long moment of shocked silence.

208

"And how exactly do you know how to do that?" Astrid finally spoke up.

Tommy smirked, looking more like the cocky and self-assured guy I knew from Sekhmet. "Because my dad is the one that created it."

There were so many questions that were spiraling through my head. This new revelation was just another piled on top of all the other new information he'd provided. I cradled my face in my palms, rubbing my temples with my fingertips. My head was beginning to pound and I was feeling only slightly overwhelmed.

"Zoey?" Liam sounded worried. I looked up, pushing my hair back and managing a small smile.

"Do you really think this is possible? You guys really think that we can sneak into Sekhmet, save Ash *and* shut down the entire Awakened operation?" I asked, my voice small, glancing around the tent. Kris and Greg were watching us with interest, and while their opinions somehow mattered to me, it was Liam and Astrid that I was most concerned with.

"I wouldn't have spent the past three days discussing this with Tommy and considering how it could help you if I didn't think that it had a legitimate shot at working," Greg offered up, his hands wide.

Kris nodded. "This is true." She sighed, her arms folded tightly across her chest. "I'm not one for fools' errands. No offense. But I've heard what Tommy has in mind and I think its solid. If we're careful, I think we can do this."

I looked over at Liam and Astrid. Astrid looked unsure, but steady. Whatever happened, she was going to be ready for it. But it was Liam that calmed me. He was looking back at me without a whisper of doubt on his features. He was always confident when it came to me. He always believed in me. I sometimes wished I would see myself the way he did: strong, unwavering, a survivor. He didn't need to say anything. I knew he believed in me and I knew he believed in us.

"Okay," I agreed. "Let's do it."

***

WE SPENT ALL day in that tent, planning. Tommy wasn't lying when he said he had extensive knowledge about Sekhmet. He had spent years working for Razi. He was a lot older than I had originally thought. In Sekhmet, I'd pegged him for maybe twenty years old but he'd spent the last eight years working for Razi, starting when he was eighteen.

He had a solid plan. It was broken down in steps; sneaking in, breaking into the room where Ash was sure to be kept, shutting down the program. We went over it again and again and again. He quizzed us until I was ready to sock him in the face. It was excruciating to go over the details repeatedly but Tommy was relentless. The better that we knew the plans, including every twist and turn we needed to know inside the facility, the less mistakes that could be made.

We couldn't afford to make any mistakes.

The plan was good but it required us to be nothing less than perfect. If anything went wrong, there was little to no chance that we could accomplish what we set out to do.

So despite the fact that it was a tedious task, I tried my best not to lose my temper with Tommy. We repeated the steps again and again, only taking breaks to have meals.

It was decided, agreed upon by all of us, that we would leave the next day. We could have continually gone over the plan but we wouldn't be any more or less prepared than we already were. I was anxious to get in there and there was no use in postponing it.

We all went to bed that night, full of nerves and anticipation.

I tossed and turned in my sleeping bag for hours, unable to sleep. I felt a little like I was going into battle. I had no idea what was going to happen the next day and I had to be prepared for the worst. At the very absolute worst, I would die and even though I was prepared to do that in order to get Ash back, I wasn't keen on the actual idea of it. Astrid's uneven breathing next to me told me that she too was awake. I was tempted to talk to her, but I was afraid if I opened my mouth, I would throw up.

Eventually I must have fallen asleep because my thoughts morphed into images. Nothing about my dreams was concrete. The images blurred together, faces and places, both from before the Awakened and after. I saw my best friend, Madison, who turned into Astrid, her stomach large, tears streaming down her face. Liam and Ash fought Awakened, which became my parents and Ash's parents. I dreamt of Awakened ten feet tall. I dreamt of blood.

When I woke in the morning, I tasted copper on my tongue and realized I had bit my lip in my sleep. I wiped the blood from my lower lip, wiping it on my pants, and closed my eyes briefly. My heart was pounding relentlessly in my chest. When I had left Sanctuary in the middle of the night on a mission to rescue Ash, I'd been running on adrenaline and anger. Now, with the day upon us, I was terrified. I had fought hard to get out of that place, and now I was willingly going back in.

It's for Ash, I reminded myself. You're doing this for Ash. Ash was worth it.

I sighed, pushing the sleeping bag down my legs. I was covered in sweat, despite the cool early morning temperatures. Astrid was sound asleep beside me, but I knew I wouldn't be able to go back to sleep. I dressed quickly, throwing my dirty hair back in a ponytail. I crept out of tent, quietly, heading toward the middle of the camp.

The bonfire was still smoking slightly, and there were a few people gathered around it, despite that fact that it had to be about four in the morning. They all murmured quiet greetings to me, and turned their attention back to the pile of wood in front of them. They all looked distracted, and I knew that they, like me, probably had way too much trouble sleeping nowadays.

I stayed there for about an hour, shivering in my borrowed jacket, sitting on the hard ground. I didn't stir until I felt a hand on my shoulder. I jumped and saw Liam standing behind me. He was already dressed; the rifle he'd taken from Sanctuary strapped across his back. There were dark bags underneath his eyes and I knew he'd probably gotten as little sleep as I had. He looked ready though.

"Kris, Nathan, Erik and Tommy are waiting just outside the perimeter for us. Are you ready to go?" He offered his hand.

I nodded, taking his hand and letting him pull me up. "Wait." I stopped and looked up at him. "Where's Astrid?"

He hesitated before answering. "Zoey…"

"We're sneaking off without her, aren't we?" I said, filling in the blanks. Liam nodded. There was guilt in his eyes but his mouth was firm and stubborn. "Last time we tried to do that, she just caught up with us. Do you really think that's a good idea?"

"Of course not," he said, immediately. "Greg has someone that's going to stick to her like glue. He's already sitting in front of her tent now." He sighed. "She's going to be angry. She might never forgive me. But I couldn't forgive myself."

I ran a hand through my hair, feeling torn between the two. "Liam, I understand but…"

"But what?" He shot out and I took a step back. He looked sheepish. "Sorry. I just…I love her. And I want her to be safe. I don't like the idea of her and the baby being anywhere near…"

I cut him off quickly. "Look, I get it. It's probably the smart move. I don't like the idea of Astrid being anywhere near Sekhmet either. I don't like the idea of any of us being near there. But I'm starting to think that Razi let us all go

212

because she knew that we would be coming back to her." I sighed. "At least if she gets us, Astrid and the baby are safe."

Liam's shoulders slumped, relieved. "I'm so glad that you understand. I really didn't want to have to fight you."

I smiled. "We should leave before she wakes up then, so she can't chase after us like last time," I pointed out. He nodded and we both turned. "I will say this though, Liam, when we come back and she wants to beat the crap out of you, I will fully support her. Got that?"

Liam let out a short, barking laugh. "As you should. Let's go."

CHAPTER TWENTY-FIVE

THE REST OF our group was waiting for us, patiently, outside of the camp. They each had their own weapons. Kris had the gun I'd stolen from Sanctuary in her hands and handed it over, along with the holster. I strapped it around my waist, feeling both comfort and dread at the heaviness weighing against my hip.

It was going to take us nearly all day to get to Sekhmet, especially since we had to go through the forest surrounding the facility. It would be all about the sneak attack. It was to our advantage to arrive at Sekhmet at night; the dark would provide much needed cover. However, it meant that we'd be walking all day, so we would stop more often. We didn't want to be completely exhausted when we arrived.

We passed the Hoover sentries right away. They didn't know the details of our plan or even where we were going. Greg had informed them that we were on our own mission and that details were on a need to know basis. They didn't need to know, so they didn't. They only needed to let us through. The two men on duty nodded to us, before turning their attention back to the forest around us. Everything was quiet and calm so when a voice rang out, it startled me.

"No! Dog, come back!"

The six of us turned around at the voice and I spotted a tail darting toward us in the tall grass. I took a step back as Dog launched himself at me, leaving drool all over my legs as he licked me. One of the sentries came running after him, looking exasperated.

"Sorry. Doesn't really seem to understand most commands," he said, reaching for the dog.

I shook my head, waving him off. "It's fine." I patted Dog on the head a couple times, feeling another pang in my chest at the memory of Bandit. "You want to go with us, boy?" Dog smiled up at me, his tail beating a heavy rhythm on the ground beneath him. "Sorry buddy, you gotta stay behind. We wouldn't want you to get hurt."

The sentry grabbed dog by the mangy scruff at his neck and held on tight while we walked away. I glanced back once before we disappeared into the thickness of the trees and then sighed. Soon, hopefully, I wouldn't have to keep leaving anything behind.

It took us more than a day to reach the forest that surrounded the Sekhmet compound. There was a buzz of nervousness surrounding us but it seemed like none of us wanted to talk about it. Instead, we talked about everything else. We told each other stories of life before the Awakened. Kris and Erik told us stories about their first year of college. Even Nathan spoke up a couple of times, talking about his job in a coffee shop back in Denver. It felt good to talk about those times, about simple things like school and jobs. At one point, the topic of conversation turned back to food and my mouth began to water. There was so much I missed. I was grateful to have a full belly at the end of each day but I missed things like pizza and tacos and hamburgers and cupcakes.

It felt like the first normal conversation I'd had in ages. Everything nowadays was about survival and the Awakened. At Sanctuary, conversations rarely ever happened and people looked uncomfortable when you brought up old times. It felt good to talk about it. Everyone had lost something. Everyone had lost someone.

These people understood what that felt like. And it only made me want to stay in Hoover more.

I could feel an ache building in my legs the more we moved. It had been so long since I'd done this much physical work. I'd lost a lot of the strength and resilience I'd had back in New York, taking various self-defense classes every single day. The sun was blazing and my poor skin was taking a beating. I knew I'd be sunburnt by the end of this trek. The sun setting was bliss and I welcomed the cool night breeze on my burning skin.

I noticed the difference right away. I couldn't quite place my finger on it but I could feel it. The hairs on my arms stood on end and I was more careful as I walked, my eyes shifting around the endless forest. I knew the others noticed it too. Without saying anything, we all slowed, taking each step more deliberately than we did before. My eyes met Liam's more than once as we scanned our surroundings.

That's when I heard it. I held my hand up and everyone came to a halt. It was hard to hear, barely there, but I would recognize that sound anywhere. The low raspy breaths that warned of an Awakened attack haunted me in my nightmares every night.

"Where are they?" Kris whispered, her eyes darting about. It was hard to pinpoint where the sound was coming from. The moment I thought I figured out what direction they were in, I heard heavy breathing in another direction. The six of us created a circle, each facing a different direction. Liam slid his rifle off his shoulder, and the others reached for their weapons, ready.

There was a long moment where the only thing you could hear was the sound of our breathing and the slight movements of the Awakened hidden somewhere in the trees around us.

A burst of movement came from my left side, heading right toward Tommy "Tommy, duck!" I screamed, as no less than a dozen Awakened came sprinting out of the trees.

Tommy rolled out of the way, just as an Awakened went soaring toward him. He scrambled on his hands and knees for a moment before regaining his footing. An arm reached toward me and I whirled, grabbing the knife tucked into my boot, slicing through thick blue skin. The Awakened howled, staggering backward, and I took the opportunity to reach forward, my knife carving a clean line through his throat. His weight pitched forward and I kicked out, my foot landing squarely in the middle of his chest. He went down in a heap and I turned to face the next foe.

Two came at me at once, and I faltered for a moment. They were children. They couldn't have been more than about thirteen years old when they had been alive. They even looked alike; they could have been brother and sister. My hesitation cost me. They attacked from both sides and I dragged myself out of my shock too late. My left arm rose just in time to block the boy but the girl's arms latched around me and we went crashing to the ground.

We wrestled back and forth. She was smaller than me, slim, but Awakened were strong and heavy. I remembered what the trainer back at Sanctuary had said about using my legs, how I always underestimated my strength. I always relied on my hands and arms to fight back and it always ended with me on my back and scars riddled across my skin.

I flexed my hips and pitched my body upwards. The girl's black eyes widened in surprise and I just managed to see the flash of anger across her face before she fell backward. My gun was in my hands and I shot both of them. I hit the girl square in her forehead but I missed the boy, barely scraping the skin on his shoulder.

He smirked at me, his first and last mistake. I took that opportunity to shoot again and this time I hit my mark, blood spraying everywhere. I wiped it out of my eyes and turned to face my next opponent.

My heart was pounding by the time it was over. There was thick dark blood everywhere and I grimaced. There were bodies strewn across the ground but I was relieved when I saw that none of them were my companions. We all stared at each other, grim looks on our faces.

"That happened a lot sooner that I had expected," Tommy said, his eyes roving over the mess around us. He had a cut on his arm that didn't look too bad, but seemed unharmed otherwise. I was impressed. He had obviously learned to fight since leaving Sekhmet.

"What do you want to do about this mess?" Nathan said, wiping his blade on his jeans. He frowned.

"Just leave it," Liam sighed. "If anyone's around to find this, then they probably already heard us fighting. Let's not waste any more time."

"Zoey, you have a cut on your face," Kris said, wiping her hand absently on her left cheek.

I reached up and wiped, smearing blood all over my fingertips. My stomach churned but I cleaned my fingers off on my pants and shrugged. "It'll match the rest of my face."

Erik laughed and everyone looked over at him. "Sorry. I'm exhausted. It's just sort of…refreshing that you don't wallow. Wallowing gets old fast."

A corner of my mouth turned up. "If I don't find the humor in it, I'll just hate it." It was actually becoming a source of comfort for me. It was a reminder that I was still alive. It was permanent proof that I was surviving.

"God, I hate fighting these things," Kris said, staring down at the bodies in disgust. She spotted the two kids lying next to me and her face drained of all color. Our eyes met and she nodded. "Let's get the hell out of here. I have a feeling these won't be the only ones we'll encounter."

CHAPTER TWENTY-SIX

AFTER WE'D CLEANED ourselves up and choked down some food, we continued on. The smell of blood lingered under my nose for miles, and I knew it was more than just the blood staining my skin and clothes. I had killed so many Awakened in the past year but it had never gotten easier. Their faces still haunted me. The Awakened wanted nothing more than to kill me, devour me, but before Razi Cylon had gotten to them they'd been living people. They had been people going to work, going to school, loving their family, living their lives. It was hard to forget that.

We remained in silence for the rest of our journey to Sekhmet. The conversation that we had easily fallen into felt wrong now. The encounter with the group of Awakened reminded us of our mission and how truly dangerous it really was.

Tommy stopped us a couple of miles away, letting us regroup and eat before we went in. The first part of the plan only involved him and Erik. We ate in silence, all of us too nervous to say anything. The only sounds were the quiet chews as we consumed our food and the beating of my heart in my chest.

No one said anything as Erik and Tommy packed up their things and disappeared into the trees. Tommy's eyes met mine and he nodded, looking confident. I hoped he felt as confident as he looked, as I felt like I was going to lose everything I just ate.

The rest of us sat in silence while they were gone. I hated this kind of silence. This kind of silence was loud and it got into your head. There was nothing else to do except listen to the screaming worries and doubts.

I didn't know a whole lot about forests but I knew they weren't quiet. You could hear the rustling of tree branches in the wind and the sound of animals moving around. It wasn't like that anymore and it put me on edge. Ever since the Awakened had come to be, silence had become normal. People – and animals too, it would seem – were too nervous to make any noise nowadays.

After about an hour, I couldn't take it any longer and I stood up, pacing the forest floor. Nathan glanced up at me every few minutes or so, before returning to his intense study of his hands at his knees. After another 30 minutes of this, I looked up at Liam, unsurprised to see him staring back at me.

"Shouldn't they be back by now?" I asked, running a hand through my hair. My eyes met Kris's and I saw the same anxiety coursing through my veins mirrored in her eyes. "They've been gone a long time."

"They haven't been gone that long," Liam assured me. "These things take time."

Taking out the guards, disabling the cameras and sneaking back here with a key card to get us through Sekhmet? Yeah, I supposed things like that took time.

"What if they got lost? Or worse, caught? What if people are heading this way right now? What if…"

"Does she ever just shut up?" Kris burst out, tugging at the end of her ponytail.

"No," Liam said and I shot him a dark look. There was a low chuckle behind us and all four of us whirled around, reaching for our weapons.

I sighed in relief when I saw Erik and Tommy standing in front of us and I resisted the urge to launch myself at them.

"Can you maybe not shoot us?" Erik asked, a smile across his face. "Considering we're the ones with the goods." He held up a slim black card, with a familiar stamped logo on it. The Egyptian goddess adorned nearly every surface in Sekhmet.

"You got it?" Nathan asked, lowering his weapon.

"Did you doubt us?" Tommy asked, his arms crossed over his chest. They looked a little roughed up, but other than a cut across Erik's eyebrow and a bruise blooming along Tommy's jawline, they looked okay.

"Well, for a moment there..." I trailed off.

"Are you ready for the next move?" Tommy asked, checking the ammunition in his gun before sliding it back into the waistband of his pants. "We won't have much time while those cameras are down so we should get a move on."

The unwavering fear that had sat simmering in my veins since we had left Hoover had disappeared for a moment, replaced by the worry I'd had for Erik and Tommy. Now it came rushing back and I felt paralyzed. I was about to willingly enter Sekhmet. There was no turning back now.

Liam seemed to get my train of thought. "Zoey, you don't have to do this. You can stay behind. No one would blame you."

I shot him a disgusted look. "I am *not* staying behind, Liam. I'm going through with this. I'm not going to keep hiding." I pushed past him, heading in the direction Erik and Tommy had gone earlier. "Let's just do this."

The hallways of Sekhmet were freezing, just like I remembered. The hairs on my arms stood up, and I rubbed my arms, trying to chase off the chills that were running up and down my skin.

"What is this entrance anyway?" I whispered. "Why didn't we use this to escape?"

Tommy shook his head. "It's a back entrance. Most of the people in Sekhmet don't even know it exists. It's for Dr. Cylon, if she ever needed a quick getaway. She barely keeps it guarded, which is her first mistake. She would never expect someone to try to exit this way, if they needed to." He sighed, running a hand through his hair. "But I couldn't take the chance that she would know I would send you here. So we didn't do that. But she's gotten lazy. Complacent. She would never think that anyone would sneak in this way."

"Are you sure about that?" Erik said from behind us.

"Well, I'm counting on that," Tommy admitted. "Let's continue."

We made our way slowly through the hallways, stopping occasionally to slide the keycard through another door or to disable the cameras in the next sector. It felt torturous to go that slow. Ash was somewhere within these walls and everything in me was screaming to run, to burst into every room and tear the place apart until I found him.

But I kept myself contained. I followed Tommy as we made our way through the bright hallways, twisting and turning until I was so dizzy that I knew there was no way I could make it out without his help. For a moment, dread filled me and I wondered if he was purposefully bringing us back in here, but I had seen the scars he had from his gunshot wounds. For some reason that I couldn't even begin to explain to myself, I trusted him.

We came to a fork and Tommy held a hand up. We all stopped, exchanging looks. He took a couple moments to disable the cameras in this corridor. "This is where we split up," he whispered. Liam and I would sneak to the detention level, where Ash was sure to be held. It seemed stupid for Razi to keep Ash in the same place she did last time but it wasn't like she was trying to hide him from us. She wanted us to come here. She wanted us to find him.

Liam and I looked at each other and I suddenly felt safe. Whatever happened next, I had my best friend with me. I had someone who would help me get Ash back. He was the only one I trusted to have by my side during this. We would succeed. I knew it. We started to walk down the left fork before Tommy reached out and grabbed my arm, spinning me around toward him.

"What?" I asked him, pursing my lips.

"You have an hour, Zoey. That's it. Once we shut down that program, all hell is going to break loose and we're going to need to get out of here. They won't have the Awakened but there are still plenty of men with guns in this place."

"I know," I barked out, impatiently.

Tommy hesitated before letting go of my arm. He pressed an extra black key card into my hand. It felt slim and cool in my hand, and I tucked it in my back pocket. "Be careful. We'll see you in an hour."

Liam came back over to me, slipping his hand in mine. It filled me with warmth and comfort. "We'll see you then." He nodded toward his friends. "Good luck."

We reached the stairwell quickly, pausing every so often to listen for any footsteps approaching. My heart was beating like a drum underneath my ribs but despite that, I felt calm. I was thrust into my worst nightmare but I was finally here. I was finally able to find him.

We raced down the stairs, getting lower and lower into the depths of the compound.

"Level five, level five, level five," I whispered to myself as we thundered down the stairs. My sweaty hand slid across the handrails. I skidded to a halt when I came face to face with a number five. "Liam."

"I know, honey. Let's do this," he said, pulling the rifle off of his shoulders. I reached for my gun, clutching it tight in my hands. "I'll go first. And don't argue with me."

The moment we pushed our way through the door, the shots began to fire.

"Shit," Liam said, shoving me backwards and closing the door. "Well, there goes the idea of sneaking in there."

"Damn it," I said, clenching my fist. "They were totally expecting us."

Liam peeked through the small window in the door. "There are only about four of them, maybe five. It's hard to tell. But we can take them out." He sighed and looked down at me. "They knew you'd come for him, Zoey. That's why they're stationed down here. They didn't have guards down here before."

"What are the chances that she still wants me alive?" I joked, a weak smile on my face.

"Well, we're about to find out," he said, shaking his head. "Cover me, okay?"

I started to protest but he didn't wait for me. He pushed the door forward again, his rifle at the ready. I cursed, loudly, and followed him, staying ducked behind the open door.

There were five of them, standing together to block passage down the hallway. They had their guns raised but they didn't shoot again. I saw more than one uneasy look as they stared at Liam. He stood, unprotected in the hallway, his rifle raised toward them. He didn't fire a shot, just stared them down.

"Let us pass," Liam said, firmly, not taking his eyes off of them. "We'll shoot each and every one of you dead and I'm not sure you'd like that. Put your weapons down and let us pass and we'll let you live."

I felt a sense of relief at his words. In the last year, I'd yet to shoot an actual person and I wasn't aiming to do so anytime soon. These guys were Sekhmet goons but they were still people.

The guards stared at us, not saying a word. I could feel my knees shaking as I crouched behind the door, wondering how long this stare-off could go on for.

"Let us pass," Liam repeated.

"And why would we let you do that?" The one in the front spoke firmly. "Who's to say that you'll shoot us as soon as we let you pass?"

"We won't," Liam promised. "We don't want anyone to get hurt."

There was a sudden movement, a hand moving. I didn't know what they were reaching for but I didn't pause, didn't stop to look. I wasn't taking the chance. I raised my gun, aiming at the man on the left. The trigger was pulled and I watched as the bullet went sailing toward him. He went down with a thump but I couldn't stop to think about that.

One of the guards on the right immediately spotted me and I ducked back behind the door, flinching when I heard the bullet strike the door. The door was heavy and I pressed my back harder against it as I peeked around the corner. Liam had shot the man who had just missed me and was aiming for the one next to him. The other two looked hesitant, unsure of whether to engage us or turn tail and run.

A shot rang out from one of their guns, just missing Liam who ducked behind the door with me. He looked down at me, crouched on the ground, before engaging again.

I aimed and missed one of them, sending a bullet ricocheting into the wall. I swore and shot again, catching one of them in the face. My stomach dropped as blood burst from the wound, and the man fell, choking, to the ground.

The last man fell, a clean shot through the throat, courtesy of Liam.

I stood up, letting the door slam behind me.

I walked over to the bodies, feeling the bile rise in my throat. "That's not the way I planned that going…"

Liam came up next to me. "Yeah, me neither." He climbed past them and offered me a hand. I took it and hoisted myself over. "It was us or them." He didn't sound happy about it. He stared at them for another moment and then reached down.

"What are you doing?" I asked him.

He yanked a gun out from underneath one of the bodies, tucking it over his shoulder. "Ash is going to need something once we find him. We didn't think of that. Now we have something."

I nodded. "Good thinking."

We continued down the hallway, more alert than before. We hadn't planned for guards down here. No one came down here. It's what had made it almost easy to sneak Ash out the first time we'd been here.

We paused at each and every door and it was like a blow to the chest each time we found it empty. I was starting to believe they were keeping him somewhere else when Liam peeked through a window and drew in a sharp breath. "Zoey."

I pushed past him, reaching for the door handle. I fumbled at the key cad in my back pocket and slid it through the slot. It flashed green and I practically threw myself through the door.

Ash stood up, quickly, and my stomach dropped. He looked awful. There was a gash on his cheek that had dried up, blood crusted at the sides. His face was a variety of colors and the side of his lip was fat and bloody. He was leaning on his left leg but he didn't' seem to notice any of that. He limped across the room, moving as quickly as he could, and grabbed me, lifting me into his arms. We went crashing into the wall, my back slamming into the hard concrete.

"I knew you would come. I didn't want you to but I knew you would," he whispered to me. His hands clutched my face tightly between them and I clung to him. It hadn't even been a week but it had felt like a lifetime since I saw him. He was here and he was whole, for the most part. He was going to be okay. He was going to be safe.

"I love…" I started to say but he cut me off with his lips sliding over mine. I welcomed them eagerly, my fingers sliding through his hair to tug him closer to me. A growl rumbled through his chest and a shiver went down my spine. He tasted like blood and sweat but I hardly noticed. Every inch of my body was pressed against him and I didn't care if he had to carry me out of this place like this, I didn't want to let him go. I didn't want to ever let him go.

Ash pulled back, his forehead pressed against mine. "I'm sorry," he said, out of breath. "I don't want to but I have to…put you down."

A jolt of concern rushed through me and I let go of him, sliding to the ground. "Are you okay?"

He grinned at me, pulling at the gash in his lip. "I'm always okay. You're covered in blood."

I shook my head. "It's not my blood. Mostly." Ash's fingers gripped me tightly, his eyes full of concern. I watched as he took an assessment of my body. When he deemed me good enough, he smiled and pressed a hard kiss on the top of my head. A shiver went through me. *He was safe. He was alive.*

He turned around, looking at Liam, who I had almost forgotten was in the room. He reached a hand toward him and Liam stared at it, before reaching for it. Ash tugged at it and pulled him into a hug. "Thank you. For being here. For bringing her. And I'm assuming, taking care of her."

I could see the surprise on Liam's face over Ash's shoulder. I bit back a smile as the two of them broke apart. "No one really takes care of Zoey," Liam managed to say.

Ash laughed, clapping him on the back a couple times. "That's true enough. But still. You came with her."

Liam shuffled nervously back and forth. "Well, I couldn't live with this girl every day if we didn't come and get you."

Ash cracked another smile, reaching his hand back for mine. Our fingers intertwined and I felt a smile stretch across my face, my first genuine one in days. "So what's the plan?"

He glanced around. "Or is it one of the kind where we make it up as we go along? Those are always my favorite."

Liam handled over the extra gun and Ash took it, nodding at him gratefully. He checked the ammunition quickly before gripping it tightly in his hands.

"Just tell me we don't have to run," Ash joked. He was still favoring his left leg, though he was trying really hard not to show it.

Liam studied Ash's leg for a moment and then looked at me. Whatever he saw on my face kept him from commenting on it. "Well, if the others did their part, hopefully not."

"Others?" Ash asked, confused.

"Yeah, we have a sort of ragtag group here to rescue," I said, opening the door and peeking out. The hallway was clear but I didn't think it would stay like that for long. "Part Sanctuary, part Hoover and part Sekhmet." Ash's eyebrows rose. "We ran into Hoover on the way to Sekhmet and picked up some of Liam's friends and ran into an old friend, who, incidentally, is not dead like we thought he was. That's how we're in here."

"Could you be any more vague, Zoey?" Liam said, rolling his eyes.

"We should probably get moving though. We, uh, deviated from the original plan a bit and I think they'll notice soon."

"Liam's eyes grew wide in realization. "Okay, I lied. Running just might come into play."

"Fantastic," Ash said, looking unperturbed. "Let's get this show on the road, then."

CHAPTER TWENTY-SEVEN

AS WE ENTERED the hallway, Liam explained what had happened since Ash was kidnapped from Sanctuary. He didn't leave anything out; Octavia's reaction, us leaving, Astrid following us, running into Hoover, learning about Tommy, everything.

Meanwhile, I walked next to them, apprehension filling me. Something about this didn't feel right. It was too easy. I hadn't felt great about the mess we had made in the hallway but I didn't expect it to be this easy. We should be surrounded. There were cameras everywhere and Tommy hadn't been able to disable all of them. It felt like a trap. It felt like a trick.

"I wouldn't call it easy…" Liam said, when I voiced my concern. "Besides, don't jinx it. We still have to make our way out of here and meet with the others, given that they've succeeded."

"So what are the others doing, if not rescuing me?" Ash asked as we made our way down the hallway. We passed the pile of bodies but Liam and I didn't say a word and Ash continued without comment.

"Disabling the Awakened program," I said, hurrying toward the staircase.

"Wait. What?" he asked, incredulously, coming to a halt. I grabbed his arm and started hauling him with me. We had no time for stopping.

Liam flung the door open and motioned us both forward. We all stepped through and started rushing up the stairs.

"You guys are kidding right?" He sounded out of breath as we raced up the stairs. He winced a couple times as his feet landed on the hard concrete stairs. He was hurt, more than just on the surface, but we didn't have time now to take inventory. We had to get out of here.

We slowed when we reached the hallway where we'd split up with the others. They weren't here. I halted, shooting a worried glance up at Liam.

"It's fine," he spoke up, answering my silent question. "Their task was harder than ours. We had to sneak down to get Ash. They had to sneak into Razi's office to shut down the program."

"This plan just keeps getting better all the time," Ash mumbled under his breath. His fingers brushed over his forehead and he winced. I zeroed in on him sharply and he smiled, dismissing my concern.

"I don't know, Liam," I said, looking around. My eyes spotted the familiar black globes that concealed the cameras around Sekhmet.

"They're going to meet us here. That's the plan. They'll be here," Liam repeated.

"You're right," I said, taking a deep breath. "They're totally going to show up."

Liam wasn't paying attention to me. He was staring behind me and Ash, his eyes wide and his face pale. "What are you doing here? Why are you here?"

Ash and I turned around. I knew who was there before I even turned. She had probably been behind us the entire time. I had known from the beginning that there was no way that she would have stayed behind.

"Astrid. Are you kidding me right now?" Liam's voice was rising and I glanced around nervously. "I left you behind for a reason. All I wanted to do was to keep you safe and you couldn't even listen to that. God, how did you even get in here?"

Astrid glared at him. "Are you going to pause for breath to let me explain or do you even want to know?"

I took in her appearance and my mouth dropped open when I realized what she was wearing. "Wait, Liam…" I said, reaching my hand out to stop him.

None of us got the chance to say anything else. An explosion shook everything around us. I crashed to the ground, landing on my elbows. The pain ricocheted up my arm and tears sprung up in the corner of my eyes. Debris covered us and I felt a hard body cover mine.

"Stay down, stay down." I could barely hear Ash's voice, though I could feel the warmth of his breath on my ear. I felt like the inside of a bell; all I could hear was ringing. I was covered in dust and who knows what else. I coughed and Ash rolled off of me. Liam was rolling himself into a crouched position. He looked around wildly.

"Where's Astrid?" he asked, frantically. My eyes scanned the chaos around us. The explosion had happened above us, judging by the chunks of wall and ceiling surrounding us.

"Liam? Zoey?" Astrid's weak voice came from our right and we all turned. I spotted an arm underneath a large slab of ceiling. We moved as quickly as we could over the mess. Astrid was trapped. I could only see a slender arm peeking out. "Ash, help me," Liam said, bending over. I opened my mouth to protest but immediately closed it at the determined look on Ash's face. The two of them bent over, grabbing the heavy wall in their hands and lifting. I raced forward, grabbing Astrid's arms and pulling her out. She was a disaster. Her hair was in knots and covered in so much dust, it looked gray.

There was blood streaked across her face and it dripped from a gash on her forearm.

"Astrid, are you okay?" I asked, feeling stupid for even asking the question. She stumbled and I pulled her closer to me.

Her small hand was trembling as she covered her mouth. She coughed and when she pulled her hand back, it was deep red. The three of us looked at her with concern but she waved us off. "I'm fine. *I'm fine, Liam,*" she insisted sharply at Liam's disbelieving look.

"We need to move. Now." I said, slinging my arm across Astrid's back.

The rubble blocked the hallway that had led us in. it should have been our way out. The four of us exchanged looks before scanning over our shoulders in the direction of the stairwell.

The stairs were blocked and it took both Liam and Ash to push enough of the plastered walls out of the way to make a path for us to climb through. We all paused when we made our way through the door. The air was clearer in the stairwell but it had not been spared from the impact.

"Ours or theirs?" Astrid managed to get out between shallow breaths. She was clutching her side in pain, leaning against the wall.

"What?" Liam asked, leaning over her. Worry was etched all over his handsome features and his hands floated uselessly in the air in front of her.

"Do you think the explosion was ours or theirs?" Ash asked, filling in the blanks.

Liam and I exchanged looks. Every part of me hurt. I was covered in blood and I didn't even know how much of it was mine. And I was worried, worried about our four companions who were floors above us. They very well could've been the cause of that explosion. They very well could have been dead.

"I don't know but we need to keep moving," Liam finally said. Astrid nodded, even as another tremor of pain jolted across her face. "I know, honey, I know but we need to keep going."

"There are…" she swallowed hard and I watched as her face grew even paler. She coughed again and blood splattered down her front. She wiped it away, impatiently, but her movements were slow and jerky. She didn't look that hurt on the outside but I was no expert. She could have been hurt on the inside. We needed to get her out of here. We needed to get her to Hoover or Sanctuary as soon as possible.

"Shh, Astrid, save your strength."

"But…" she protested weakly. She swayed for a moment and then pitched to the side. Before she could crash to the ground, Liam was there, his arms scooping her up. Her eyes were closed and relief filled me when I saw the rise and fall of her chest.

"Liam…" I started to say but I stopped immediately at the look on his face. "Up or down?"

He sighed. "We need to get the hell out of here. We can't wait for the others; we have to hope that they get out. Astrid and Ash need medical attention and they're not going to get it if we stick around much longer." He sighed again and shifted Astrid in his arms. "Up. Let's go."

Each step felt like agony. I knew we needed to move faster but I couldn't. None of us could. Ash's face was hard and white and pain flashed across it with each step. Astrid was small and light but Liam was hurt and I could see the strain on his face. Our pace was slow and impossible. We were going to get caught.

There was blood on my shoes and each step was slippery. I couldn't get a grip on the stairs and I kept losing my footing. My hand clutched the handrail. *One more step, Zoey. You can do this. One more step.*

"I need to take a break," Liam finally gasped. He stumbled into the guardrail and Ash and I both rushed forward, reaching for Astrid. The four of us were hopeless and we had barely made it up three flights of stairs.

"We need another plan, Liam," I said in between heavy breaths. "We're sitting ducks here."

Liam closed his eyes briefly, his brow furrowed. There was a streak of blood across his nose but he didn't seem to notice it.

"You need to get out of here, with Astrid," Ash spoke up. "This is the last place she should be." Ash's eyes met mine and I could see a plan brewing behind his eyes. It didn't matter what he was going to suggest; I would be there right by his side, no matter what.

Liam started to shake his head but I immediately interrupted him. "Don't argue. Get out of here."

"You'll get caught," Liam protested.

Fear sat like a lump in the back of my throat. I would rather die than be in the hands of Razi again. "Maybe we will. Maybe we won't. But if we continue like we are, we'll all be caught and I won't be able to live with that."

"Go," Ash insisted. "Get the hell out of here. Get her out of here." He held his hand out for Liam's rifle. Liam stared at the both of us for a long moment before handing it over.

"Guys, I can't…" He looked helpless as Ash took the rifle and slung it across his own back.

"Don't say it," I said. I hugged him, the best I could with Astrid in his arms. He kissed the top of my head and I squeezed him tighter. People who loved and cared like Liam existed so rarely and they were even more rare in this world. "Go."

Liam stepped away and looked down at Astrid, still passed out in his arms. His eyes were red but his face was set and determined. He readjusted her and turned back to us. "I love you guys," he said, his voice hoarse.

I pressed my lips together and grabbed Ash's arm. "We'll see you in Hoover. I promise." The two of us faced the door with a large number 3 printed on it. I took a deep breath and pushed my way through it, Ash at my heels.

It was time to make some noise.

CHAPTER TWENTY-EIGHT

THE HALLWAYS WERE quiet except for the squeak of our shoes on the slick floor. We took each step carefully, listening for anyone approaching. There was no way to hide our trail. Both of us were a mess, covered in blood. Each bloody footprint left behind a calling card right to our location.

Nothing looked familiar. I had no sense of direction in here. I had only spent time in a few rooms when I was here and I never went anywhere without an escort. We took turns at random. They knew we were here. They had run into the others and they had to know that Ash was missing out of his room by now. So why weren't they attacking?

We had to make a scene. Liam and Astrid were making their way out of Sekhmet and we had to make it easier on them. What I wouldn't have done for a pack of Awakened or Sekhmet guards at that moment.

"Did you see what Astrid was wearing?" Ash finally spoke up, his voice barely above a whisper.

I nodded. "She was in a Sanctuary uniform. When she left, she was in normal clothes. She was in normal clothes the entire time we were in Hoover. Where did she get those?"

Ash hesitated as he checked around the next corner. He nodded and we both continued down the hallway. "You don't think…you don't think they're here? Sanctuary?"

I nearly laughed. "When they told me that you had been taken and Liam asked them what they were going to go, they just looked at him. They looked at him like he was crazy." I made a face, mimicking Octavia's voice. *"We will not risk the lives of Sanctuary citizens for one boy."*

Ash snorted, shaking his head. "That sounds about right. So where exactly are we going if we get out of this situation?"

My face lit up for the first time since I had walked into that room and seen him alive. "Hoover. We are going to Hoover."

He looked confused for a moment. "As in, Liam's Hoover?"

We came up to a fork and we stopped for a moment. "Yeah. We ran into them on the way here and we stayed with them for a couple days. And Ash, it's amazing. It's this incredible community. They're like a family. It's not a prison like Sanctuary. Everyone there is actually living, not just surviving."

Ash's arm reached for me, sliding around my waist and he tugged me toward him. His eyes searched mine for a moment and the crooked smile I loved so much stretched across his face. "We'll go. We'll make it there. You and me, always."

"Always," I repeated, my fingers gripping him tightly before he let me go.

"Are you ready to go home?" he stepped back.

I smiled up at him. "Yeah, let's get the hell out of here."

It was at that moment that there was a loud bang to our left. We whirled around, just in time to see a door swing open. Several Awakened came bursting into the crowded hallway. Our weapons were in our hands immediately. Ash looked down at me, a grin on his face, and I couldn't help it. I grinned back.

"I love you," he told me.

"I love you too," I said, as the Awakened spotted us and came sprinting down the hallway. Nothing else needed to be said. We didn't hesitate. We didn't wait for them to come to us. We threw ourselves into the fight.

The fight was pure chaos. They outnumbered us four to one. I ducked and dove and shot round after round of bullets. The hallway was narrow, an advantage as they couldn't bombard us but we were getting tired. This was nothing like either of us had seen before. They just kept coming.

My feet slipped in the dark blood of an Awakened at my feet and I fell into the wall, sending a shock of pain through my spine. I winced as a hard body collided with mine. My elbow jabbed into my assailant's stomach and I heard a groan. Placing my palms against the wall, I pushed myself off kicking out with my leg. I felt it land and he went sprawling to the ground. I ducked a blow from another and my knife went six inches deep into the neck of my fallen assailant. I yanked it out, ignoring the sick noise it made as it was pulled from the flesh, and stabbed the one I had just avoided right in the face.

I was getting tired and I was losing count of how many I'd taken down. There was a pile of bodies and we had to back up to keep ourselves on solid fighting ground. We were going to run out of space soon and I didn't know where else to go. I was exhausted and they kept coming. My wish for attacking Awakened had come true and I cursed myself for even thinking it. This wasn't like an Awakened attack in the woods. This was right in the heart of Sekhmet. I had no idea what kind of numbers Razi had under her command. She could have thousands, millions even.

With each Awakened that came bursting into the hallway, my heart sank. Something had gone wrong. The Awakened program should have been down by now.

Ash went flying to the ground. An Awakened landed on top of him, large and strong. Ash's face was pale and he was covered in blood. I'd lost track of how much was his own. He was struggling against the Awakened and he'd lost the rifle at some point.

I moved toward him but another, smaller Awakened blocked my path and I stopped short. Her arms reached for me and I ducked, sending a kick into her stomach. She growled, angry, and punched in my direction. My hand wrapped around her arm and I flipped her. She landed hard, blinking several times, and I shot her straight in the forehead before she could recover.

I spun around and aimed at the large Awakened wrestling with Ash. He had gotten the upper hand and I shot at him, missing him completely, the bullet lodging itself into the plaster wall behind him. I cursed loudly and shot again, landing it this time, straight in the back of his neck. He collapsed on top of Ash and I helped him push the heavy body off.

The two of turned toward the hallway, where more Awakened were heading our way. We were both breathing heavily. "Are you okay?" I asked.

He nodded, looking like he could vomit at any moment. His shirt was sticky with blood and his hand was pressed tightly to his ribs. He couldn't do this much longer. He was already injured before the fight and this was just making it worse.

I spotted the door to the stairs. We would have to get to it fast. We couldn't keep fighting. There were too many of them and we weren't as strong and resilient as them. "Ash, you have to be ready to run, okay?" His head bobbed up and down. He looked like he was going to pass out. "When I say so....go!"

I shouted the last part and the two of us took off sprinting. Even injured, Ash kept a good pace. The Awakened were coming straight at us. We just had to beat them by a few seconds but they were faster and they weren't tired like us. I didn't even know if they got tired. We slipped and slid on the blood-coated floor and collided with the door.

"Go, go, go!" I screamed. I yanked at the handle, pulling the door open, and we slipped our way through. We took a moment to take a breath and then, without a word, went running up the stairs.

Ash stumbled a few times as we made our way and I reached for him each time, pulling him to his feet. His eyes fluttered open and closed. He was getting slower. I cursed myself for letting him come up with this plan. We should have just gone with Liam and Astrid. Everything about this was stupid.

We made our way up to the first floor and practically fell through the door into the hallway, colliding right into someone. I reached for my gun but halted when I saw who was in front of me. It was Tommy, Nathan, Erik and Kris, looking fairly beat up but thankfully alive.

"Fancy meeting you here," Erik said, cheerfully wiping a smear of blood out of his eyes. "I see you were successful." He looked over at Ash and his brows furrowed when he saw the state he was in.

"Yeah, and apparently you weren't," I retorted. "We met some of our scary friends downstairs."

Tommy sighed. "Yeah, they're everywhere. We've been running circles trying to get onto the 7th floor, to Razi's office, but Awakened keeps stopping us. She's always had a lot of them stationed here but this is ridiculous. They're everywhere. Not to mention she tried to blow us up."

"Yeah, we were right below that," Ash spoke up. His voice was weak. I hoped he could hang on just a little big longer.

Tommy winced. "Sorry about that." He looked around and frowned. "Where's Liam?"

"Astrid somehow made her way in here," I explained. "She got hurt in the blast, badly, and we told them to get out of here."

"Fantastic conversation we're having here," Kris cut in and I could hear the distress in her voice. "But we sort of came here for a reason and now that they know we're here, I really don't think we should linger."

"Good point." Tommy nodded. "Let's move." He looked at Ash, concerned. "You okay there, buddy?"

Ash straightened up, grimacing. "I really wish everyone would stop asking me that. Let's just do this, okay?"

Tommy looked up at me and I nodded.

"All right then." The six of us started moving down the hallway. Tommy ushered us in the direction of the elevator. He slid the black key that he had stolen from the guard through the slot and the elevator immediately opened. We all piled inside and I was grateful not to be on those stairs again. Ash slumped against the wall, taking deep breaths, and we all watched the numbers as we descended to the 7th floor.

As soon as the doors opened, we were met with the growling faces of a pack of Awakened.

"Awesome," Nathan joked, his brow furrowed. He gripped the large knife in his hand tightly. "I was really missing these guys."

"I know," Kris piped up. "I just haven't killed enough of these guys today."

After that, we didn't hesitate. We threw ourselves into the fight. I had no idea how we were still going. Everyone was exhausted and injured but we kept going. We kept fighting.

My muscles burned as I sunk my knife into the thick flesh of a foe, and I yanked it out, feeling sluggish. A part of me wanted to stop fighting and just let them take me. There were just too many of them.

I tripped over a fallen Awakened and went sprawling on the ground. I lay there for a moment, staring up at the bright lights in the ceiling above me. I blinked, once, twice, three times, trying to clear my vision. Every single part of me was screaming, protesting any further movement.

A hand was suddenly in my vision and I reached up for it, missing it once before my fingers latched on and I felt a familiar palm against mine. Ash pulled me up and I clung to him, breathing heavily. The fight was continuing around us. I saw Tommy punch an Awakened in the face before slitting her throat. I watched as Kris and Erik tag teamed a pair of Awakened, sending them flying. The two of them moved together so in sync. I sighed, closing my eyes tightly and pressing my forehead against Ash's hard chest.

"We're almost done," he whispered to me. "We're almost home, baby. Just a little bit longer."

His words were met with an unexpected, immediate silence. I pulled away from Ash, grabbing his arm tightly. The remaining Awakened were still and silent. My heart skipped a beat and I took a step back, my eyes wide.

"No." The word was low and shaky but it carried in the silent hallway. Ash stepped in front of me, but he couldn't shield me from Razi Cylon. No one could. We were done.

She stood in front of us, looking satisfied. She was surrounded by her oversize goons. They seemed to have doubled in number since the last time I had seen her. I didn't care about them though. I cared about the boy who was handcuffed on his knees in front of them and the girl passed out in the arms of another.

"Let them go," I told her, shakily, taking another step back.

Razi Cylon smiled, the thick red scar on her throat gleaming in the light. My stomach churned at the sight of it. "Now, why would I do that, Miss Valentine? You brought them straight to me, just like I knew you would." She looked over at Liam and Astrid with a satisfied look on her face. "I knew all it took was taking your precious boy and all of you would come bursting in here. You were always so careless."

"She didn't come alone," Tommy spoke up from behind me. "You're always underestimating her."

Razi's eyes narrowed when they landed on her former ally. "You were supposed to be dead. It's incredibly inconvenient when people don't stay dead."

Tommy rolled his eyes but his body was taut and ready, his hand fluttering ever so slightly near the gun strapped around his waist. "Inconvenient," he scoffed, shaking his head.

Razi stared at him, studying him, leaving the rest of us holding our breath. My fingernails were digging into Ash's skin. Liam was barely conscious, swaying back and forth. He'd been a little beat up after the explosion below but now he was almost unrecognizable. Both of his eyes were red and puffy and his lips were bleeding profusely.

Eventually Razi looked away and her eyes met mine. A shiver went up my spine as she regarded me carefully. There was a gleam in her eye and the corners of her lips were slightly upturned. "I'm so glad you are back, Zoey. We have missed you here at Sekhmet."

"I'm not back," I whispered fiercely. I cleared my throat and my voice came out stronger. "I'm here for Ash. That's it."

"I knew all I had to do is was take the boy and that you'd be here. I knew it."

"You used him," I accused her. "You used him as a tool to get what you want, like he doesn't matter. Like he's not even a person."

Her eyes narrowed and when she spoke again, her voice was sharp. The hairs on my arms stood up. "When are you going to understand? People are expendable. People do not mean anything to me. I take what I can get from them and that's it. People make mistakes, hurt people, create messes."

I looked at her, disbelieving. "Then why do you care? Why do you kidnap us? Why are you obsessed with getting us pregnant and perfecting the world if you think this?"

"Because I can control them. Because I can make it better. Humans can't be left alone to their own devices. They need someone to guide them; they need me. Without someone to keep them in line, they could destroy everything."

"People don't destroy everything," Ash cut in. "You destroy everything. There is nothing left because you destroyed it all. People have died. Cities have burned. And you hide yourself in a hole in the ground and pretend like you're fixing the world."

For a moment, she looked as if she was going to lose her temper. Her eyes burned black and her fists clenched. Then, it was gone, and her features were smooth again. She turned to her nearest bodyguard. "This one has served his purpose. I have no use for him anymore."

The words took a moment to register and everything moved in slow motion. We all reached for our guns as the bodyguard raised his own gun and pointed it at Ash. I dove in front of Ash just as a shot rang out. The two of us tumbled to the ground.

Large hands reached for me but I pushed them off. I threw out my limbs, in furious and messy punches and kicks, anything to keep them off of me. Ash was beneath me and he wasn't moving but I couldn't think of that. I had to stay on top of him. I had to keep him safe.

A hand reached around my neck, yanking me back, making me choke. I dove forward but it was too late. I was trapped. I looked down and the world began to spin. My body went slack in my captor's arms.

Ash was lying on the ground, unmoving. He looked almost peaceful, like he was asleep. I could almost believe that he had passed out. He was bruised and bloody and he had been so exhausted. I could almost believe it.

The hole in the middle of his forehead told an entirely different story.

Loud, gut-wrenching screams filled the hallway and it took me a minute to realize that they were coming from me. There were horrified gasps and reactions from my companions but we were trapped, captured. The big ugly goon who had hold of me started dragging me away but I fought. I kicked and screamed, tears bleeding down my cheeks, anything to keep from leaving Ash.

Ash, who was the love of my life. Ash, who I had come to save.

Ash, who lay dead on the cold hard floor.

A hard punch landed in my stomach and I blacked out briefly from the pain. I stopped struggling and tried to regain my sense of direction. I felt something pierce my skin, a needle, and I screamed, locking my eyes on Ash one more time before I slid into complete darkness.

CHAPTER TWENTY-NINE

WHEN I WOKE up, I was on a soft bed. The room was spinning and I immediately rolled over and threw up over the side of the bed. There wasn't much left in my stomach and I dry heaved for a couple minutes. The corners of my eyes were crusty from all the tears I'd shed.

I rolled back over onto my back and stared up at the ceiling. The reality of the situation hit me like a ton of bricks and I covered my face. Each breath that came out of my mouth felt hard. Each breath was careful and shaky.

Ash was dead.

Ash Matthews was dead.

I let out a frustrated scream, preparing for the tears that didn't come. I felt empty, even more so than when Octavia had called me into her office. He was gone. The whole reason we had broken into this stupid facility, had risked our lives, was to save his life and it hadn't mattered. He was dead. He was gone.

I sat up and looked around. A new realization hit me and I closed my eyes briefly.

I was in the same room that they'd kept me in the last time I was here. Of course I was.

I was still in the same clothes that I had arrived in. I was covered in blood and my hands shook as I held the fabric of my shirt under my fingertips. There was the deep red of human blood and the even darker black blood of Awakened. There was a stack of clean clothes on the table across the room but I made no move to go near them. I didn't want to see them. I never wanted to be in those beige clothes ever again.

There was also a plate of food next to the clothes. I didn't know how I had missed the small before but it made my stomach churn. I was pretty sure they had laced my food when I had been here before to make me sleep most of the time and I didn't want to sleep.

I wasn't even sure I wanted to survive.

Ash was dead.

It didn't matter how many times I repeated myself. It hadn't registered with me. It didn't feel real. The image of Ash laying on the ground, eyes wide open, with a bullet in the center of his forehead kept flashing through my mind and I squeezed up. I dry heaved a few more times, my fingers clutching the blanket beneath me.

I wished I wasn't alone.

I had no idea where everyone else was. Astrid. Nathan. Erik. Kris. Liam. They could be in other rooms somewhere or they could all be dead. I wasn't sure which one I preferred. It wasn't that I was eager to end my life but I wasn't eager to be back here. I wasn't eager to be poked and prodded.

I wasn't eager to have a baby in my stomach, which was sure to be Razi's next plan.

Time passed by slowly. There had been a clock in the room before, but it seemed to have disappeared in the months since I had stayed here. I had no idea how much time was passing. I thought of Greg and everyone waiting for us in Hoover and my stomach clenched. We were supposed to be on our way back by now. They had known that we might not return, but I had hoped, we had planned. Everything had fallen apart.

I started counting but I lost count somewhere past three thousand. I tried to name the starting line-up for the Mets but I couldn't remember their names. Everything was blending together and Ash's face kept flashing behind my eyelids.

The food kept tempting me, even though I knew it'd be cold by now. I hadn't eaten in so long and I had lost so much blood. They couldn't keep me in here forever.

After what felt like hours, I heard something and sat up, the hairs on the back of my neck at attention. My eyes were pinned on the door as the handled turned. Someone stepped through and I thought of Tommy. But it was a face I didn't recognize. Of course. Tommy didn't work for Sekhmet anymore. He was on our side now.

The boy that stepped through the room was young though, probably not too much older than I was. He looked wary as he came into the room and I didn't blame him. I probably had a bad reputation for punching people around here. Not completely unwarranted, but I wasn't going to fight him. When he crossed over to me and placed handcuffs on my wrists. He hesitated, his cold fingers lingering on my skin.

"I'm not going to fight you," I said, my voice low, and he jumped. I almost laughed. This was the person they had sent in to handle me? He pulled me up and I nearly fell over. My body was so exhausted. Maybe they weren't so far off.

I followed him through the hallways, feeling an overwhelming sense of déjà vu. I had been in this hallway before, repeatedly. I knew exactly where we were going and I knew exactly what was behind that door.

The boy slid the card through the slot and the door popped open. He pushed it open and practically forced me into the room. My heart sank and I entered the all too familiar room. The work out equipment, all the medical tools. They had been my worst nightmare just six months before.

The worst part of those nightmares was sitting right in front of me, looking quite pleased to see me. "Zoey. Sit down."

I looked at her and the chair and remained standing. I wanted nothing more than to collapse in that chair but I wouldn't listen to her. Not anymore. Not like I did before.

Razi finally looked up from her notes and raised her eyebrows. "You're suddenly disobedient?"

"You killed my boyfriend," I said. My voice wavered but my eyes remained on her. I would not show my weakness. I would not show her my tears.

"Zoey, you are nineteen years old and you put way too much stock into a person that would have not been important in less than five years, guaranteed, if you had continued to date him in the normal world. You are blinded by the fact that this world leaves you with a smaller selection than before. He was familiar. He is also easy to replace. You'll see that."

Anger burned through me and I pictured launching myself at her and wrapping my hands around her throat until she stopped breathing. I glanced over my shoulder and saw that her bodyguards were still very much in attendance. "I won't see anything. I won't see anything other than the fact that you're a bitch."

The vein in her forehead throbbed and she dropped her eyes back to her notes. I wanted to throttle her for everything she had done. She had tortured me. She tortured Liam. She had made Astrid pregnant. She had killed and killed and killed.

I wanted to kill her. The cold metal of the handcuffs digging into my skin reminded me that I could do no more than get under her skin.

"Sit down," was all she said in return.

I sighed, and sat down in the chair. "I hate you," I spat at her.

She nodded. "I would be surprised if you didn't." Her eyes met mine. "You're so much healthier than the last time I saw you. I'm proud of you.

My fingernails were biting into the skin of my palms.

"We are going to get started right away, Zoey. I won't let you get away like you did last time," her voice was clipped and impatient. She stood up, handing her notes off to one of her doctors that were standing to the side.

I felt my heart sink into my toes. She would do to me just as she did to Astrid. She was going to make me pregnant. I sunk further into the chair as if it could just transport me out of the room. I wished it could take me away, anywhere but here.

One of the doctors reached for me, and I put my hands up to block him. He clucked, irritated, and motioned for one of the bodyguards. He made eye contact with me and my vision went red. He was the same one who had killed Ash. I recoiled from him.

"Stop fighting," Razi said, bored.

I stepped backward and then there was a loud boom, not unlike the explosion that had happened the day before. I lost my footing and sprawled to the ground. My hands were still locked together and I couldn't catch my fall. I landed hard and rolled onto my back.

Razi was up on her feet, looking panicked, turning to her bodyguards. They reached her in no time and started tugging her towards the door. Everyone was running out of the room. This was clearly not expected. This was not on Sekhmet's agenda for the day.

I could hardly believe it. I had always thought I was important to Razi, important enough to go through all this effort just to get me back. But in a moment of panic they'd left me behind. Sekhmet was not the place it had been when I was here – Razi wasn't the same person and this realization gave me hope. This place could be taken down, maybe it would not be done by me, but someone would succeed.

I waited until everyone left the room before trying to regain my footing. I pushed myself up just in time for another explosion to rock the entire floor. I fell again, catching myself clumsily with my palms. I grunted, crawling across the floor. I just had to make it to the door. That's all that made sense to me, making it to the door. Everything would be okay if I could just reach the door.

The door swung open just as I was reaching up for the handle and I skittered backwards to avoid being hit.

"Oh shit, Zoey, I'm so sorry."

I lay on my back for a long pause, staring up at the two people who had come bursting in through the door.

"K…K…Kaya?" I asked, disbelieving. I looked from her face to Bert's. "What on earth are you guys doing here?"

Kaya looked at me, and her expression switched from apologetic to fierce. She was dressed in in the sleek black Sanctuary uniform and had a gun in her hand. She looked nothing like herself, at least not the Kaya that I'd known when I first arrived at Sanctuary. She looked confident and sure. She looked strong. "Did you really think that you could just leave and I wouldn't come after you?"

I opened my mouth to reply and shut it almost immediately.

"You left in the middle of the night. You snuck out without saying goodbye. You had no idea if you'd be coming back or whether you'd see me again. Actually, I think you had a pretty good idea that you wouldn't be coming back." She offered me a hand and pulled me to my feet.

"Kaya…"

She shook her head. "We've been sharing a room for months. We've shared so much. I've heard you cry and scream. I've heard your nightmares and you've heard mine. I thought we were friends, Zoey. Screw that, I thought we were family."

Tears pricked at the corners of my eyes. Family was a word that I didn't' get to hear very often lately. "Of course we…"

She continued. "There was no way I was going to let you storm into this place by yourself. I wasn't going to let that happen. So I don't know what exactly is going on but we found you and we found the others so let's take this stupid place down," she said, her voice rising.

Silence fell between us as her words sunk in. Her eyes fell on my handcuffs, and to my surprise, her face lit up. She turned to Bert, who had stayed quiet during the entire exchange – not that this was unexpected. She smiled widely. "See, I told you that axe would come in handy."

I took a couple steps back as Bert raised a large axe in his hands. It was red and I recognized it as one that would have been kept in those glass cases with a fire extinguisher. "I think that sounds like a really bad idea?"

"You don't trust me, Zoey?" Bert asked, a gleam in his eyes.

I looked back and forth between the thick silver chain that was keeping my hands locked together and the axe in Bert's hands. "I always trust you," I said, swallowing hard. The two of them laughed and dragged me over to an empty table. Within moments, and after I had squeezed my eyes tightly shut, my hands were separated. My wrists were still encased in silver circles but it didn't matter to me at the moment. My hands were free and I wanted a weapon.

I wanted to kill Razi Cylon.

"We found almost everyone else," Kaya explained, handing over a gun that she'd tucked in the back of her waistband. It was a small handgun, just like the one I had stolen from Sanctuary.

"Do you have anything else besides a gun?" I asked, anxiously. I didn't always trust myself with a gun. Even after

252

years of training back in New York, even after the training I'd received at Sanctuary, I didn't feel confident enough unless I was able to kick or punch something.

She patted herself down, before reaching for a large knife tucked in her vest. She looked so prepared compared to me. She had the appropriate Sanctuary soldier uniform on, and she carried several weapons. This was how someone was supposed to storm the castle. I sighed, reaching for the knife.

"Anyway, we found the others. We were looking for you, and we sort of stumbled on everyone else. Luckily we found Liam first or we would have never thought to release the others. But we haven't found Ash and Astrid."

The loss flushed through me. Impossible as it seemed, I kept forgetting. My hands folded into tight fists. "Razi took Astrid. I assume she's alive, probably close to the doctor herself. She's not letting her go." I swallowed hard and looked away. "Ash is…Ash is…"

I couldn't bring myself to say the words out loud. I hadn't said it out loud yet. It wouldn't…it couldn't be real until I said it.

Kaya strode forward and wrapped me into a hug. Her tears were dripping onto my clothes but her cries were silent and when she pulled away, she still had the look of determination of her face. "He would never forgive me if I didn't get you out alive. So I'm getting you out of here."

When we left the room and entered the hallway, I was surprised at the amount of people there. I was also surprised at the utter chaos that was taking place. There was a loud shrilling noise filling the hallway, as alarms went off. People in Sekhmet uniforms and Sanctuary uniforms were engaging each other and the three of us dashed across the slick linoleum floor to the adjacent hallway.

Someone hard and tall collided with me and I nearly fell from the surprise. I felt arms wrap around me and I nearly collapsed with relief. I would recognize these hugs anywhere. "You're safe," I said, my voice low.

"Zoey, I'm sorry," Liam whispered back.

I took a step back, releasing him. I didn't want to talk about Ash. Not now. Not ever. "What's the plan?"

Kaya was reloading the gun that she had strapped to her waist. She looked up. "Our plan was simple: Get you the hell out of here and maybe take out a few of these assholes while we were it. But Tommy here says you have a plan to take the entire Awakened system out."

I made eye contact with Tommy. He, like the rest of us, looked terrible. Compared to Kaya and Bert, who were clad in clean, crisp Sanctuary uniforms, we looked like a ragtag group of misfits that had gotten lost and somehow ended up here. "We do. But we need to get into Razi's office to do it."

"So we've heard," Bert cut in, his deep rumble easily heard over the chaos behind us. "We're going to tackle that while the rest of the force keeps the Awakened and the guards occupied."

I took the ammunition he handed me and tucked it in my back pocket. "How many of the Sanctuary soldiers are here?"

She sighed. "Despite what Octavia thought, there were a lot more people at Sanctuary that were willing to fight. Most of them were people who had lived out here before everything had happened. They're pissed. It's not a full force. But it'll be enough. We'll take this system down and then we'll make sure Sekhmet is gone for good."

She looked up at us and despite the soldier that had taken over, you could still see the Kaya I knew well underneath. She looked a little embarrassed as she continued. "Of course, all of this is unauthorized. She'll be pretty pissed once we return…"

Liam looked at her, his brow furrowed. "Damn, Kaya," he whistled, sounding impressed. "But how the hell do you plan on making that happen?"

She smiled devilishly up at him. "Trust me, we have a plan."

Kaya did a quick scan of all of us, making sure we were all armed and ready to go. Since we were all at least standing, I figured she approved. She nodded at Tommy and the two of them started leading the way down the blaring hallway. The alarms were distracting, loud and flashing and I winced with each shrill call.

I couldn't help but stare at Kaya as she and Tommy led us down the corridors and around corners, and through the minimal amount of guards left in the area of Sekhmet that we were in. She was so different from the girl I had met six months ago. She was sure of herself. She was confident. She was a leader. I would have laughed at the idea of going into battle with her months ago. Now I followed her without hesitation.

We moved quickly. The corridors we made our way through were empty, except for the occasional guard. We knocked them unconscious and moved on. It seemed most of the fight was away from this section, which made me nervous. I was unafraid of what we would find when we reached Razi's office.

"Do you still have the key card?" I asked Tommy as we continued to make our way deeper into Sekhmet. Even though we were underground and there was no way of telling, I still felt the descent. It felt colder and more terrifying. I felt it in my bones.

Tommy shook his head. "They took it as soon as they took us away." He sent a sideways glance my way. "Zoey…"

The hairs on my arms stood at end at the mere mention of my name and I shot him a dark look, trying to keep my emotions at bay. I couldn't cry now. Not now. "No."

He looked like he was ready to proceed anyway so I continued. "I don't want to talk about it. I don't…" The sob caught in my throat and I swallowed it, feeling its descent all the way into stomach, where it sat like a rock. "I can't. We have to finish this. I can't think about anything else." Tears were forming at the corners of my eyes and I swiped at them angrily.

A hand enclosed mine and I found myself looking into Liam's deep blue eyes. They were so full of emotions that it was hard to pick out just one. Hurt. Concern. Worry. Exhaustion. Determination. I loved this boy so much. I had lost everyone, but I had gained a new family and he was such an important part of it. "Let's take this bitch down."

I nodded, feeling the rage and grief boiling beneath the surface of my skin. I felt like I was burning, like at any moment, I could burst into flame and take out everyone in this place.

"Let's go kill the bitch."

CHAPTER THIRTY

THE MAIN FLOOR was absolute chaos. We entered confidently and drew back almost immediately. The entire place was crawling with Awakened and Sanctuary soldiers. The fight had made its way onto Razi's floor. My eyes zeroed in on the door at the end of the seemingly endless hallway. I recognized it right away. I had been in that office. I had seen the true expanse of what this place was about from the woman herself, right in the place where she had created it.

Now I was ready to go in there and take it all down.

There was just the small matter of taking out the never-ending army of Awakened that were blocking our path.

"We might have to split up," Liam yelled over the noise. "Some of us should take these assholes out while the rest sneak into Razi's office. "

No one spoke up to disagree.

"I need to get into that office," Tommy pointed out. "I'm the only one that can take it down."

"I'm going with you," I demanded, immediately. Several mouths opened and I put my hand up to stop them. "No. I'm going. I deserve it."

No one answered. Kris and Erik looked as though they wanted to argue with me but they must have seen the defiant look on my face, because eventually they nodded in agreement. We split the group up just as the Awakened in the hallway began to notice that we were standing there.

Liam grabbed my arm before we split up. "Be careful. Come back to me, okay?"

I nodded, afraid to use my voice. I wasn't sure what would come out if I tried. And I couldn't make promises that I wasn't confident I could keep.

It was going to be hard work to make our way down the hallway to Razi's office. The Awakened were everywhere, their raspy voices shouting over the blaring alarms. They were coming out of the walls, the floor and the ceiling. There was absolutely no way we were going to make it through without having to fight.

I was tired. I couldn't remember the last time I had slept normally. I couldn't remember the last time I had eaten. I couldn't remember the last time I hadn't felt worried or anxious or scared and I was so sick and tired of it.

I was so tired of living my life afraid. I wasn't going to do it anymore. I was done.

I dove into the fight. I forgot all about the gun strapped to my waist. All that mattered was my strength. All that mattered was the knife clutched tightly in my hands and the anger coursing through my veins. Each and every single one of these bloodthirsty creatures had been a person. They had been mothers and fathers and daughters and sisters and brothers. They had been people. They had taken my best friend, my mother and father, everything I had known.

But it wasn't their fault. They were exactly what that bitch at the end of the hallway had created. They were programmed this way. I didn't believe for a second that they didn't deserve to die but they deserved to die because they were better than this. They were better than the monsters they'd be turned into, just to serve one woman's purpose.

This was what was coursing through my mind as I weaved my way in between opponents, taking out as many as I could.

I could feel their fingernails sinking into my skin. I could feel their teeth biting into my flesh. I wasn't invincible. But I wasn't going to stop. I was going to keep going. My body was a constant blur of motion as I fought my way through. Every once in a while, I would catch a glance of one of my friends and feel a sense of relief before I threw myself at my next opponent.

Our progress felt slow and impossible. With each batch of Awakened defeated, a new one appeared. They were endless. When you turned a third of the population into an army of incredibly fast and intelligent monsters, you ended up with an army that was never ending. Razi Cylon had known what she was doing.

We had to shut down the program. We could never hope to defeat them all. We had to shut it down. It was the only way to end this.

I slammed my fist into the stomach of an opponent and she stumbled away from me. My knife sunk into her forehead before she even had the chance to recover. I wiped the blood splatter out of my eyes but it was pointless. I was covered in blood, my hands and arms, all over my clothes. Fresh blood covered old blood and I knew some of it was my own.

There was no one around me. I had lost Tommy somewhere in the fight; I'd sworn he had been right behind me. I spun around to find a group of Awakened blocking my path to Razi's office. They regarded me carefully. There was a tall, thin man in the front. He looked like he could fall over with just a breath of air but I knew better. Appearances meant nothing when it came to the Awakened. They were strong, period.

"Get out of my way!" I cried, angrily.

Laughter rumbled its way through the group. Not one of them broke their eye contact with me and I felt unnerved with so many of those blank eyes on me. There was nothing natural about those pure black eyes.

"Now, why would we do that?" the thin Awakened asked me, casually. We might as well have been talking over a cup of coffee.

"Because I will take out every last one of you if you don't."

He laughed, and the hairs on the back of my neck stood at attention. This was not a sound I ever wished to hear again. "You're planning on doing that anyway, sweetie."

"True," I said, shrugging, faking a confidence that I most definitely didn't feel. Instead, the panic was rising in the back of my throat. There were way too many of them and I had lost my friends in the pack behind me. "But trust me, the way I planned is much less painful than the way I'll be forced to if you don't let me pass."

There was a long silence as they took in my words. I didn't dare breathe or move as I waited for them to do something.

Finally, one of them spoke. They were hidden in the back and I could barely hear their voice over the battle going on behind me, but I heard them.

"I don't believe you, Zoey Valentine."

My heart stuttered in my chest and I stumbled backward at the familiarity of the voice. No. There was no way. It couldn't be...

The Awakened that had spoken pushed his way through the group, until he was at the front. He smirked at me and tears flowed down my cheeks. I felt an ache throughout my entire body at just the sight of that smirk.

"You won't do it. You're a scared little girl. You'll always be a scared little girl."

The blue eyes I had once known so well were gone. Staring back at me were a pair of endless black orbs. Gone was the reassurance. Gone was the comfort. Gone was the love.

There was no way that this could possibly be happening. I had to be dreaming. This was a nightmare. I was still in my room, locked up, waiting for Razi to come and impregnate me. This couldn't be real. I refused to believe it. My eyes closed briefly but when I opened them again, the scene in front of me hadn't changed. He was still there. He was still so very real.

The grin on Ash Matthews' face grew larger and he took a few steps closer to me, his pale blue skin glowing under the florescent lights. "Are you ready to run, Zoey?"

I was going to kill Razi Cylon. She had killed my boyfriend.

And she had turned him into a damn Awakened.

Ash bent over in a crouch, like a cat ready to pounce. My heart pounded harder in my chest and I started staggering backward. His tongue darted out between his lips and he licked them, his expression hungry and dangerous. The look on his face was nothing less than pure, unadulterated desire. But this desire was different than anything I'd seen on his face before. He was going to kill me. He was going to tear me to pieces.

I didn't think I could stop him.

"Run, Zoey," he cooed at me. "Run, baby."

I didn't hesitate. I turned and ran.

***

MY SIDES WERE burning as I ran but I couldn't stop. If I stopped, he would catch up to me. If I stopped, he would be on top of me and what would happen then?

My running wasn't graceful. I was soaked in blood and I slipped, colliding into walls and falling a few times. I could hear the hard falls of Ash's feet behind me. I knew he could catch me easily. The Awakened were so much faster than a normal human and I wasn't at my best right now. He should have been on top of me already. He should have me already.

He was playing a game with me. He was he cat and I was the mouse. I was a toy to play with before being devoured.

"Run, little Z. Run, run, run!" Ash's voice sang its way after me. This was not the boy I knew. This was not the boy I loved. Everything was telling me that I had to stop him, that he wasn't Ash Matthews.

But he looks just like him. It is him, I thought as I glanced over my shoulder and caught a glimpse of him. He was practically skipping down the hallway after me, looking unconcerned and unhurried. My lungs burned but I picked up the pace, taking a sharp right.

This level was an endless maze of twists and turns. The rights and lefts were impossible to navigate. I had no idea where I was going and it would be so easy for him to cut me off.

"Are you lost, Zoey? Can't find your way out?" His voice was coming from all directions and I whirled around, unsure of where he had disappeared. "You know I'll catch up to you eventually."

"Shut up, shut up, shut up!" I screamed, covering my ears with my hands.

Ash's laughter filled the air around me and it sent shivers through my body. It sounded so much like him but it wasn't. His laugh was cruel and harsh, and that wasn't Ash. Not at all. He had been a bully at times but he had never been cruel.

He had also never been a bloodthirsty zombie before either, I reminded myself.

I had to stop talking to myself. I was losing my grip.

I'd idled for too long. A finger traced the line of my shoulder blade and I froze. Ash's cool breath washed over the back of my neck. I had never been afraid of Ash, but at that moment, I was terrified.

"I see your weapons, sweetie," Ash whispered in my ears. His fingers left my skin and found their way to the knife clutched uselessly in my hand and the gun tucked into my waistband. I waited for him to take them away from me but instead he just brushed his fingertips over them. "Why don't you fight me? You were always my little fighter. My little survivor."

There was a lump in my throat and I swallowed hard. The blood in my veins had turned to ice and I didn't think I could move even if I wanted to. "I don't want to hurt you," I whispered, my voice shaking.

"That's your first mistake." He spun me and I was against the wall in a split moment, my head knocking against the hard plaster. I saw stars and I blinked, trying to regain my sight.

Ash was staring down at me, his arms braced on the wall behind me, locking me in. The unfamiliar black eyes bore into mine and I shuddered. His fingers reached for me, brushing my hair out of my face. "Christ, Zoey, why do you have to be so goddamn beautiful?"

His head lowered toward mine and I flinched, my eyes squeezing shut. "Just get it over with already," I demanded, quietly. "Just kill me."

His voice was just a whisper on my jawline. "Soon," he promised. "But not yet." His lips lowered and his teeth found the soft skin of my collarbone. His tongue made circles and he moaned slightly at the taste of the blood. He broke the skin there and I gasped, the pain rippling through my chest and into my stomach.

"Ash," I pleaded, softly. "Stop. Please."

He yanked himself back and his expression darkened. There was anger burning in his dark eyes and he snarled at me. He pulled me away from the wall and shoved me. "Run, Zoey. I want to see you run away from me."

I stared at him, at the growling monster in front of me.

"Run!" he screamed, spit flying from his mouth.

CHAPTER THIRTY-ONE

MY HEART WAS threatening to break out of my rib cage and make an escape. I tripped over my own feet as I hurried away from him, colliding with the wall before I found my balance and sprinted faster than I had before. There were no taunts this time, no songs, no teasing. All I could hear was his frantic breathing behind me as he chased me. He was right at my heels and I was confused. Why was he letting me run? Why didn't he just stop this now?

We had reached a crowded hallway. There were no people. In fact, it didn't look like it was used to foot traffic often. There were cardboard boxes and carts overflowing with everything from tools to medical supplies crowding the hallway. I weaved my way in between them as best as I could. But my foot got caught and I lost my momentum, crashing into a cart. It tipped over. I was tired of playing this game.

I sunk to the ground, spent. There were several things biting and poking into my skin but I didn't care. My eyes struggled to stay open. I heard him coming closer but I couldn't bring myself to get up. It was over. I was tired of playing this game.

Ash had caught up to me and he threw himself at me. I barely managed to raise my arms to keep him from burying himself into my flesh. We struggled back and forth and more than once, his teeth found his way into me. I screamed, the sound filling the empty hallway.

"Ash, please," I sobbed as the pain ripped through me. He didn't answer. He didn't seem to hear. He was obsessed. Every time I tried to block him, he found an opening. I was suffocating and I didn't know how much longer I could fight him off. He was everywhere. His tongue was making a pattern across the scar on my face and I flinched away from me. "Stop, stop, stop, stop."

He pulled back and his eyes grew wide, like he was surprised to find me below him. I took advantage of his hesitation and knocked my head into his, forcing myself up. He cursed, rolling backward. I landed on top of him and I pulled my knife out, pressing it tight against his throat. His eyes grew wider and his mouth twisted into a snarl.

"You stupid bitch," he barked at me. I flinched at the words, and pressed the tip deeper into his flesh. Dots of blood began to appear. "Just give up. You keep fighting. You keep trying to survive. When are you going to realize that you're not going to survive? There are too many Awakened. We fight and we fight and look what happens. They kill us and they turn us into monsters. Just let it happen, Zoey. Stop fighting."

Every word hit me like a punch to the gut. My breaths were come out shaky and uneven and I knew I wouldn't be able to hold him down for long. "No. Never. I'm here to survive. That's what the Ash Matthews I knew would have wanted. He would have never wanted me to give up."

"He doesn't exist anymore."

My grip on the knife was slippery and I faltered. "No, he doesn't. But I knew him better than anyone and he would have wanted me to survive. He would have told me to keep surviving." The tears were flowing freely now and I didn't care. I didn't care that they ran down my cheeks and landed on his chest. "He would have never wanted to become...to become this."

"Stop talking, Zoey," he growled. "Just stop."

I shook my head. "Never. I love you, Ash Matthews. I won't let you live like this."

I lifted the knife, ready to drive it straight through his neck but he was too quick. His hands gripped my arms and he lifted his hips, throwing me on my back. My head cracked against the hard floor. The knife flew out of my hand and went skidding across the floor. His fingers plucked the gun from my waistband and tossed it away into the unknown. His eyes were darker, if that were even possible, rimmed with red. His anger was rolling off his body and I felt the heat of it.

"Don't you ever say that to me again."

He had my arms pinned to the ground and his knees had my legs immobile beneath me. There was nowhere to go. I met his gaze. "I love you," I repeated.

An angry and impatient roar erupted from his lips and his fingernails bit into the soft skin of my arms. I hissed in pain but didn't waver.

"I won't ever stop saying it. Ever. I love you, Ash."

He relinquished one of my arms but before I could do anything with it, his hand was wrapped around my throat, cutting off all my air supply. I choked, my hand reaching for his fingers uselessly. They were stone, unyielding. My focus faded in and out as I tried and failed to fight him off.

I was going to die. Razi was going to let him kill me and I didn't understand why, after everything she had done. She wanted us, and she was letting us die. I had held onto the fact that she wanted me alive but now? Now I wasn't so sure.

My eyes closed and it took everything that I had to pry them open. I barely recognized the face floating above me. He was a monster. His razor sharp teeth were bared and his deep, endless eyes were narrowed as he tightened his grip around my throat. I felt lighter and weightless and I knew I wasn't far away from losing it. I stopped fighting, my arm falling to the side. My fingers brushed against something, the handle

266

of…the handle of something familiar. My brain fought hard to make the connection. What was it? It was…it was a tool of some kind. It was just out of reach but I stretched and pulled, straining for it.

My hand enclosed around the grip and it registered in my brain. It was a screwdriver. A goddamn screwdriver. It couldn't be my knife. It couldn't be a weapon. It was a damn useless tool and it was all I had left.

I didn't hesitate. My arm flew up and I drove the screwdriver as hard as I could in the back of his neck, right in the sweet spot, right where that special little chip sat. Ash's grip released and I coughed and gasped, each breath burning through my chest and throat. His eyes met mine in surprise. His breath caught and I dropped the screwdriver, as if it had burned my palm. It didn't move, staying lodged into the back of his neck.

"Ash," I whispered, reaching for him. "I'm sorry. I love you. I'm so sorry." My fingers found the soft strands of his dark hair and even though it wasn't him anymore, it felt like him and I held onto him.

"Zoey," he whispered, and then he was gone. His breathing stopped and his eyes drifted closed.

I pushed him off of me and skittered backward, my back colliding with a cart behind me. My trembling hand met my mouth and it barely muffled the sounds of my crying and screaming. I covered my eyes as the scene replayed over and over in my mind.

I didn't know how long I sat there, letting myself fall apart but eventually I raised my head and was almost surprised to find myself still alone. I used the back of my hand to wipe away the tears and snot and blood that covered my face and managed to pull myself into a standing position. Ash's body lay in a heap next to my feet and I took a deep breath. I forced myself to turn away from it. This was not how I was going to allow myself to remember him. I wouldn't remember him as an Awakened. I wouldn't even remember him as the boy I saw just a day before.

Instead I would remember the boy who shot spitballs at me during third period and filled my locker with glitter so I walked around looking like an anime character. I would remember the boy who invited himself over when my dad and I watched Mets games on TV. I would remember the boy who threw touchdowns on Friday nights and could throw a fastball like it was effortless. I would remember the boy who kissed me and held me and protected me. I would remember the boy who loved me.

I stepped over him, keeping my eyes on anything except him. I found my knife and my gun and shoved both of them in my waistband. I started walking down the hallway. I paused at the end, before I was completely gone. My eyes squeezed shut. "Goodbye," I whispered.

I straightened up before continuing on my way. I had a mission.

There was a certain woman who was due a visit from me.

CHAPTER THIRTY-TWO

UPSTAIRS WAS STILL a mess of blood and bodies and fighting. I walked through it, barely noticing it all. No one else existed. I dimly recognized the faces of my friends in my peripheral vision. I knew I felt relief but it was so dim compared to the burning desire I had to get through the crowd and into that office. I spotted Tommy in the crowd. He was covered in blood and was fighting a pair of Awakened by himself. I had wondered why the Awakened were still fighting, why he hadn't shut down the program yet, and now I had my answer.

No one was paying attention to me as I moved through the fight. It was like I didn't even exist.

It was almost too easy. She hadn't even stationed Awakened at the door. Instead, there were two men, two breakable and fragile human boys. Before they could react, my gun was in my hands and I had shot both of them. My aim was off, as it had always been, but they both went down. I didn't stop to check if they were dead. I knew later it would catch up to me. I didn't like taking lives. But nothing mattered right now. I didn't care.

I stole a black key card from one of the fallen men and slid it through the slot in the door. It flashed green and a wave of satisfaction swept through me. My hand closed around the door handle, which was cold under my palm. I turned it and it swung open easily. I took a deep breath and stepped through.

Razi Cylon stood with her back to me and she didn't even turn as I entered the room. She had to have heard me open the door but she was focused on what was in front of her. The entire back wall of her office was made of glass and I knew exactly what she was looking at. She had brought me in here before, shown me the labs that had created the Awakened. I didn't know what she saw now but I hoped it was everything she had worked for bursting into flames.

I took a couple steps forward, my blood-coated shoes slipping against the slick floor. Razi glanced over her shoulder as I made my way into the room and her eyes registered surprise. I expected her to attack but she merely turned away from me, facing her labs again.

I scanned the room and my heart stopped when I spotted Astrid. She was awake, her hands bound and a gag shoved in her mouth. Her eyes widened when she saw me, she looked exhausted and starved and it only fueled my fire more.

I was on her before she could even move. My knife was applying just the slightest bit of pressure on her ribcage and my gun was bruising her temple. She jumped, but she could not have been that startled. She seemed resigned and it made me angry. After everything she had done, I didn't want her to take this easily. I didn't want her to lay down her weapons and wave the white flag. I wanted her to fight. I wanted her to beg. I didn't want this quiet, defeated Razi. I wanted the angry woman who had burned down the world in her quest for redemption.

"I didn't expect to see you here," she admitted. Her hands were shaking uselessly at her side. It was just me and her, and she knew she was at the disadvantage. She would lose this fight before she even tried. But, god, I wanted her to try. I braced myself, waiting for some sort of defense but nothing came.

270

"You never seem to expect anything from me," I said, calmly. "You always underestimate me."

"That is the furthest thing from the truth," she protested, lightly.

"Turning...Ash into an Awakened and sending him after me? That was a stroke of genius, truly. I applaud you for that plan." I dug the knife deeper into her ribcage and she gasped in pain. "I bet you didn't expect me to survive that. I'm sure you thought I wouldn't be able to kill him. But guess what? I did. I left his body to rot and you're next."

I could almost feel her heart stutter in her chest. She swallowed hard and there was a slight tremble in her voice as she replied. "I don't know what you fight for, Zoey. There is hardly anything in this world worth living for. There is no love. There is no life. There is only destruction."

"Then what do you fight for?" I asked her.

"Control," she whispered. "I fight for control."

I let this sink in. "Well, you're wrong," I whispered in her ear. "There is love and life and so much. The only destruction is you." My finger was at the trigger of the gun. I was ready. "And you won't be able to destroy anything anymore. You won't be able to control anyone anymore."

The shot rang through the room and I stepped back as her body went crumbling to the ground. I gulped down air and leaned against her desk. She was so small in death and it was hard to believe that I had ever been frightened of her, that she was the monster that had haunted my nightmares for so long. It felt so anticlimactic. After all of this, it was so simple. A bullet to the brain and she was dead.

The door burst open behind me and I whirled around, raising my gun. Tommy and Liam were there, their arms held high. I sighed, and slumped against the desk. The adrenaline and burning desire for revenge leaked out of me.

Liam practically ran across the room and scooped Astrid into his arms. He tore at the cloth keeping her bound. I could see tears streaming down his face all the way from where I was standing.

Tommy picked his way through the room to me. He came to a halt when he spotted the body lying at my feet. His mouth was an O when he was finally able to look away and up at me. "Zoey...Zoey, you did it."

I nodded, my head bobbing up and down sloppily. I raised an arm and pointed to the computer weakly. "Do it already."

He shook his head. "Right. Of course." His eyes fell on Razi again and he shuddered. He switched his focus on the computer. I watched as his fingers flew over the keys, becoming a blur. I didn't know if he was really that fast or if I was losing track of everything around me. Everything was starting to catch up to me.

"Are you ready for this?" Tommy asked, quietly. "Hell yes, I am," Liam spoke up. Astrid was breathing heavily and she definitely needed medical attention, but it looked like Razi had fixed the worst of her problems. She looked dazed, as if she wasn't quite sure what was going on around her. "Do it."

Tommy looked at me and then back to the computer. He pressed a few more buttons. The four of us held our breath, as if waiting for a signal that it had succeeded. We didn't dare move. This was it. It either worked or it didn't.

"Does anyone want to volunteer to go take a look?" Liam said, under his breath.

"It does seem quiet out there...right?" Tommy asked, uncertain.

Just then, there was a blast of noise and Kaya came running into the room and her face split into a bright smile when she saw us. "I have never loved four people more in my life," she said, sprinting across the room and wrapping Tommy in a hug. "You did it! They're just...they're done. It was incredible. They all collapsed at the same time. They're dead. Tommy, you did it."

Tommy didn't answer. He was staring at the computer in front of him as if he could hardly believe it. His fingers ran through his hair and then he looked back up at all of us with a shaky smile. "It worked."

"Hell yes, it worked!" Kaya shouted, moving backwards toward the door. "I should say though, we should probably get going. We, uh, may have planted some bombs and it won't be long before they all go boom."

The four of us groaned. "Of course. It would be much too easy to just walk out of here, wouldn't it?" Tommy said, pulling himself to his feet. "Let's get the hell out of here."

At his words, an explosion rocked the entire floor, sending us all flying. The ceiling caved in on us. I coughed, rolling under the desk as quickly as I could. Tommy was already in there and his arms wrapped around me as things crashed around us. When the ringing in my ears stopped and it grew quiet, I kicked the ceiling that was blocking me in and the two of us crawled out. I spotted Liam and Astrid, and my eyes searched frantically around the room for Kaya.

"Where's Kaya?" I asked, my voice shaking. The four of us searched the debris piled around us, calling out her name.

"Zoey! I found her!" Liam called out to me. I started moving over to him. His face paled and he held out his hand out to stop me. "Shit. Zoey, don't...shit."

I didn't care what Liam said. I pushed pieces of ceiling and wall out of my way, desperate to get over to them. Tommy stopped in front of me and held me against him. "No, Zoey, you don't need to see that."

I screamed, my throat raw, beating my fists on his chest. "I am so tired of people dying. I'm done! No more!"

"I know, honey," he whispered to me, his palms firm on my back. He raised his head. "Liam, we need to go. There could be more."

Liam must have nodded because suddenly Tommy was grabbing my arm and dragging me from the room. The hallway was a travesty. The bomb must have been set off further down because there were holes in the walls everywhere and a fire was burning brightly. Bodies littered the floor, a mix of Sanctuary, Sekhmet and Awakened. My lips trembled and I turned away. None of these people had deserved to die.

"Come on, this way," Tommy shouted, steering us in the opposite direction. We moved quickly and soon we were in the stairwell. I was so damn sick of this stairwell. "It's only seven flights. You can do this, Zoey. You got this."

Only seven flights. It might as well have been a million. Each step sent flames of pain through my body but I pushed my way through, climbing, using the handrail to haul myself up. Astrid tired quickly and Liam lifted her into his arms without hesitation.

We had scaled about three flights when another explosion rocked the compound. I grabbed onto Tommy, who had a firm grip on the handrail and we managed to stay upright as the shaking continued around us. "Hurry," he insisted. "We're almost there."

I nearly collapsed with relief when we reached the top floor. Another explosion went off but we barely registered it, running through the large warehouse that housed all the transportation for Sekhmet. With one last burst of energy, I sprinted in between cars and vans and small planes. I could see the sun just through the large doors.

Almost there, Zoey. You're almost there.

There were others running beside us and I didn't care who they were. The mix of tan and black blurred to me and I just ran. Fifty more yards. Forty more yards. Thirty. Twenty. Ten.

I burst through the door. I wanted to stop. I had made it but I knew I wasn't far enough away. The bombs continued to go off, and I realized they were climbing up the levels. It wouldn't be long before something went off here and I wanted to be as far away as possible. I stumbled, landing on my knee, but a hand was there immediately, dragging me to my feet. I made eye contact with Erik briefly as the two of us ran.

The last bomb went off and Erik threw me to the ground, covering my body with his. The ground underneath us rumbled. I didn't think I would ever be able to get back up again. I just wanted to stay there, let the ground swallow me up. I was slipping in and out of consciousness. I had hit my head too many times and I had lost way too much blood.

Erik rolled off of me and helped me to sit up. His hands held my head firmly between them and he looked back and forth between my eyes. "Zoey, are you okay? Zoey?"

I shook my head and my eyes started to slide closed. He shook me hard and I cried out. "Stop," I said, trying to push his hands away.

"You need to stay awake. You need to look at me. Don't close your eyes," Erik pleaded with me. "Come on, Zoey, stay with me."

My eyes were heavy and it was so hard to keep them open. I could hear Erik and I wanted to tell him that I was trying but everything was fading away. I turned my head and saw nothing but flames and smoke coming from where Sekhmet had stood. It was gone. It was done.

We had lost so many people in there. So many unnamed people that hadn't deserved to die. So many people. Kaya.

Ash.

The last thing I remembered before the darkness overwhelmed me was Erik screaming my name.

***

THE SUN WAS bright when I woke up. I was in a tent, the tan fabric rippling slightly in above me. I realized that there was a person in the tent with me and I sat up quickly, reaching for a weapon that wasn't there. The world spun and I pressed a palm to my forehead. I closed my eyes again, taking deep breaths, trying to fight off the dizziness that had come on so fast.

A hand reached for mine and I jerked back, my eyes flying open.

"You should take things slow and easy," came a deep voice.

Bert's hand reached for me again and this time I let him take hold of mine. "Bert," I said, softly.

"Yes, its me."

"Where are we?"

"You're back in Hoover." The voice was different this time and I looked over Bert's shoulder. Greg stood in the entrance of the tent. "You've been out for three days. We were worried. Everyone will be glad to know that you are okay."

There was a long silence as the three of us regarded each other. I took in my surroundings and I realized with a start that I was in Greg's tent. I looked back at him, startled, and there was a smile on his face, clashing with the sadness in his eyes.

"What happens now?" I asked.

Greg told me what happened after we escaped out of Sekhmet. The Sanctuary forces had placed enough bombs in the place to effectively destroy it. It was a wasteland now and no one would be going near it again anytime soon.

There were a lot of survivors, mostly soldiers from Sanctuary, though there were a few from Sekhmet as well. Greg had welcomed them but they were being monitored around the clock. They hadn't proved to be trustworthy in the past and they'd have to earn trust in the future.

Tommy had led everyone back to Hoover. Everyone who was mobile helped the injured and about fifty people had made the day's journey. I didn't ask who had made sure I had returned. I already knew who had carried me all the way back.

Out of the six of us that originally set out from Hoover, only four of us had returned. Kris had died at the hands of an Awakened and Nathan had been a victim of one of the bombs. I knew it would be a long time before the image of him blowing to bits would leave my mind.

Some of the Sanctuary citizens had returned. Octavia hadn't been pleased but according to Liam, she couldn't very well punish all those soldiers for taking down Sekhmet, especially since her dad had basically been the one to lead them into battle. Sanctuary and Hoover had struck an alliance, an uneasy one, but both communities knew the benefits of it. In the end, it was all about survival.

"We're going to live now, Zoey," he said, softly, taking one of my hands in his. "We're going to survive and it's all because you were brave."

I shook my head, trying not to let the tears fall. I had lost too much in the last year and I didn't know how much more I could take.

Greg stood up and Bert quickly followed, both of them giving me the courtesy of privacy. I appreciated that more than they could know. I needed time to cry. I needed time to grieve.

I knew I would never be the same again. I needed this moment to accept that.

Greg stopped just before leaving the tent. "You are always welcome here, Zoey. This is your home. This is your family. I know it doesn't feel like it yet but it's true. We'll be here. Don't let yourself fall into sadness. The world is going to start over. It's been given a second chance. Let's grab onto it."

I considered his words in the silence of the empty tent. There wasn't much of a world left. There wasn't much of my world left, but it was something. I had spent so much of my life surviving.

I would just have to keep surviving. For my dad and my mom. For Madison and Bandit and Kaya and every single person out there that lost their lives. I would do it for Liam and Astrid, who fought harder than anyone else I knew. I would survive for Ash, who would want nothing less for me.

But I would survive for myself. I was still alive and, like Greg had said, the world had been given a second chance. I wasn't ready yet but I would be. I'd be there for whatever happened next.

EPILOGUE

LIFE IN HOOVER was exactly the way I had expected it to be. I had fallen in love with it the moment I saw it months ago and it was the place where I'd wanted to return. It was the place where Ash and I could be together and be happy and safe.

I was safe. I wasn't happy.

I knew that it was going to take time. I knew that eventually the ache in my chest would dull and that I would be able to take a breath without it feeling like it took effort. Breathe in. Breathe out. I hated having to remind myself.

Now that Sekhmet had been taken down, and the Awakened all across the country had been eliminated, it was possible to settle down and be safe. There was no government and there were plenty of survivors still looking for places to live, things to steal. We would never be truly and completely safe, but things were better.

Greg and the rest of Hoover still didn't want to stay at Sanctuary and I didn't blame them. It felt good to be outside, to remember that despite everything, the world was still moving, still turning, still growing and changing. Instead, they picked an abandoned town nearby, finally ready to stop and put down roots, instead of being constantly on the move. It worked out in everyone's favor. Some of the people in

Hoover decided to go underground, take in what Sanctuary had to offer, and a few of the Sanctuary citizens moved out with us, into the small houses that we had created a community in. The two communities supported each other.

I also knew that Liam was grateful to be so close to Sanctuary, close enough that when Astrid was ready, they would go back and she could have the baby. We had been so worried after everything that had happened in Sekhmet. Astrid had been injured so much but she was strong and so was their baby.

I spent most of the time on my own and the rest of Hoover respected that. Everyone was working. This town hadn't been bombed, not like most towns across the country, probably because it was so small. Despite that, it was still a mess and there were weeks spent on cleaning and foraging and making the new Hoover a place where we could all live. I threw myself into the task, working and sweating until night fell, and I was too tired to think of anything else but my bed.

I shared a house with Liam, Astrid, Corbin and Erik. Corbin had left Sanctuary immediately after word from Hoover came in. He didn't want to be there. "Too many memories," he told me. I knew what he meant.

Corbin and I spent a lot of time together, not talking, just taking in the comfort of each other's company. Everyone had experienced loss and the only thing to do was pick ourselves up, move on and try to survive the best we could.

Often times I snuck out of the city. There was a large hill just outside of it and I would climb it, taking out all of my stress and all of my grief on the physical activity. There were small pleasures in the burning in my legs as I climbed. I hardly ever stayed there alone. More often than not, someone would come and find me.

Most of the time, it was Erik that came to find me. He never asked anything of me. He sat next to me, sitting in silence until I was ready to descend. I knew over the short time we had known each other, he had grown to have feelings for me, and perhaps one day I could grow to feel something back for him.

Right now, it seemed impossible. I was only filled with Ash. I could think of nothing but Ash.

Maybe one day.

Liam found me one cold afternoon. He climbed up the hill and his face fell when he saw me, tears streaming down my face. I had been hiding my tears from them for months. I knew it hurt them to see it but I had to. There were days when I woke up from nightmares, screaming into my pillow and all I could remember was Ash and how he couldn't climb into bed to comfort me. The reality of it made moving on harder than I could have imagined.

My knees were folded tightly against my chest. "I never meant to fall in love in the middle of all of this, Liam. I didn't. But it happened anyway and I lost him too. What am I supposed to do about that?"

His arm reached out and wrapped around my waist, tugging me closer to him. I flinched at the contact before relaxing against him. "You remember him. You love him, even though he's gone. That's all you can do."

"I killed him." Even months later, the feel of the screwdriver in my hand as I drove it into Ash's neck was still painted in my memory. I relived it every night.

Liam sighed. "You saved him. If he could have asked, he would have. He would have never wanted that. He's in a better place. You know that."

I didn't. I didn't know anything else but the hurt and pain but I clung to it. I had to believe this or I would fall apart. Ash was in a better place. He wasn't suffering anymore. That was the best I could hope for.

Hope was the only thing that was left in the world. Hope and love. As Liam slid his hand into mine and squeezed, I held tight to this idea. Hope and love. This would be what got us through it all. This was how we would survive.

In the end, it was the only thing that mattered.

ACKNOWLEDGMENTS

IF I THOUGHT writing the first book was incredibly tough, it was nothing compared to writing the sequel. So that means there are quite a lot of people to thank.

A huge overwhelming amount of love to my family. My parents, who always support me, even when I'm stubborn and headstrong and overly opinionated. My siblings, Robby, Jessica, Dink, Joey and Stevey, for being the best five people in my life. My dog, Scout, who is the best writing company ever.

Love and thanks to my best friend, Daniel Boulanger. Thank you for loving me and supporting me and dealing with me when I cry and introducing me to incredible people and most importantly, for being my Liam.

To Shelby, Nathan, Erik, Allison, Lauren, Alyssa, Jenna, Allison, Holly and all the rest of the incredible friends that I've met this year. You have reminded me what true friendship means and this book would not have been finished without you guys coming into my life. Thank you for loving me for just being me.

Huge shout outs to Chris, for constantly pushing me forward on days I wanted to give up, and Emerson, for helping me through the hardest scene to write in this book. To

Sydney, who has read all my books and loved them and believed in me on days that I didn't.

To all the amazing friends I've met in this community, both in real life and on the internet. Thank you for supporting me from reader to blogger to author and for just being my friend. Mina and Jade and Nicole and Astrid and Alyssa and Isabel and Natasha and Meghan and the list goes on forever. Book friends are the best.

To Logan, for always believing in me and helping me edit my books when being an author was just a dream. To Xina, for editing and re-editing my books, and making sure I sent out the best book possible. To Claire, for making this cover gorgeous and unbelievable.

To all of the following music loves: Set it Off, Our Last Night, Issues, As It Is, All Time Low, anything and everything Andrew McMahon has ever done and the entire cast of Hamilton…thank you for keeping this girl sane during the late nights of writing.

To Courtney Saldana, the most badass librarian I've ever known. Thank you for your never-ending support and taking a chance on me, when I was a newborn blogger. The Ontario Teen Book Fest is so important to me and I'll be a part of it, in whatever way I can, as long as you'll have me.

A huge hug of love to my OfTomes siblings, Gabriella, Freedom, Claire, Esther, Jorge, Jennifer, Laura, Emily, Hilary and all the authors that keep joining the family: I am honored to be on the same shelves as you. Thanks for the support, the advice, the late night writer talk and more.

To all the authors that I have loved and been inspired by and who have supported me right back: Leigh Bardugo, Jessica Brody, Morgan Matson, Gretchen McNeil, Andrew Smith, Melissa Landers, Cora Cormack, Jennifer Armentrout, Cassandra Clare, Rainbow Rowell, Aaron Hartzler, Tonya Kuper, Robin Benway, Lauren Miller, Mary McCoy, Michelle Levy, Nicole Maggi, Mary Weber and yeah, this list could go on for ages too. I am forever indebted to your words and your advice and your inspiration and your friendships.

I will never have enough thanks in the world to give to Mr. Benjamin Alderson. Thank you so much for taking a chance on me and the world I built. Thank you for believing in The Awakened, and for allowing me to bring The Survivor and The Sanctuary to life. You have made my dreams come true and I will never be able to thank you enough for it. You are an inspiration and a good friend.

Lastly, to you, who have made it through The Awakened, The Survivor and are now here, in The Sanctuary. You are my favorite people in the world. Thank you for reading my books and thank for you for always supporting me. You are the literal best.

ABOUT THE AUTHOR

SARA ELIZABETH SANTANA is a young adult and new adult fiction writer. She has worked as a smoothie artist, Disneyland cast member, restaurant supervisor, photographer, nanny, pizza delivery driver and barista, but writing is what she loves most. She has an obsession with baseball, cupcakes, tattoos and green iced teas. She runs her own nerd girl/book review blog, What A Nerd Girl Says. She lives in Southern California with her dad, her nana, five siblings and two dogs. Her debut novel is *The Awakened*.

CPSIA information can be obtained
at www.ICGtesting.com
Printed in the USA
FSHW010045281018
53282FS

9 780995 679290